AMERICAN RACCOON DOG:

The Extraordinary Saga of an Ordinary Gaijin

A Novel
By
Timothy Regan

SHOGANAI PRESS
Eureka, California

ISBN-13: 978-0692514511
First Edition

Library of Congress Control Number: 2015951365
Shoganai Press - Eureka, CA

10 9 8 7 6 5 4 3 2

INTRODUCTION

Minzoku Shiryō: Japanese Folklore

Japanese folklore is very rich and imaginative in both its traditional and contemporary forms — from the beloved *maneki-neko*, the beckoning cat, to the evil-spirited *kappa*, the nasty riparian-dwelling blood-sucking goon.

The maneki-neko is the paw-raised cat figure that is omnipresent in stores of every description. If the maneki-neko has its left paw raised, the icon is said to be encouraging customers to shop. A maneki-neko with its right paw raised is said to signify an inward flow of money into the business, or in the setting of a home — an inward flow of good luck and wealth.

It has been suggested that the legend of the kappa is based on the giant Japanese salamander. The Japanese salamander can grow to a length of five feet or more and obtain a weight of close to sixty pounds. One fascinating rendering of the giant salamander was brought to life by Japanese artist Utagawa Kuniyoshi (1797 – 1862). The painting depicts a samurai in battle with a particularly ferocious specimen of the giant amphibian in a torrential sea.

Whether or not the legend of the kappa has any connection with the giant salamander is unclear. What is clear is that the mythical creature lives in rivers and among the lush vegetation that lines the banks of such rivers in hope of overtaking some unsuspecting human. According to legend, one can easily recognize a kappa by the spherical depression located on the top of its head. When the bowl-like depression is filled with water, the creature is particularly dangerous and prone to its blood-sucking agenda. If confronted by a kappa, it is recommended that a person politely bow to the beast at a 45-

degree angle. The creature will invariably bow in kind, thus effectively spilling the source of its powers. At that point it is best to immediately flee the scene, as the creature becomes "recharged" once its head-depression becomes replenished with water. There is, however, one other option that can be called upon if one finds himself in a particular bind with a kappa. Kappa are so crazy for cucumbers that they will adhere to promises of nearly any description made to people who furnish them with one or more cucumbers. According to legend, cucumbers are the only food that kappa prefer over young children.

Lodged between the purely evil kappa and the purely benign Hello Kitty is a host of creatures of comparable importance and social relevance. One particularly important legend is related to the real-life Japanese raccoon dog (the *tanuki*). In reality, the tanuki is neither a raccoon nor a dog, but rather its own unique species, the nocturnal mammal — *Nyctereutes procyonoides*.

Tan Tan Tanuki

The tanuki is known as a mischievous and jolly master of disguise and for its ability in taking (or assuming) the identity of another being or entity. From a physical perspective the tanuki is most known for its ridiculously over-sized testicles. A schoolyard song chimes:

> *Tan Tan Tanuki no kintama wa,*
> *Kaze mo nai no ni,*
> *Bura bura.*

Roughly translated, the verse reads: tan tan tanuki's bollocks ring, the wind stops blowing, but they swing, swing.

In Japanese folk tales, both foxes (*kitsune*) and tanuki are known to trick or deceive people. It is said that both of these entities possess the ability to change their appearances to trick travelers. In this sense, there is certain reason to be wary when encountering either creature. Where the kitsune is considered to engender a certain amount of fear in people, the tanuki is known more for its humorous variety of trickery.

The tanuki is also known to be somewhat gullible and absentminded. Tanuki statues are often found outside of Japanese restaurants. They are typically depicted wearing over-sized straw hats, in tote of a bottle of sake in one hand and a ledger or promissory note in the other.

Bunbuku Chagama is a somewhat amusing and popular tale of a tanuki that has been caught in a trap. As the story goes, a kind, yet monetarily poor gentleman comes along and releases the grateful creature from its predicament. In an expression of gratitude, the tanuki wants to do something for the man in return for his kindness. Towards spreading happiness (bunbuku), the tanuki transforms itself into a tea kettle (chagama) and makes the man wealthy — that is, before the tea kettle transforms back into the tanuki, whereby the man becomes understandably angry and disenchanted with the chain of events.

An important aspect of the legend of tanuki is his enthusiasm for drinking sake. Tanuki, according to folklore, often change into human form, where they pay for their drinks with currency that eventually transforms into ordinary tree leaves.

The most notable aspect of the tanuki's mystique concerns his so-called ability to shapeshift, sometimes through the act of blowing air and pulling on his scrotum. According to legend, the tanuki can expand this skin-structure to the size of roughly eight tatami mats or to a size large enough to form a shelter that protects him from the rain and other elements. An 1841 watercolor by Takehara Shunsen depicts exactly such a scenario.

In Japan, the size of a room is often measured in tatami mats. With the average area of a *Nagoya-size* tatami mat being around 1.65 square meters — eight tatami mats would have an area of approximately 13.2 square meters or 142 square feet. If this area were to form the ceiling of a room, the room would have nearly 12 feet by 12 feet of floor space. In a room of this size a lot of good or a lot of evil can take place.

A tanuki variant known as the *mame-danuki* is said to be able to transform its scrotal skin into rooms where humans are invited to take part in various business activities. One popular means of the dematerialization of the "room" involves dropping a lit cigarette onto the "floor," an event that restores circumstances to their more earthly state and which sends the then revealed creature fleeing and howling in great pain.

Bunmei Kaika: Cultural Enlightenment

The fall of Edo (modern day Tokyo) in 1868 marked the end of Japan's feudal system of government and the beginning of the Meiji Era (1868 through 1912), an important catalyst in the transformation of Japan from an agrarian isolationist nation governed by war lords to a modern nation poised to eagerly consume global enlightenment on a grand scale. Quite suddenly, foreign information on many subjects was greatly esteemed by the government of Japan and its people.

No longer were the collective interests of the Japanese people administered by scattered warring syndicates secured by legions of soldiers bound by honor, battle, and swordsmanship. The samurai followed a code of conduct known as bushido (literally, the way of the warrior), which stressed the mastery of martial arts, frugality, loyalty, courage, and honor — until death. Tempered by Confucianism and Zen Buddhism, the samurai were expected to be educated, refined, honest, and wise. The samurai way of life effectively came to a close, absolutely, with the restoration of Imperial governmental control, which resulted from the overthrow of the Tokugawa Shogunate during the summer of 1868.

Japanese isolationism during the Edo Period (1603 through 1867) was promoted by several factors, most notably: Shogun Iemitsu's 1633 prohibition of Japanese travel abroad; a 1639 Shogunate edict that severely restricted Japanese trade, effectively limiting Japanese commerce with only China and the Netherlands; and a complete ban on foreign books and literature. Early in the Meiji Period, a complete reversal of these trends was realized.

The fall of the Shogunate Era changed the social structure associated with the people of Japan. The Edo Period is marked by a strict four-class system. At the top of the social hierarchy were the samurai, followed by the peasants, the artisans, and the merchants. In reality, there was a fifth class of citizens, this group consisting of outcasts or individuals with professions that were considered to be "impure."

The emergence of the Meiji Period coincided with a shift in the social hierarchy associated with the people of Japan. No longer were the samurai at the top of the social structure; in fact, even before the end of the Shogunate Era, merchants began moving up though the hierarchal ranks. The end of the Shogunate Era created a whole new class of Japanese citizen — the purposeless samurai, men without a reason for being; and, unfortunately, men without a means of respectfully attending to even their most basic needs.

Hyaskusho Ikki: Peasant Uprisings

Included in the traditional peasant designation were Japanese farmers. Leading up to the Meiji Period were many uprisings waged by the people against the feudal system and its patterns of taxation on the populace. Peasants were not happy with government policies, corrupt officials, famine, inflation, or taxes. The entire fiscal system was based upon a tax on the people in the form of rice. Tax collectors of the day, physically, collected rice from each village or enclave. Rice was of such importance as a monetary surrogate, during the Edo Period, that even the salary of a samurai was paid in the form of rice. After the onset of the Meiji Period, bands of master-less samurai ramped-up the plunder they imposed on farmers and their crops, ultimately placing many of those who worked the soil in dire straits. Trained only for war and the use of the sword, these derelict samurai helped themselves to the products of the farmers' labor. The end of the Shogunate Era promoted great amplification of this practice and left many Japanese farmers looking toward other opportunities through which they might eke out a living.

Atarashii Hajimari: A New Beginning

As conditions would dictate, both the samurai and certain classes of peasants were looking for new opportunities during the Meiji Period. Where many of the samurai discovered options in organized crime, some peasants took their skills as farmers, fisherman, and the management of such pursuits to locations abroad. As early as 1868, Japanese farmers immigrated to Hawaii to work in the sugarcane fields. In 1869, Japan discontinued this practice, due to the perceived fear by the government that Japanese workers were degrading the reputation of the Japanese race. In 1885, the Japanese government resumed its policy of allowing Japanese workers to secure agricultural work in Hawaii.

The Chinese Exclusion Act of 1882 greatly increased United States demand for Japanese migrants to work in agricultural positions that had been previously filled by Chinese workers. By 1900, there were some 24,000 Japanese immigrants residing in the United States, most of which had come from small rural Japanese farming communities. The majority of these immigrants held agricultural jobs that were located in the California delta regions of San Joaquin and Sacramento counties.

For the ex-samurai, the transformation of livelihood involved a certain amount of retooling. Hard times transformed many of the samurai into social misfits and delinquents who often assumed vocations suggestive of the criminal trade such as gambling, swindling, loan sharking, or extortion. Many of these ex-samurai joined existing criminal gangs or started new ones. Collectively, Japanese criminal syndicate groups are known as *the yakuza*. Traditionally, yakuza groups have been divided into two dispositions — those involved in gambling (*bakuto*) and those involved in peddlery (*tekiya*).

Fushigi: Strange, Wonderful & Fantastic

It didn't take long for Cynthia Martin to become settled in her English teaching position at the Ikemoto Academy. Cynthia had her mind set on teaching in Tokyo and was certain, from the start, that she would land a teaching position at the prestigious academy. She had mapped out most of it in her mind — and the remainder in her heart and on paper.

Cynthia had been raised with the privilege enabled by her private-school upbringing, the spacious freedom of her lakefront home on Mercer Island in Washington State, and parents who invested their heart and soul into rearing their only child. She had everything and needed nothing more, that is — until the summer of 2012.

Cody Fletcher never quite understood how he was granted a position at the Ikemoto Academy. His grades were unremarkable in college, he was uncomfortable in his own skin, and he scarcely knew a word of Japanese. In fact, the only thing that he seemed to have going for him was his Japanese ancestry. On most days, Cody wondered how much longer his luck would last, what little luck he had.

Cody was a fourth-generation Japanese-American, the son of an Oakdale, California sweet potato farmer. He majored in agricultural studies and received his teaching credential at California State University, Stanislaus. With his years spent working in the potato fields, young Cody could identify no other response to his father's mandate that he become "educated" than to become formally schooled in the only skill-set with which he had any personal knowledge or involvement.

By the time that Cynthia Martin had arrived in Tokyo, Cody had been working at the academy for more than two months — a period of time in which he had failed to integrate himself into the community of his placement in any meaningful manner. During the summer of 2012, Cynthia was twenty-three years old and Cody was thirty-one.

Cynthia Martin arrived at the Ikemoto Academy nearly coincident with her graduation from the University of Minnesota, with her major study in the Japanese language and a minor subject of Japanese history. She was a young lady of many talents. In addition to speaking nearly flawless Japanese, she was very skillful in the art of *anime*. As a child, she spent many hours breathing life and form into the fantastic ideas and visions that played upon her mind. As an adult, her forms were vibrant, wild, and fantastic, much as if they might at any point step from the page and into the consequential world where ideas become tangible, real, and inevitable.

Cody Fletcher was a very curious fellow indeed. He was a tall, gaunt man with long scraggly black hair that served to widen his narrow head. Cody spoke plainly and with great word economy and he knew little more concerning social graces than what could be assembled from his interactions with the farm hands that turned the soil in his father's sweet potato fields. He was a hard worker concerning his every undertaking, whether assisting his father in the fields during harvest season or preparing a lesson for the classroom. At the academy he stood out among all of the other *sensei* (teachers). Each day, without deviation, he wore black slacks, black shoes, a white button-up shirt, and a double-breasted black sport coat that made him look more menacing and important than was in his best interest.

Cynthia Martin was a tall, svelte young woman, whose once dark hair was bleached to a very pleasant blond color. With the exception of the classroom environment, she exclusively wore round dark sunglasses, a tendency that made her look more like a rock-star than a sensei at the venerable Ikemoto Academy. In the months leading up to being granted a teaching post at the academy, Cynthia created a particularly phantasmagorical piece of anime where she walked out of her Pacific Northwest life back-dropped by Mount Rainier and flying Chinook salmon, and into her life at the academy where she is greeted by the video-game character Mario, Hello Kitty, Maneki-neko (the beckoning cat), and a rather wild-eyed, yet apparently harmless, tanuki.

CHAPTER ONE:
CALIFORNIA

Greener Pastures

For more than one hundred years, Cody Fletcher's family had been in the business of agricultural production. When Cody's great-grandfather, Takaharu Yoshitaku, first worked the rich fertile soil of the San Joaquin Valley in 1912, he labored in the production of strawberries, russet potatoes, and Tokay grapes.

The russet potato was developed in 1872 by Luther Burbank, and by 1900 it was a top spud-product from California to Idaho. The Tokay grape, a grape that has been around for centuries, was first planted in Lodi, California in 1847, one year before the discovery of gold at Sutter's Fort and three years prior to California's admission into the Union. The strawberry, in one form or another, has been propagated in North America since at least the latter half of the eighteenth century. By all indications, California agricultural ventures of the day were remarkably profitable for all participants, regardless of their race or individual stakes in the various agricultural operations of the time.

Still, at least for Japanese immigrant farmers, something was missing, that missing element being suitable marriage partners. Traditionally, Japanese men never brought along their wives when they ventured to other lands in search of new horizons or opportunities. For unmarried men who longed for wives, few pathways were available toward remedy. One means of attracting and securing a suitable wife involved the so-called "picture bride program." As the term implies, Japanese men wishing to marry Japanese women sent photographs of themselves to family members in the hope that they would pass the photographs along to prospective candidates for marriage. Once the bride's name was entered into her husband's family registry, the marriage was considered official in Japan, and the woman was eligible for travel documents to the United States.

In addition to finding a suitable wife, Japanese farming men had a desire, as all men do, to attain a plot of land that they could call their own. Discrimination, in its root form, is nearly always associated with competition among unlike groups for a perceived common resource or resources. Competitive entities very often develop relationships that become of such toxicity that the more established group works tirelessly toward making the livelihood of the other as precarious as possible.

The Chinese Exclusion Act of 1882 was designed to bar the immigration of Chinese into the United States. This law not only came into being from racism, but spawned additional racism toward people of Chinese descent. This law also facilitated a seamless transfer of oppression that could be readily channeled to Japanese immigrants. Such racial animosity congealed into coherent efforts that were designed to prevent individuals of Japanese descent from owning land and, in some cases, from becoming citizens. Despite governmental pressures designed to disengage the Japanese spirit and to upturn their successes in agrarian pursuits, present and future, many Japanese farmers became quite successful.

In 1913, California passed the Alien Land and Naturalization Act. This law prohibited Japanese immigrants from becoming established as citizens and landholders. This act was nothing short of a hurtful response to the economic successes of Japanese truck farmers in California during the early twentieth century. The essence of such a response seems to be that it was okay to live and prosper in America, just as long as you were a member of the white ruling race. A product of this act was that it brought about land leases that were limited to three years. This forced the frequent relocation of many Japanese families.

To circumvent the Alien Land and Naturalization Act, successful Japanese farmers often tried to purchase land through their American-born children. By 1920, this loophole was closed with revisions to the Act. The new amendments prohibited Japanese immigrant parents from serving as guardians of their minor childrens' properties. A further blow came to unmarried Japanese farmers when the Japanese government, in an effort to maintain positive relations with the United States, discontinued the practice of issuing visas to picture brides in March of 1920. The end of the picture bride program left more than 20,000 bachelors unable to return to Japan towards bringing back to the United States Japanese wives. The Asian Exclusion Act of 1924 completely closed the gates to Japanese immigration into the United States.

Executive Orders

With virtually no specific evidence of collusion with "the Japanese enemy," Executive Order 9066 forced the relocation of 120,000 United States residents of Japanese ancestry. It is said that perhaps as many as sixty to seventy percent of the interned population were legally American citizens. Nonetheless, on February 19, 1942, just over two months after the Japanese bombing of Pearl Harbor, President Franklin Delano Roosevelt placed into motion an order that would lead to the establishment of ten war relocation centers. Onward from December 7, 1941, in the eyes of the American populace, every aspect of the Japanese race — everything connected with the Japanese race — was characterized as despicable; and now the United States government was preparing to place every single individual of Japanese heritage into internment camps that resembled prisons.

On March 18, 1942, Roosevelt signed Executive Order 9102, which created the War Relocation Authority (WRA), the organization that would engineer the relocation, maintenance, and supervision of the interned Japanese. Within six months, centers sprouted up and were in full-operation in Arkansas (two), Colorado, Wyoming, Idaho, Utah, Arizona (two), and California (two).

An important objective of the two orders was to remove United States residents of Japanese ancestry well away from the western seaboard. While the majority of those of Japanese ancestry from the San Joaquin and Sacramento delta regions were shipped off to one of the two relocation camps in Arkansas, of particular relevance to the Yoshitaku family were the two relocation centers located in California.

The state of California had within its borders internment camps located in Modoc and Inyo counties. The Tule Lake War Relocation Center was reserved for Japanese individuals, and their families, who were suspected of strong-loyalty to the Japanese nation, as inferred from responses to two specific items on the WRA intake questionnaire. The Tule Lake War Relocation Center was the largest of the ten camps, with a peak population of close to 19,000 detainees.

Those interned at the Tule Lake facility were referred to as the "no, noes" and their relocation facility as the "no, noes camp." What this distinction referred to was specific candidate responses to items 27 and 28 of the War Relocation intake questionnaire. Question 27 asked draft-age men whether they were willing to serve in the armed forces. Question 28 asked whether detainees would "swear unqualified allegiance to the United States" and "forswear any form of allegiance or obedience to the Japanese emperor, or any other foreign government."

A "no" response to either query meant that the respondent and his family were destined for placement in the Tule Lake encampment.

These questions presented strong dilemmas for many respondents and their families, and not infrequently led to incidents of estrangement among family members. No Japanese detainee wanted to be labeled as subversive, and no detainee desired to be interned at the Tule Lake War Relocation Center. The camp contained twenty-eight guard towers, was surrounded by seven-foot-high barbed-wire fences, and was patrolled by Army tanks. Fortunately for the Yoshitaku family, their destination was the Manzanar facility.

The word *Manzanar* is Spanish for apple-orchard, and up until the 1920s, the location was a pleasant farming community that drew its water from the Owens River drainage. Well before the 1940s, Manzanar was rendered an arid wasteland by virtue of water diversions designed to provide water to the City of Los Angeles and its burgeoning population.

Cody's grandfather, Takahiro, was born in Stockton, California on June 20, 1923. He was the youngest of four children to Takaharu and Kotori Yoshitaku. Takahiro was just shy of his nineteenth birthday when the bus carrying his entire family passed through the gates of the Manzanar War Relocation Center on April 27, 1942. By the time the Yoshitaku family arrived at Manzanar, the WRA had slapped up row after row of barracks that were not much more than unfinished hulls offering little more than shelter from the desert sun and wind-breaks from the frequent gales that moved the omnipresent dust and sand back and forth, repeatedly. Nearly every activity that the Yoshitaku family engaged in during the ensuing three years took place within the barbed-wire fences that defined the boundary of their world and their bleak existence.

The WRA set up schools for the children, dining halls and food preparation facilities, and workshops to service the maintenance needs of the encampment. By day, most of the men and women found activities, of one sort or another, to busy themselves. During the more pleasant months of the year many of the men spent their time working in the center's various gardens. In the heart of the summer, however, the detainees soon learned to complete their agrarian pursuits early in the day, being driven out of the gardens daily by scorching temperatures and/or the winds of late afternoon. Many of the women occupied their time toward fashioning garments or mending existing ones. Throughout their ordeal, everyone wondered what would become of the interned masses once the war ended.

Perhaps the most tragic aspect of the internment proceedings were the material losses that were suffered by detainees and their families. Some families were luckier in this area than others. A rare few were able to transfer their belongings and acquired wealth to trustworthy associates or friends who were not subjected to the internment operation. After the war, for the great masses of the interned Japanese there was no one waiting in the wings to assist them towards reestablishing themselves. For this reason, it was essential that every family group develop a concrete plan to facilitate them in their quest to reenter society.

When the Manzanar camp closed during the summer of 1945, Takahiro Yoshitaku had proposed marriage to a fellow detainee, and through the family of his wife-to-be, he found employment working as a hand on a large produce farm south of Turlock, California. Shortly after moving in with his wife's family on their farm, Takahiro Yoshitaku took Emi Tanaka as his wife.

After several years, through hard work in the fields, Takahiro was able to purchase a plot of land where he built a home and a life for his young bride. By 1951, Emi had given birth to a boy and to twin girls, whom she named Peter, Alice, and Gail. Cody's mother, Gail, was born in 1951, and his Uncle Peter was born in 1950. Takahiro and Emi had decided to give their children American-styled names toward the hope that it would facilitate the integration of their children into their community and into greater society in general. Unfortunately, the distrust of Asians lingered well after the close of the war in the largely Caucasian-populated Central Valley region of California. In result of this unwelcoming climate, the assimilation of the newly liberated Japanese became additionally hindered by factors that were out of the control of these repeatedly oppressed groups of now-American citizens.

While *Issei* (first generation in America) and *Nisei* (second generation in America) largely believed that acceptance into American society could be achieved through actions that made them a credit to their race and their adopted country, this belief underwent regular degradation in the two decades that preceded Japanese internment in the War Relocation Centers. Still, the majority of Japanese immigrants held that through hard work, diligence, and dedicated study their individualized American dreams could be achieved. Once interned, this disillusionment transformed into confusion, fear, and inner turmoil for many Japanese, to the point that many of the interned felt they might never gain acceptance or ever be on the receiving end of a fair deal or equal opportunity. In short, it was long becoming clear that the playing-field wasn't level and that difficulties in the efforts of Japanese-Americans to integrate into American society were hampered not only by their race and the stigma of their internment, but as well by cultural differences that contributed to the uniqueness of the Japanese people. The desire to integrate into American society forced many of Japanese ancestry to abandon aspects of their culture and Japanese identity. This included the adoption of American names for their children, modeling their habits and appearance after the white-bread templates associated with mainstream culture, and avoiding most activities and habits that accentuated Japanese-ness. Above all, the Japanese in America knew that there was no turning back. They were in America to stay, and sacrifices needed to be made for the greater good, whatever that meant.

As children, Peter, Alice, and Gail Yoshitaku distinguished themselves in their public school education to a substantial degree, enough to make their parents proud and to be accepted into the University of California. While Peter and Alice did, in fact, go on to attend school in Berkeley, Gail chose to follow up on the offer made by San Francisco State College, her second choice school, an act that caused quite a ruckus in the Yoshitaku household.

Gail, who had always seemed quite different from her siblings, had a strong predisposition to follow paths of her own, regardless of the consequences. Gail's parents long realized that her passion and strong will were not always qualities that worked to her advantage. As far as Takahiro was concerned, the closer tabs he could keep on Gail — the better, and her attending school in San Francisco greatly reduced that hope.

Gail entered San Francisco State College in the fall of 1968, too late for the summer of love, yet just in time to take a front seat towards experiencing and participating in the social turbulence that was to at first confuse — then cloud — the minds of many American young people.

To describe San Francisco as a "dynamic place" seems wholly inadequate. To suggest that it was a "dynamic place in the 1960s" is a gross understatement. Without any doubt, the era provided to the American people the greatest cultural-revolution since the 1920s. Emergent wrinkles in the social climate spawned new liberties for minorities and women, and a new sense of consciousness for nearly everyone. The times were marked with violence in Southeast Asia and confusion amongst youth and others as to why the Vietnam War was worth sending young men into harm's way in a distant land about which few Americans knew anything. It really was a perfect climate for revolution, and American youth missed few opportunities to express their disgust for the war and their distrust in the United States government. The general mantras for legions of American youth was that "If you're going to San Francisco, be sure to wear some flowers in your hair," and the quick-to-become-cliché: "Make love not war!" and "Hell no! We won't go!" Almost anything went in San Francisco. It was a time of protest of the over-reach of government. It was a time of personal exploration relative to new freedoms that offered insights into the human psyche and intrapersonal expression.

For Gail, being on her own in San Francisco was the most exciting experience that she had encountered in her young life. In San Francisco, Gail felt answerable only to her college professors and to the well-ingrained sense of right and wrong that her parents had worked tirelessly to instill in her mind. While getting good grades and properly attending to her studies was a personal nonnegotiable, a certain evolution took place in her mindset regarding the social constructs of law, order, and justice. She first began to examine, and then to question, nearly every aspect of her American experience. Before long, Gail found herself in active protest of her government and its apparent oppression of ideals associated with the prophetic soul of her generation.

Humble Beginnings

By most any standard, the housing accommodations for the visiting faculty of the Ikemoto Academy were humble, if not outright meager. Each apartment in the housing facility possessed a chair, a writing desk, a twin bed, a small refrigerator, a small stove, a wash basin, a baseboard heater, and a bathroom. Each housing unit possessed forty square meters of floor space, and no frills. Women faculty members were housed on the second floor, and men were housed on the ground floor.

For Cody, the units reminded him of a college dormitory room, albeit being slightly larger and better equipped. For Cynthia, the apartments reminded her of the accommodations that were afforded to the housekeeper in her parents Mercer Island home, a space that was roughly twice the area occupied by the walk-in closet attached to her childhood bedroom. Both Cynthia and Cody made the best of the less than optimal housing arrangements.

Cody adorned each of the four walls of his nook with taped sheets of paper that were scrawled with Japanese words and phrases that he wished to learn. Cynthia decorated her walls with framed pastel drawings that illustrated various important milestones in her recent life. Two drawings were particularly outstanding. One involved an anime sketch of her and several others, with their backs to the viewer as they walked in lock-step through the front entrance of the Ikemoto Academy. The drawing was dated July 2011 and illustrated Cynthia's petite figure, accompanied by Hello Kitty, Mario of video-game fame, and a lean dark-haired individual of unknown identity. The other standout drawing had the appearance of a fruit packing-label with the words: RACCOON DOG SWEET POTATOES emblazoned across a wooden box loaded with what appeared to be sweet potatoes possessing strikingly deep-amethyst flesh. The latter drawing was dated May 20, 2012, the week after Cynthia arrived at the Academy. Other drawings stood out, but none, at the time, seemed quite so fanciful.

It was fair to say that Cynthia's mind was a breeding ground for the fantastic and the preposterous, yet her heart and intent were pure and kind, throughout. Cynthia was spirited, sometimes forceful, and unmistakably conscientious and responsive to human impulses and their auras.

CHAPTER TWO:
FINDING ALCATRAZ

Early Turbulence

Ever since having moved to San Francisco, Gail had pondered Alcatraz Island through the often thick fog that wafted to and fro from the Golden Gate Bridge to locations inland, but she never gave much thought to taking a closer look.

There is no doubt that Alcatraz Island acquired its name from early Spanish maps that labeled the island: *La Isla de los Alcatraces*. A complex retracing of the origin of the word Alcatraces suggests that the intent of Spanish mariners was to describe the island as little more than a haven for pelicans. Located less than two miles off San Francisco's Fort Mason, Alcatraz Island might as well be one of the Farallon Islands to those wishing to leave the island without strong inclination or proper authority. Alcatraz Island is a wind-swept, rocky outpost surrounded by the sometimes treacherous cold waters of the vast San Francisco Bay. The isolation and inhospitable nature of the island for many years provided safety to pelicans and confinement to those incarcerated. In 1868, Alcatraz Island was developed into a military prison. During October 1933, control of Alcatraz Island transferred to the Federal Bureau of Prisons, where between its inception as Alcatraz Federal Penitentiary and its March 1963 decommissioning, it housed some of the most notorious criminals incarcerated in the federal prison system.

Alcatraz Island started the next chapter of its being beginning in March 1964, when several dozen Native American activists endeavored to retake the island under the color afforded to them by an obscure Indian treaty, signed nearly one hundred years previous, that mandated the return of federally held facilities to Native Americans once such installations had outlived their usefulness to the federal government. Swiftly and effectively, the federal government thwarted the advances made by the poorly organized band of protestors and aspiring occupiers.

In November 1969, a variant group of wannabe occupiers arrived at Alcatraz Island with fortified zeal and renewed vigor. On this occasion, the landing party was somewhat more organized, and group members were able to hang their hats and create a presence upon the rocky outpost.

It was clear to Gail that something of importance was brewing on Alcatraz Island. It was less than clear to her, at the time, that her family's struggle to become accepted in American society possessed much of the same abhorrent threadwork as did the historic treatment of Native Americans by the United States government. Between campus war protests and escapades associated with the Native American occupation of Alcatraz Island, a new sensitivity slowly began to emerge from what Gail thought was her collective soul, and little by little she became estranged from anyone who failed to share her sympathies.

The initial party of occupiers in the November 1969 conquest was assembled from a tribally diverse group of charismatic Native Americans from several western states, many of whom were students with strong backgrounds in activism. Toward the termination of the occupation in June 1971, many of the occupiers were found to be non-native opportunists, drug users, and social misfits looking for refuge.

During the spring semester of 1970, Gail met a fellow student named Dwight Fletcher and they quickly became inseparable. Twenty-year-old Dwight was a tall, sturdy, and handsome fellow who was raised in Oakdale, California, where his father worked a large plot of land upon which he grazed cattle and grew alfalfa. Dwight spent many years of his youth laboring on the farm, in which time he developed a strong work ethic that he was able to parlay into academic success once in attendance at San Francisco State. Dwight had a very strong personality and, as Gail soon learned, could be gruff in his disposition, especially when he felt frustrated or underappreciated.

One of the first commonalities recognized by the pair was their shared distaste of the Vietnam War effort exercised by United States forces. Both watched in utter horror as National Guard troops mowed down four protesters at Kent State University on May 4, 1970. That spring Gail and Dwight *heard the drumming* — four shot dead by the U.S. government machine in Ohio. Right or wrong, this is what they heard. Nightly, they followed news reports of the latest casualty figures of the war, and with each day their collective bitterness toward the heavy hand of the U.S. government deepened, widened, and refluxed.

By August 1970, both Gail and Dwight were seriously considering dropping out of college, but only Dwight took the plunge into the limbo of what would appear to most to be a structureless existence. For several weeks, Dwight's roommates allowed him to remain in the residence — which was just about the time that the money from his campus work-study program became exhausted. Finally, realizing that his head was in a really bad place, Dwight worked up the courage to ask Gail if he could move into the small Japantown apartment that her father had rented for her. Reluctantly she agreed to honor his request, with the stipulation that he would immediately find employment.

The first few days of Dwight's job search were marked with disappointment. For the most part he spent his days sitting around Gail's apartment sipping green tea, reading through job listings in both the *Chronicle* and the *Examiner*, and making phone calls when he identified opportunities that had potential. Each evening when Gail returned from school, she became increasingly upset with Dwight's apparent lack of diligence regarding his quest to locate employment. On the fifth night she gave him the ultimatum: "Get a job tomorrow, or be prepared to spend the night out in your truck!"

The next day Dwight found a temporary job unloading container ships on San Francisco's Pier 23. The work was extremely vigorous, even for a strapping young man who had hefted 100-pound bales of alfalfa, from dawn to dusk, during his high school years. For three weeks, Dwight maintained the regimen of unloading cargo ships for twelve hours a day, six days a week. For hours on end, Dwight lifted and walked boxes, bales, and barrels of every description from point A to point B. Most every night, when he got off his shift at 5:00 p.m., he was never too exhausted to venture down to a local longshoreman bar where the stevedores, dockworkers, and various wharfies mingled until it was nearly time to wake up for the next shift. Since this arrangement kept Dwight off of Gail's turf, it didn't seem to occur to her to give him a particularly hard time about the matter.

One evening at the Long Wharf Tavern, Dwight met a longshoreman by the name of Joseph Norris. Norris was a Native American of Blackfoot bloodline who, when not on longshoreman duty, operated a small slip off of Pier 40 from where he launched a ferry and small cargo transports. During their initial meeting, the two talked about the Native American occupation that was taking place on Alcatraz Island. According to Norris, something close to 100 people were regularly occupying the encampment with numbers surging close to 200 with increasing frequency. Norris went on to bring Dwight up to date on the current state of the occupation and its history.

The current occupation had started the previous November when five Native Americans jumped into the waters

off Alcatraz Island after a boat had brought them into range of
the shoreline. Once stepping onto dry land, the quintet claimed
the island by *Right of Discovery*, a particular strain of land
claim that had reference to the manner in which Colonial
powers usurped control of newly discovered lands during the
so-called *Age of Discovery*. Without delay, the Coast Guard
removed the group with force. That same day, a larger group
gained a foothold on the island, fourteen of whom remained on
Alcatraz overnight. The next morning the group left the island,
but not before the men laid an additional claim to Alcatraz by
the Right of Discovery proclamation. Ten days later, a much
larger contingent set foot on Alcatraz Island. This time,
seventy-nine Native Americans were members of the landing
party. This action and the resulting occupation were announced
to the world in what became known as the *Alcatraz
Proclamation.*

In this declaration, leaders of the Alcatraz occupation
and reclamation effort notified the federal government of their
willingness to purchase Alcatraz Island for twenty-four dollars
in glass beads and other trinkets, roughly what had been paid to
the Lenape Indians for Manhattan Island some three and a half
centuries earlier. The decree went on to state that
administrators of the proclamation would place a portion of the
island's land into a trust to be administered by the *Bureau of
Caucasian Affairs* (BCA). In closing, the group offered to
share their religion, their education, and their way of living,
toward delivering to the white race a level of civilization
whereby all white brothers could be brought up from their
savage and unhappy state.

What Joseph told Dwight moved him to a degree that
he started to shake and break out in a rash. At one point, Joseph
became so concerned about Dwight's wellbeing that he insisted
that the pair take a walk along the waterfront. It was this night

that Dwight first spoke to anyone about his own Native American heritage.

"Joseph, I'm really hearing you man, what you have to say. It really cuts me deep. My grandmother was a member of the Pit River tribe up near Modoc. So, I guess I'm one-quarter Indian myself."

At that point, Joseph stepped back from Dwight and took a good long look at him, much as if he were looking directly into Dwight's soul. "Hey, I knew something was eating at you, man, at the Long Wharf," Joseph said. "You know this fight, this cause, this movement, is important, don't you?" With a silent nod from Dwight, Joseph continued. "At first I wasn't sure that I could trust you, man, but now —"

Looking puzzled Dwight said, "Trust me for what?"

Passing over Dwight's inquiry, Joseph detoured, "Hey, Dwight, have you ever been to Alcatraz Island? Do you want to go with me to Alcatraz Island?"

Thinking that Joseph was either drunk, insane, or just kidding around, Dwight backed up to appraise whether Joseph was pulling his leg, saying, "I don't know, Joseph. I'm really not up for a swim."

"No, no, you don't understand. I can get us a ride out to Alcatraz this weekend," said Joseph.

"Yeah, I really don't know about this weekend. I promised the ol' lady that I'd hang out with her. I've been working a lot lately, you know."

"Dwight, the invitation is open, and your gal is invited too. Plan to stay the night. Things get real interesting at night out on the rock."

"Yeah, man. I don't know, and I don't want to inconvenience you if the plans fall through."

"Don't even worry about it, man," said Joseph. "A boatload of people and supplies will be headed over to the island whether you and your gal come along or not. Hey, what is your girlfriend's name?"

"Gail, Gail is her name. And, uh, I think she might be into going. No, no — I'm sure that she would want to go."

As expected it didn't take any prodding, whatsoever, to get Gail energized for the trip to Alcatraz Island. She could hardly wait to meet Joseph, or Indian Joe, as most people called him. The only thing that seemed to trouble her was that Dwight had never taken the time to talk with her about his Native American heritage, but she decided not to make an issue of the matter since the dialog was now wide open.

It was October 3, 1970. Dwight and Gail arrived at Pier 40 well before sunrise. The pair was tremendously eager to start their adventure, and that included experiencing every conceivable or inconceivable manifestation and nuance that the day might bring. Gail brought a writing tablet in which to record her experiences and other important information that would likely come her way during the weekend, but she resisted bringing a camera as she well knew that the event was not to be a sightseeing outing. The fall morning possessed a slight chill in the air, yet the air was relatively dry. This allowed for easy passage of the sun's rays, as the yellow-orange orb hovered low in the sky, above the hills to the east, before making its sharp skyward dash towards the heavens. The couple held hands and kissed just as Indian Joe drove up in his beaten-up work truck.

"Hey, Dwight! I'm glad you could make it! Is that your gal, Gail? Or should I say, I hope that your name is Gail. Never mind. I'm Joseph. You can call me Indian Joe."

"Yes, I'm Gail. Thank you so much for inviting us."

"Well, we won't be leaving for an hour or so, not until the others arrive," said Joseph. "Can I get the two of you to help me load some supplies from my warehouse?"

"We would be happy to help," said Dwight.

By 9:00 a.m. the boat was fully loaded with supplies, and the skipper had completed instructing the passengers concerning personal safety and offloading procedures. "All aboard!" said the captain as the converted fishing trawler slowly pushed away from the dock.

Close to forty people were crammed on the deck and in the boat's cabin. Probably everyone wondered whether they'd be able to make the twenty-minute trip out to the island without attracting the Coast Guard, as the vessel was surely in violation for having exceeded its passenger limit. Slowly, surely, from side-to-side, the boat waddled like a massive elephant seal skirting across the sand, as it moved across the cold bay toward Alcatraz. As the boat approached the rocky outpost, the motor fluttered and stopped whereby the boat's momentum was just adequate to slowly glide itself alongside the dock.

"Hey, throw us a rope," said Indian Joe to the contingent of men, women, and children who clambered down the pathway to the dock to greet the incoming group of visitors to the island.

"Hey Joseph, did you bring my package, man?" said a tall lanky blond-haired fellow wearing a Native American headdress, cut-off jeans, and blue-tinted sunglasses.

"Hey, I don't know, man. Who are you?" said Joseph.

"They call me Waldo, as in Emerson, man," said the fellow.

"Hey, all I know is that some guy dropped off a big heavy package of something and said there'd be a guy to pick it up on the other end."

Up on the landing of the rocky fortress was a carnival atmosphere. People were playing basketball, singing, and dancing, while others simply mulled about, looking much as if they were waiting for something consequential to happen. In the background were the various prison buildings, structures with their window glass long broken-out, paneless apertures where sheets and other makeshift curtains billowed and furled with the nearly constant breeze that swept the island. If any of the newcomers had hopes of laying claim to a piece of virgin wall or water tower on which to spray paint some prophetic scrawling, they were out of luck, just as were the multitude of adventurers and glory-seekers who flooded into California following John Marshall's gold discovery in 1848. Just as then, not a single piece of viable territory was left unclaimed.

It wasn't clear what Dwight and Gail hoped to gain from their first-hand exposure to what had the potential of becoming a very important chapter in the American Indian movement, nor was it clear how they might transform what they learned into a unique sense of personal enlightenment.

By noon all of the boat's cargo had been unloaded and carried up to the landing that marked the level ground from which the various prison buildings were erected. As the boat pulled away from the dock, a very powerful sense of isolation and uncertainty overtook Gail, and then Dwight. The pair was now immured to twenty-two acres of land on an island that was little more than a mile from the northern-most portion of San Francisco. Here they were to remain in isolation and confinement until the following morning, when the vessel that delivered them to the outpost would return to shuttle them back to the pier from which they'd departed.

There is something ironic about the choice of the Native American contingent to have chosen to occupy or claim Right of Discovery to Alcatraz Island; after all, local Native American groups historically shunned the island, almost entirely. The general consensus seems to have been that Native Americans thought that Alcatraz was cursed. Known oral histories suggest that the Indians referred to the island as "Evil Island," well before the arrival of the white race. Furthermore, perhaps not coincidentally, the way that things were so far shaking out, it appeared that modern times had done little to improve the island's image. If the island had a history of misfortune for the Indian race, other races of men who had come to the island, over the years, didn't appear to fare much better. From what it appears, finding Alcatraz didn't particularly seem to be in the best interest of any of those who'd stepped onto the isolation of its treacherous windswept precipices. The truth seems to be that a trip to the rock doomed the lives of many men, many of whom would never be able to shake from their minds the sense of helplessness and isolation that the Island of the Pelicans delivered mercilessly with frequent recurrence.

The bleakness of the island and its accommodations — particularly with the decrepit buildings silhouetted against a world-class city like San Francisco — really seemed to dampen some of the energy associated with the moment. Throughout the day, Gail and Dwight could hear ceaseless drumming, which as the day progressed into night became accompanied by chanting, howling, yelling, and cursing. Dwight later learned that Waldo's large package contained a case of Jim Beam, a bunch of strong Columbian herb, and a bottle of pills called *screamers*. In fact, it had been Waldo's package that served as fuel for the rowdiness that carried on until dawn.

The next morning Gail and Dwight were on their feet at sunrise, having never really fallen asleep that night, instead opting to take turns on the lookout for shadows coming their way. After rolling up their sleeping bags, they groggily surveyed the now quiet ruins for signs of life. *Where was Joseph?* they wondered. Surely he must have heard all of the night's proceedings.

Gail and Dwight could see people starting to walk toward them after exiting a distant building. They could just barely make out Joseph's robust physique among the figures that were progressing toward them. Apparently, there was a large contingent of the occupiers that had barricaded themselves in one of the machine shops on the far periphery of the complex.

"Hey, Dwight, where did you and Gail sleep last night?" Joseph asked.

Squinting his tired eyes in the direction of Joseph and trying to focus, Dwight said, "We didn't sleep a wink. We spent the entire night just trying to stay out of the line of fire."

"That damn Waldo Emerson! He's responsible for all of this. Some of the folks that come out here are coming for the wrong reasons or are falling to the ill virtues of a few bad apples. I'm really sorry that you had to see this, Gail. It makes it close to impossible to get support for our cause with this sort of nonsense going on. We will need to work to banish Mr. Emerson."

Absorbing much of the disheartenment and frustration that accompanied Joseph's words, Dwight and Gail let the stark silence of the moment do their talking. Picking up their gear before ambling down the pathway to the dock, the pair just gazed at poor, old, good-hearted and good-intentioned Joe and broke into half smiles.

That afternoon, subsequent to arriving at Gail's apartment, Dwight said to Gail, "I've been thinking about going back to Oakdale and helping my dad on the ranch."

Gail, genuinely surprised by Dwight's revelation, stepped back, looking deep into Dwight's eyes. "When do you have to go?"

"I don't know, but soon. I want to stay together, but there just doesn't seem to be anything for me here anymore."

"What do you mean, there isn't anything for you here? I'm here," said Gail.

"Listen, Gail. I just think that I'm a distraction in your life right now. I mean, I don't want to get in the way of your goals. We can still see each other, and Oakdale is only two hours away."

"Yeah, you're right. We can still see each other on weekends, or every other weekend," Gail said with surprisingly little attachment. "It is probably best this way, until I complete my degree."

Into the Abyss

For some reason, Dwight believed that the best way for him to get his head together was to bring himself back to the family homestead in Oakdale. He felt that this little corner of the world was the only venue that he felt he had ever conquered. To come back to the location of his roots seemed like a logical place for him to reconnect with himself and to serve as a launch pad from which to bring some clarity into the next chapter of his life. As Dwight expected, his mother welcomed him back into the family home with open arms. His father, however, was considerably less keen about the idea as he felt that such an arrangement lacked sufficient opportunity for the personal growth for his eldest son. He felt that by now Dwight should either be completing his college education or settling into a career pathway.

In accepting Dwight back into the family household, his father not only expected him to assist with the day-to-day chores on the sprawling property, but to gain a foothold in another employment venue such that he could begin to develop some sense of personal identity as a productive community member. Dwight's father was not so much concerned with the variety of employment that his son selected, as much as he was solicitous to Dwight that he find something soon and stick with it.

In the meanwhile, Gail settled into her junior year at San Francisco State. Most days she immersed herself in her studies to a point where she didn't allow herself to become distracted by Dwight's absence from her life. Early on in their physical estrangement, she would write Dwight a brief note most every day, if for no other reason than to let him know that she was thinking of him. Since Dwight recognized the letters to be lacking in content that required immediate response, he felt it acceptable to dispatch a single letter on a weekly basis. For the most part, the letters seemed to only serve as a means to prolong or to prop up an intimate association that would most surely die.

Towards satisfying his father's employment mandates, Dwight secured a job transporting freshly harvested almonds to a local processing plant. He found the job uninteresting, but he felt that the position carried more prestige than laboring with the migrant workers in the orchards. Dwight also appreciated the fact that trucking produce to the various processing plants allowed him to network with some of the workers and foremen regarding other employment opportunities. In his first week on the job he was able to secure future work transporting oranges and lemons, in a position that would likely last from late November until late February or early March. For the first time in quite a while, Dwight was beginning to feel like he was in charge. Not only did he have a job, but he had another one lined up that would start a month down the road.

With his new sense of contentment, Dwight felt inspired to write Gail a brief note. In that letter he shared the news about his new job and discussed the possibility of making a trip to San Francisco for a visit during the Thanksgiving recess.

In the three short weeks that had elapsed since Dwight had left San Francisco, Gail had largely resumed her independence. She was happy to hear from Dwight, but she was aware that their lives had taken different paths. Gail felt strongly that she wanted a man who was college educated, and in her heart she felt that Dwight had made an error that would likely haunt him for the remainder of his life.

Several days after Dwight mailed his note to Gail, he received not only a communication from her that looked a lot like a "Dear John" letter, but as well a letter that he had hoped he would never see.

The very official dispatch read:

SELECTIVE SERVICE SYSTEM
ORDER TO REPORT FOR
ARMED FORCES PHYSICAL EXAMINATION

To: Dwight Fletcher
        893 Wainwright Road
        Oakdale, CA 95361

You are hereby directed to present yourself for the Armed Forces Physical Examination by reporting to:

ASSEMBLY ROOM – 2nd FLOOR FEDERAL BLDG.
401 North San Joaquin Street
Stockton, CA 95202

on: November 10, 1970   at: 7:00 AM

IMPORTANT NOTICE:

Read Each Paragraph Carefully…

After reading and absorbing the gravity of the contents of the letter from the Selective Service System, Dwight jumped into his truck toward the delivery of the information to Gail with much the same urgency as a dying man with only hours to live. As he motored westward, Dwight pondered: *Those bastards don't think that they can send me off to war, do they?*

His mind raced with such fury that he couldn't even reason his way through the matter. *They can't do this to me — I have rights! They can't ship me off to Vietnam. My work is of national importance in the food supply chain. The government can't get in the way of the American people's right to eat almonds. It's just plain wrong! Hey — I'm a lover not a fighter. Almonds — not war! Does that work? What am I thinking? They don't care about me. I'm just a pawn, a nobody. The government doesn't care who they send to be slaughtered. Maybe I can hide out on Alcatraz Island with Joseph Norris and Waldo Emerson. That's what I'll do. They'll maintain my cover, won't they? Man, I've got to get to San Francisco to talk with Gail. She'll know what to do.*

The trip to San Francisco was the most excruciating two-hour drive Dwight ever knew. When he reached Oakland he felt a great sense of relief. He was almost where he thought he needed to be. All he had to do now was make it over the Oakland Bay Bridge, cross over Van Ness Avenue, and then turn onto Laguna Street, and he'd be in Japantown and then at Gail's door.

While dodging the draft might have been an acceptable response in very liberal San Francisco, especially with Dwight's chosen circle of friends and acquaintances, such avoidance would never receive any support in a very conservative rural community such as Oakdale, or for that matter — in any Central Valley community. Above all, Dwight knew that such a move wouldn't gain any traction with his father. In his short life, Dwight had never been as conflicted as he was between his moral distaste for the war effort and his government, and the sense-of-duty lecture that he knew was forthcoming from his father. Gail, dear, sweet, thoughtful Gail, seemed to be the only sense of reason that he could tap into during this time of great internal turmoil.

As Dwight exited his truck and headed through the heavy wrought iron gate leading to Gail's apartment, he experienced great uncertainty regarding exactly what he had to say about his predicament. But here he was at Gail's door, at 8:30 p.m. on a Friday night, unannounced. After several false starts and stops, Dwight's knuckles finally impacted Gail's apartment door. Rap, rap, rap. "Gail, open up. It's me, Dwight."

Gail, who largely felt that she was over Dwight and moving on, was particularly pleased that her estrangement from him had been initiated so amicably and that it ultimately had caused so little pain. She maintained fairly strong feelings for Dwight, but allowed the idea of reconnecting, from where they'd left off, to occupy only a very small portion of her reality. As such, she was somewhat stunned to see him at her door.

"Dwight! What are you doing here?"

Having prepared what he was going to say to Gail for close to three hours, Dwight couldn't seem to induce a single word. He just stood in the doorway — vacant and voiceless, looking much as if his world were collapsing about him, his eyes glazed over and his body language aggravated.

"Please come in. What's wrong? You do not look well." Clearing schoolwork and books from her couch to the floor, she said, "Sit here! Tell me what's going on."

Following Gail's directive, Dwight just sat and stared deep into Gail's beautiful eyes for a moment. "Gail, I've really missed you."

"Surely you didn't drive all the way out from Oakdale just to share this with me?"

"No, you're right. I just wanted to see you, to talk with you. I just wanted to tell you —" Dwight said, pausing, as he grappled with the difficulty of accepting that what he had to say, had to exit from his mouth.

"What do you want to tell me, Dwight?"

Sitting up and leaning forward, with his elbows at his knees and his hands clasped, Dwight's eyes made the journey from his feet to Gail's eyes. While slowly looking up from the floor towards Gail, he said, "I think that I'm going to Vietnam. I received an order to appear in Stockton for a physical exam in a couple of weeks."

"No, no! Dwight. Please tell me that you are kidding," Gail said as she stood and placed her hand on Dwight's cheek.

"No, Gail, I am serious. Here is the letter from the Selective Service."

Taking the letter into her hands, with her mouth agape, Gail carefully examined the content of the document, before exclaiming, "Oh, no, Dwight. Those corrupt bastards are going to send you off to their dirty little war. Oh, my God. What are you going to do?"

"I don't know. My dad would totally freak if I didn't go. He's kind of gung-ho about this sort of thing. He was in Normandy, and he still tells stories about the gallantry of his unit."

Throughout that evening and into the next day, Gail helped Dwight come to grips with the reality that unless he failed his physical examination, there was a substantial likelihood that he'd be drafted into military service. After a breakfast with little fanfare, Gail sent Dwight on his way back to Oakdale with a promise that she would continue to write.

Dwight reported for induction in the United States Army on December 11, 1970. And after nearly eight weeks of boot camp he was in the jungles of Cambodia. His assignment was to serve in the 101st Airborne Division directly in support of the First Army of Vietnam's 1st Division. Dwight's specific duty was to serve as a helicopter fueling technician at Firebase Vandergrift.

On February 8, 1971, Operation Lam Son 719 and its companion operation Dewey Canyon II commenced in the southeastern jungles of Laos. While this operation was extremely complex and politically charged, the U.S. objective was to push close to 20,000 South Vietnamese soldiers into southern Laos to disrupt the supply lines that were feeding the aggressions of North Vietnamese forces. In short, the goal was to shut down the flow of men and materials that moved down the Ho Chi Minh trail. Since U.S. troops and advisors were prohibited from stepping onto Laotian soil by the Cooper-Church Amendment, the military was limited in service to support-roles that facilitated the South Vietnamese advancement into Laos. This largely turned U.S. involvement in the offensive into an air support mission, a mission that involved supplying continuous aid and evacuation to the poorly trained, incompetent, and incapable South Vietnamese Army. In the end, the lives of close to 10,000 members of the South Vietnamese contingent were lost, and the supply lines remained largely intact.

The entire undertaking and the outcome of the Lam Son 719 mission was a complete disaster, just as was the pattern of things to come out of the Vietnam War for the remainder of Dwight's tour of duty. Dwight's first and most important mission during his enlistment occurred in February and March of 1971, during a befuddled operation that became a metaphor of his life for the remainder of the decade. The frustration and ineffectiveness of the Vietnam War effort became a template and a figurative vehicle for the internal frustration and fecklessness that Dwight sensed in his life.

The long and the short of it was that Dwight remained out of harm's way during his entire tour of duty and that his assignments were largely *hurry-up-and-wait* missions. In Dwight's eyes, nothing about his tour stood out as being particularly interesting or important. The only good thing

Dwight could say about his service was that he didn't directly harm anyone or anything. Other than having the opportunity to travel to another part of the world, the experience, in his mind, was entirely worthless. The lack of meaning that Dwight experienced during his time in the army seamlessly blended with the six years of emptiness that would follow once he returned to Oakdale, California.

When Dwight was discharged in the spring of 1973, he was greeted by his parents at Sacramento's McClellan Air Force Base with a fanfare that resembled a hero's welcome, his mother jumping up and down gleefully as he came into view. During the drive back to Oakdale, Dwight's father wanted to know all of the details of his son's adventures in Vietnam. He wanted to know about the weather, what the people were like, what foods they ate, and the various dangers that he was subjected to. "Don't tell me about how many gooks you killed, not in front of your mother," Dwight's father said, in a ribbing manner, referencing his son's well-established aversion to the war effort. During the two-hour drive, Dwight's father did most of the talking while Dwight sat slumped in the back seat, staring blankly out the window at the miles upon miles of green grass that formed the highway's boundary. "We'll have to set you up with a job pretty quick, buster," counseled Dwight's father.

Dwight was soon to learn that public perception of the war was at an all-time low. Visions of the Mei Lei Massacre were still on the minds of many of the American people. Many Americans pictured U.S. Armed Forces marauding through villages, setting homes ablaze, raping women, and murdering the defenseless. For many veterans, finding a job became a real challenge.

After returning to the family home, Dwight spent the first couple of weeks being catered to by his mother. She made his breakfast, washed his clothes, sorted his socks, and even made his bed. During the third week, after his mother launched an effort to trim his toenails, Dwight decided it was time to visit the packing company where he worked prior to his service in Vietnam. He was sure that his old boss, Mr. Reynolds, would hire him back as a truck driver.

On that sunny day in late April 1973, Dwight pulled into the Valley Distributors Inc. plant, where he flew up the staircase leading to Mr. Reynolds' office. The door was open and he stuck in his head, "Hello, Mr. Reynolds. It's me, Dwight Fletcher."

"You're that boy who went to Vietnam, ain't you?"

"Yes, sir, I am."

"Have a seat for a spell. Well, I'm glad to see that you're still in one piece and that the Japs, I mean the gooks, didn't hurt you none. What can I do you for, Mr. Fletcher?"

"I was wondering if you might have a position for me."

"Well, son, we're kind of between production lines now. We start tomatoes in early June, and then peppers, and then more tomatoes, and ... I don't think that nothing's going to come around until June, boy. Come back in June. I might be able to set you up then."

"Well, Mr. Reynolds, do you know anyone who might be hiring now?"

"You might try Central Packing — they're always looking for fellas. And I hear they pay good too. Hey, boy, I wish you well in your pursuits. And welcome home, son. Welcome home!"

In the back of his mind Dwight had heard of Central Packing, but he wasn't quite sure where it was located. It seemed to him that it was just south of Highway 108, set back along the foothills to the east of town. Dwight's hunch was right, and before long he was pulling into the parking lot of the plant's front office. Upon entering the establishment and requesting information regarding available positions, the receptionist handed him a job application that he quickly filled out and returned.

"It says here that your most recent work history was in the U.S. Army," said the receptionist.

"Yes, I just completed a tour of duty in Vietnam," Dwight said with an unexpected sense of pride.

"Were you honorably discharged?"

"Yes, ma'am, I was."

"Okay, can you start tomorrow at 7:00 a.m. sharp? We pay $7.50 an hour."

"Yes ma'am!" said Dwight. "I'll be here early!"

During the drive home Dwight reflected with amazement how he was able to line up a job so fast — no interview, no background check — just his friendly outgoing nature and his good military service record, he thought. The only thing that didn't occur to Dwight to ask, while at the facility, was the type of work he'd be doing. But for $7.50 an hour, he wasn't much concerned other than to make sure that he didn't wear any clothes that he didn't mind soiling.

At 7:00 a.m. the next morning, he met his foreman, Duke Billings. Duke instructed Dwight to put on a pair of rubber boots and a pair of elbow length rubber gloves, and to fasten a full-body-length vinyl apron around his torso.

The pair then went to the adjoining room where Duke stood in the doorway. "DWIGHT, THE PROCESSING ROOM CAN BE VERY LOUD. ALWAYS WEAR YOUR SAFETY GEAR AND GOGGLES WHEN YOU ARE IN THIS ROOM, IS THAT UNDERSTOOD?"

"Yes, it is understood," said Dwight.

"I CAN'T HEAR YOU."

"YES, SIR. IT IS UNDERSTOOD!"

Dwight still remained unclear as to what his particular job in the plant was. All that he could be sure of was that cattle walked into one end of the building, and dressed and processed beef rolled out on carts from the other end.

"OKAY, DWIGHT. WE'RE GOING TO PUT YOU ON THE STRIPPING LINE. YOUR JOB IS TO STRIP OR PULL THE SKIN OFF THE HANGING CARCASSES AS THEY MOVE DOWN THE OVERHEAD CONVEYOR LINE. IS THAT UNDERSTOOD?"

"YES, SIR. I UNDERSTAND, MR. BILLINGS."

By 8:00 a.m. Dwight was stripping the thick sheets of hairy skin from each carcass as it moved down the line. The work was bloody and physically demanding. By the end of his twelve-hour shift, Dwight was so exhausted that he could barely remove the various layers of his protective gear. Completely beat, he climbed into his truck and headed home where he showered and immediately went to bed.

The next day, and for many months thereafter, he repeated the task of stripping carcasses. Grip, pull, twist, re-grip, pull, twist, and yank — for twelve hours a day, four days a week. After six-months of exemplary service, Dwight was offered a job on the bleeding line, which he jumped at as the position was jointly less strenuous and of greater compensation.

After two years at the plant he was able to put away enough money to place a down payment on a piece of land that his father offered to sell him at a good price. Immediately, Dwight set into working his property, settling upon sweet potatoes as his primary crop. Four days of the week, it was the gruesome task of draining blood and other bodily fluids from bovines, and for the remainder, it was enriching soil, turning soil, preparing plots, and planting sweet potato slips. By the fall of 1977, Dwight was harvesting his first crop of Hannah sweet potatoes, and by the following year he was experimenting with a not-so-productive variety of Japanese sweet potato.

In the late spring of 1979, Dwight decided to see if he could locate Gail. After coming up empty handed, he realized that he'd tucked the contact information of Gail's parents, Takahiro and Emi Yoshitaku, into an old text book that he'd kept. Immediately, Dwight made the phone call.

"Hello, Mr. Yoshitaku. This is Dwight Fletcher, and I'm trying to reach Gail."

"Oh, Dwight, yes we have heard Gail speaking of you. You joined the Army, didn't you?"

"Uh, yeah. Actually, I was drafted. Can I please get Gail's phone number from you?"

"Yes, Dwight, let me get the book. Oh, here it is."

"So, Mr. Yoshitaku, what is Gail doing these days?"

"Well, she is still living in San Francisco, but I think that I should let her give you the details."

"How are you and Mrs. Yoshitaku?"

"We have been very blessed. We have been successful with our farm and now we have five grandchildren."

"Oh, that's great. Well it is very nice talking with you, Mr. Yoshitaku. Thank you for providing me with Gail's phone number."

"Okay, Dwight. Goodbye."

After getting off of the phone with Mr. Yoshitaku, Dwight couldn't help but wonder whether any of the grandchildren that Mr. Yoshitaku referred to were Gail's offspring.

The next day Dwight worked up the courage to give Gail a call. One ring, two rings, three rings, click. "Hello," Gail said.

"Hello, Gail?"

"Who is this?" said the voice on the other end of the line.

"It's Dwight, Dwight Fletcher."

"Dwight! Dwight Fletcher," Gail screamed into the phone.

"Yes, it is me, in the flesh."

"Dwight, it has been a very long time. How are you?"

"Oh, I've been okay, I guess. I didn't lose any body parts over in Vietnam, anyway. What have you been doing? Did you finish your degree?"

"Yes, I completed my degree. Now I'm working as a bookkeeper for a mail order Asian-oriented seed company located in Oakland."

"I have to ask. Are you still single?"

"Boy, that is really to the point, Dwight," Gail laughed. Yes! I am just a single girl living the dream. How about you?"

"Well, since you asked, I'm a bachelor with no current love interest. I live in Oakdale where I have a home and five acres of sweet potatoes, including a very tasty, albeit not particularly productive, strain that was developed in Japan."

"I do like sweet potatoes, Dwight, but five acres? I guess I've just become accustomed to the home-gardener level of production."

"Gail, I'd like to see you, if you are willing."

"Well, I don't know. This week I need to rearrange my bookshelves and the following week I was going to make sweet bean pastries, and, well, I've been meaning to Turtle Wax my car ... Dwight, I would absolutely love to see you, and honestly no time could be soon enough."

"I see you've maintained that acid-sharp sense of humor."

"Don't get your expectation set too high. I just spooled off eight years' worth of stored humor in a single stroke."

"I'd like to come and visit you in San Francisco."

"Dwight, I can't wait."

Dwight was absolutely in heaven. Not only was he making good money in his regular job at the meat packing plant and experiencing some success in his farming operation, but he was going to see Gail in San Francisco. The synergy, of all that seemed good in Dwight's life, was intoxicating.

Dwight made a date with Gail to meet in the lounge on the 19th floor of the Mark Hopkins Hotel on July 7, 1979. It was Dwight's hope to capture Gail's beauty against the background of his favorite city. In the moment, the event was magical for the pair. They laughed, measured each other's personal growth, discussed the past, and spoke about the potential of a future together. At the close of the evening, the pair separated. Dwight retired to his hotel room and Gail to her apartment. After the second evening spent together, Dwight returned to Gail's apartment, where the pair talked late into the night, and where he ultimately fell asleep on the couch. By the time the weekend came to a close it was quite apparent to the pair that they had again become a couple.

The couple became man and wife on February 23, 1980, at a small ceremony that took place at the Yoshitaku family home. From that moment on, Gail was the loving wife of Dwight Fletcher of Oakdale, California. And from that moment onward, Dwight devotedly attended to his loving wife's every perceived want or need. In May, Gail announced to Dwight that a new arrival was expected in the Fletcher household early the next year. Cody Hoshi Fletcher was born January 23, 1981.

Cody's early upbringing was loving but uneventful. His mother doted on him nearly around the clock until he entered kindergarten. She then augmented his education at home and encouraged his most every healthy impulse. Gail loved her son and her husband as fully and completely as any mother and wife could. She taught Cody songs and Japanese words and phrases, and tickled his fancy with many of the stories that her parents had told her when she was a child.

One such story that Cody particularly enjoyed was the Japanese folktale, "Momotarō." Momo and tarō, respectively mean "peach" and "eldest-boy." The tale is quite charming.

In this classic tale, an old man and his wife, living in what is now known as the Okayama Prefecture, go about the drudgery of their day-to-day existence with the weighty void of being childless until one day the wife, while washing laundry in a creek, finds a very large white peach floating downstream whereby she brings it home as a supper treat for her husband. Just as the old woman takes a knife to the flesh of the grandiose orb, a boy springs from the fruit, protesting "No, don't cut me."

Much to the amazement of the couple, before their very eyes is the most beautiful baby boy they have ever seen. The child makes the old man and woman's life complete, and they are very happy. As the story goes, the couple raises the boy to be kind, honest, thoughtful, brave, and strong.

When the boy, whom they name Momotarō, becomes fifteen years old, he convinces his father and mother that the time has come for him to rid his country of the threat of the ogres, a particularly unpleasant assembly of mean-spirited savages. In preparation for the trip that Momotarō must make to Ogre Island, his mother prepares him a batch of millet dumplings, and his father supplies him with armor and a fine sword to use in his imminent battle with the ogres. As it turns out, the millet dumplings prove instrumental in their ability to serve as enlistment incentives for his ever-growing army. Three dumplings later, the boy has added a monkey, a spotted dog, and a pheasant to his regiment.

When the boy and his recruits reach the vast sea, they build a boat and proceed across the water to Ogre Island. By the end of the day, the four brave souls have conquered the ogres with very little bloodshed. The enemy's casualties were limited to dog bites, monkey scratches, peck-wounds from the pheasant, and a couple of minor flesh-wounds from Momotarō's sword. In settling battle reparations, the ogres agree to abandon their wicked ways and to forfeit a great treasure consisting of gold, silver, and precious jewels.

Once the quartet has loaded the spoils of their triumph onto their boat, they head back across the sea to the mainland where they build a cart to haul the treasure to Momotarō's home. And, forever thereafter, Momotarō, his parents, the pheasant, the monkey, and the spotted dog live a life characterized by happiness, comfort, and material wealth.

As most boys would, Cody naturally identified with Momotarō and his quest.

Regardless of the personal sacrifices doing so might entail, Gail's life was fully and completely dedicated to her husband and their young son. Her primary objective was to provide Cody with the love and support necessary to be healthy, happy, successful, and fulfilled in every conceivable manner. Gail very well recognized the utility and power of story-telling as an instrument for imparting good judgment, morals, self-discipline, and generalized personal growth.

Another of the many stories that Gail shared with Cody was the tale of "The Mountain Kami and the Fish."

This story involves a specific mystical deity known as a *kami*. In this story there is a very spiritually powerful kami who lives in the mountains by winter and in an agricultural village from spring through fall. After many years of experiencing good crop yields and the company of the kami during the planting, growing, and harvest seasons, it becomes evident to the peasants that it is the kami who is responsible for the village's prosperity.

Then one spring day the kami, while drinking from a particularly calm stretch of water, catches a glimpse of his reflection in the water. By the time he rises to his feet he becomes absolutely horrified with his appearance and bellows across the valley, "I am ugly. I am the ugliest thing alive," before running off into the hills toward his mountain retreat. As the kami makes his break toward the mountains, the people of the village yell: "Don't leave! We love you. We honor you." But it is too late; the Mountain Kami doesn't hear the pleas of the peasants.

In the kami's absence, the crops soon fail, the trees begin to wither, a drought ensues, and all looks entirely hopeless for the people of the village. Realizing their dire state, the peasants consult a very wise old woman about their predicament. Standing aback and thinking for a long, long while, the wise old woman finally offers, "I am very old and have lived a very long life, and I do not recall anyone as ugly as this kami.

Thinking about the old woman's observation, the peasants reply, "His looks do not matter to us. He is our friend. We need him."

At that point, the old woman resumes her deep thought, and finally advises, "Then it is your task is to find someone who is uglier than the kami. You need to find the ugliest soul in the world. You see, the kami is shy, and for all of these years that he has visited the valley, he has never known that he is ugly."

After dedicating much effort and thought to the matter, the peasants come back to the old woman and confide, "We have searched the village and neighboring villages, but we have not found anyone who is uglier than the kami."

After remaining in deep thought for some time, the old woman finally speaks. "What you need to do is go up into the hills and catch a mountain fish." Hearing this, the peasants' faces took on a confused look before the old woman continued, "Think about it. There is nobody as ugly as the mountain fish, with its bugged-out eyes and flapping gills."

Upon catching a mountain fish, the peasants laugh, "Ha ha he he he ho ho. Oh, how perfect. This is a magnificently ugly beast. There could be no more perfect an ugly being in existence. The kami will be so pleased." So the peasants take a bucket containing the live mountain fish high-up into the mountains where the Kami had his home. "Kami of the mountain, please open up the door for us. See what we have brought for you."

When the kami comes out of his house he looks into the bucket and a smile overtakes his face. Then he becomes consumed with laughter. "You have brought me a beast that is uglier than me. Look at her eyes all bugging out and her mouth opened, closed, open. Ha ha ha. What a ridiculous looking creature."

After sharing a hearty prolonged laugh with the peasants, the kami returned to the valley with the peasants where life became eternally good, forever.

Oakdale, California

Just about one hundred miles due east of San Francisco on Highway 120, lies the town of Oakdale. Since the time of Cody's birth in 1981, Oakdale has grown from a town of 9,000 residents to its 2012 population of close to 21,000 residents. The vast majority of those in the greater Oakdale area derive their incomes from agricultural pursuits of one sort or another.

Overall, Oakdale continues to be the same sleepy little town that it has been for much of the last fifty years. In fact, many long-time residents continue to refer to Oakdale as the "Cowboy Capital of the World," a title that makes you wonder if Oakdale is moving in the direction of progress, moving away from progress, or is just a town in a state of prolonged dormancy.

The racial makeup of Oakdale is roughly 68 percent Caucasian and 26 percent Hispanic, with no other race contributing more than 2 percent of the total population. This racial composition has been largely consistent over the last twenty years. Overall, town life is peaceful and characterized by racial harmony. In the high school environment rivalries do though develop when a group or person threatens the status quo established by the cowboy culture. As will become evident, the cowboy culture of Oakdale was less than inviting when it came to accepting Cody as a member of the community.

In the early years, when Dwight was building his foundation in agriculture, Gail and her young son were partners in adventure. Some summer days, the pair would drive to Turlock to visit Grandma and Grandpa Yoshitaku. Other days they would follow the Sonora Pass road through the gold country towns of Jamestown, Sonora, and Twain Harte. Once the pair just kept on driving all the way to the 9,628-foot summit of the Sonora Pass where they marveled that snow was present on the side of the road, even in the depth of the hot summer temperatures that prevailed in the Central Valley.

While visiting the summit, Cody discovered an ornate plaque that referenced a man named Andrew Fletcher as the first individual who "called to attention" the utility of developing this pass through the mountains. Apparently, the current Sonora Pass road follows the initial wagon road that was proposed by Fletcher in 1862 and developed by 1865. Andrew Fletcher was able to convince state planners of the importance of connecting Tuolumne County with the isolated mining camps of Mono County. Taking advantage of Cody's surprising observation, Gail, who never missed an opportunity to build up her son, counseled, "Cody, I don't know if you are related to Andrew Fletcher, but if you are — you have pioneer blood on both sides of your family. I just know that you're going to do something big one day, son."

Not all, however, was carefree and leisurely for Cody. When he reached ten years of age, his father started the process of grooming his boy regarding the vocation of crop production. In early lessons, Dwight would simply drive along the thoroughfares that divided his fields and point to important landmarks and operations that were being attended to by his migrant workforce. As Cody learned more about his father's agricultural venues, Dwight introduced him to several of the field laborers and encouraged him to watch their processes and to learn their skills. After observing new tasks or operations, Dwight would often quiz his son regarding the depth of his learning. Dwight's overriding goal for Cody, at that time, was that he be able to understand what his father did for a living and be able to explain to a third party the mechanics of his agricultural operation. Sometimes the intensity of Dwight's lessons for Cody became a bone of contention for Gail, but as a dutiful wife she never let the issue become a wedge between her and Dwight.

And so the days elapsed. Dwight continued to work by day at the processing plant and by afternoon, evening, and weekend in his drive to build his sweet potato enterprise. Little by little he would add a half-acre here or an acre there to his operation, but it took much time and money to grow the business. Still, he prospered. He was able to build additions to his home and to provide well beyond the basic needs of his small family.

When Cody turned twelve, much to Gail's dismay, Dwight bought him a Yamaha 200 motorcycle, and that boy — well, he was in his element. He learned not only to ride the motorbike, but to become so skilled on the vehicle that it almost seemed to grow out of him, much as if it were an appendage of his being. In so doing, Cody learned every inch of every rural dirt road within miles. Having scoured the neighboring roads and fields with such frequency, he found himself able to keep his father informed regarding the agricultural pursuits of nearly every farmer in and about Oakdale.

But Cody's life was not, in the eyes of his father, to be spent merely on playful recreation. By the time Cody was a freshman in high school Dwight mandated that Cody accompany him to the fields to learn the sweet potato business from the ground up. This included developing an iron-clad understanding of all processes associated with the family business of producing sweet potatoes.

Just prior to the spring of 1997, Dwight presented a directive to Cody that he be responsible for a one-quarter acre plot which he was to manage entirely, from preparing the field prior to planting, up through the harvesting process. This required that Cody plow the field with his father's John Deere tractor, mix the plowed soil with nutrient amendments, plant each sweet potato slip by hand, manually weed the plot, provide daily irrigation, and, ultimately, to remove the mature sweet potato crop from the ground with the John Deere. Before Cody even stepped onto his plot, his father directed him to calculate the number of sweet potato slips that his operation would require. Cody based his calculation on several factors, including the square footage area of an acre, the distance between adjacent rows, and the planting distance between adjacent plants.

First Cody tackled calculating the area associated with his quarter-acre plot. Since a square mile possesses an area of 640 acres, Cody knew that he could start his calculation based on the area of a square mile in acres, and the distance of a mile in feet. Since a mile has a distance of 5,280 feet, then a square mile has 5,280 feet x 5280 feet or an area of 27,878,400 square feet. Dividing this last number by 640 acres informed Cody that a single acre of land had an area that was 43,560 square feet. Since Cody only was required to farm one-quarter of an acre, this meant that his plot only needed to be 10,890 square feet in area. Taking the square root of 10,890 square feet, Cody discovered that his plot was to be a square piece of land that was roughly 105 feet to a side. Based on a rule of thumb on the Fletcher farm, Cody would make each row of sweet potatoes five feet apart and would place adjacent plants five feet apart. This meant that Cody's plot would require something close to 440 sweet potato slips, for his plot formed a square with twenty-one slips to a side.

That spring, Cody plowed and provided amendments to his staked-off region and waited, and then waited some more, until he was certain that no possible threat of frost existed. When the proper moment came about, he picked up the stock he needed from the curing room and proceeded to plant each of his four hundred and forty slips. After an entire weekend of planting, Cody, with great care, moved and reconnected the irrigation pipes above his fledgling plants and then, with a great sense of achievement pumping through his entire body, he turned the valve, thus providing his incipient crop with the first of, by his calculations, 150 to 180 of such waterings. In this moment, as he surveyed his plot, wiping the sweat from his brow, an overwhelming sense of pride and accomplishment overtook Cody. *Yes,* Cody thought as he surveyed his field, *my father is demanding and perhaps tyrannical at times, but his intentions are very good.*

With sustained diligence and a sense of pride and care, perhaps only known to the gardener, Cody's little crop flourished and prospered. On that mid-October day in 1997 when Cody pulled the tractor up to his plot he could hardly contain his excitement. Stepping down from the tractor, Cody took a walk around the perimeter of his thriving plot for the last time. Just as he started to step up into the John Deere's cab, his father appeared and the two exchanged small talk, Dwight offering praise to Cody's work ethic and follow-through. Finally, Cody stepped into the tractor and cranked the starter, yet the engine only sputtered. When Cody restarted the engine, again it sputtered whereby Dwight motioned for Cody to exit the cab.

"Let me check out what's going on," Dwight said to his son, gently pushing him out of the way and climbing into the cab. "I'm going to crank the engine. Open up the hood and see if the belt is spinning."

Stepping up to the tractor, Cody lifted the hood and began to inspect the drive belt. "Dad, the belt isn't moving."

With the engine having shut down, Dwight said, "See if you can move the belt."

"What?" said Cody.

"SEE IF YOU CAN MOVE THE BELT!"

"What?"

"GRAB THE BELT AND TRY TO MOVE IT!"

Following his father's hastily directed commands, Cody grabbed a portion of the belt with his left hand and instantaneously the belt jumped and spun, whereby a ghastly shriek of agony shook the air. "My hand! My fingers! My fingers are cut!"

Dwight raced to Cody's aid. "Let me see. Are you all right, son? You'll be all right."

As Cody slowly unclenched his left hand, Dwight could see that portions of Cody's pinky and ring finger had been severed. With no delay, Dwight removed his shirt and tightly wrapped up Cody's injured digits.

Later that night, after returning from the emergency room, Gail comforted Cody, "You will be all right, son. You must rise from your misfortune and remain whole. You cannot let this get you down. You need to keep your head up. Your father and I love you very much, and we are counting on you to remain strong and steady.

Disgusted by the accident and its outcome, Gail spoke to Dwight in tones that were of such anger that she could hardly recognize herself. "You push too hard, and when you do — you make mistakes. I hold you responsible for this misfortune, Dwight. You must do whatever you can to help our son through this difficult time."

The next day Dwight worked on the John Deere and brought it back into running order — immediately thereafter he went to work harvesting Cody's plot of sweet potatoes. After loading up the harvest, Dwight brought the soil-laden tubers to the washing station where they were cleaned and culled. He then brought the batch to the curing room and carefully placed the lot into bins.

At dinner that night, Dwight, thinking that he'd done Cody some great favor, shared what he'd done. "Cody, I want you to know that you do not need to worry about harvesting your plot. I did it for you, and your harvest is in the curing room."

"How could you? How could you do that? I worked all season to see the product of my effort," Cody said taking a stance against his father's careless action.

"Son, I thought that you would be relieved that you didn't have to complete the harvest."

"Relieved? Dad, I didn't die! I just lost a couple of fingers."

Gail, while again disappointed with her husband for acting hastily, and again so proud of her son, simply smiled at Cody, but she had words, words that could be said at the dinner table, for Dwight. "You are so impetuous in your ways. Your heart is so good most of the time. How could you not have known that Cody would want to harvest his own crop? How could you not have known this?"

Feeling much as if he couldn't do anything right, Dwight quietly retired from the table and went out to the garage to work on one of his many projects. When he wanted to be alone, he often sought refuge in his garage, a place where he could be all by his lonesome amongst his tools and, occasionally, some bourbon. It was in his garage that Dwight developed some of his good ideas — and a number of his ideas that proved not to be so good.

Perhaps Dwight had become too intense about his desire to become successful, or perhaps it was that his job at the processing plant had led him to become desensitized towards life and/or the fundamental needs of others. Dwight had become successful, prosperous, and respected in his community, but at what cost?

Generally, Cody kept largely to himself at school. It wasn't so much that he was antisocial, but he did think that the best policy, particularly while in high school, was to avoid drawing undue attention to himself. As a result, the cowboy-majority at Oakdale High School neither paid attention to him nor felt that he posed any threat. Cody simply went to school, completed every assignment that was expected of him, followed school rules, and sometimes played chess with members of the chess club during lunch. When he returned to school, after his accident with the John Deere's drive-belt, his hand was still heavily bandaged. Unfortunately this drew some very unwanted attention from one of the campus big-shots from the clan of cowboys who often hung out in the hallway near his locker.

"Hey, what did you do to your hand, Fletcher — poke yourself with your chopsticks?"

"Hey, Welch. Don't talk to me, okay? Not today."

"What, are you too good to talk to me, Chinaman?"

"I'm not going to tell you again, Welch. Let me be."

"Hey, Welch, I think you better not push it," said Luke Binford, a member of the group of cowboys.

With Luke's comment, Pat Welch just stood and leered at Cody with a sappy smirk on his face. "Yeah, Binford, I've got better things to do than to waste my time with that wiry sweet potato farmer."

It seemed as though most everyone in Oakdale knew everyone else's business. That is, as long as it didn't concern sensitive personal matters such as an individual's race or ethnicity.

When Cody got home from school that day, his father had another surprise for him. "Cody, I've been thinking. You're really getting to know the business — the business of growing sweet potatoes, and, well, I'm not sure that I've properly let you know just how proud I am of you. You've really blossomed into quite a young man. Next spring, I want you to start to take a leading role among the farm hands. Tomas and Hector really like you, and more importantly, they respect that you were able to manage you own sector of potatoes."

"I don't know, Dad. I'm only sixteen," Cody said, as he contemplated what other surprises his father had in store for him.

Dwight put his hand on Cody's shoulder. "Cody, I know this. That is why I am suggesting that you postpone taking the responsibility until next year, next spring. A lot can change in a year, and you're almost a man now. In the meantime, I want you to be observing the process and the procedures more than ever. Eventually, I'm going to want you to train each of the new men who come to work on the farm."

"Okay, Dad, I will do as you say."

"Cody."

"Yes, Dad?"

"One more thing, let's not say anything to your mother about this yet, not now."

"Sure, Dad, whatever you say."

Over the next couple of months, Cody began to regain the use of his damaged fingers. Slowly, but surely, he began to feel sensation returning to his compromised digits. The first positive sign that he noticed involved a new awareness to hot and cold when his damaged hand was submerged in water that differed greatly from ambient temperature. Just prior to Christmas, Cody was testing his left hand in nearly every conceivable manner. The starkest difference that Cody recognized was his inability to grip tools as he once had. He just didn't seem to be able to wield hand tools with the same finesse that he did prior to his accident. In time, he found he had the courage and fortitude to dig his hand deep into the fertile soil that once nurtured his personal crop of sweet potatoes.

Cody felt optimistic about the prospect of regaining full use of his hand, but felt somewhat self-conscious about his deformed fingers. Still, Cody was able to break into a smile at the challenge presented by his misfortune. Something that always gave him comfort, when he felt ashamed of his hand, was the thought of the kami as he observed the mountain fish swimming in the bucket with his bulging eyes and strange mouth expressions.

Just after the new year, Cody's luck ran thin in his ability to stay out of Pat Welch's pathway. As Cody made his way through the hallway to his locker, he found that a large group of cowboys were focused on him, much as if he'd become the topic of discussion.

"Hey, loser, I hear that you had a little accident out at the potato patch," said Pat.

"I warned you, Welch. Stay out of my way!"

"I'm staying out of your way. I'm just saying —"

"Hey, Welch, I have an idea. Do us all a favor and don't say anything — ever."

At that point, Pat stepped back and chuckled nervously before finally noticing that his entire crew was laughing, laughing at him. "I'm going to really let Cody have it. You wait and watch," Pat informed his pals.

Later that day, Luke pulled Cody aside in their history class and said, "Hey, Cody, I just want you to know that I have nothing to do with Welch and his beef with you. I don't know why he has it out for you, Cody, but I think that you should know that he's angling to mess you up."

"Thank you, Luke, but I think I'll be okay," Cody said with a true sense of comfort with the matter.

The following week, Pat called out to Cody while he was playing chess outside the cafeteria. "Hey, Chinaman, why are you so ugly?" Pleased with his comment, Pat looked around at his clan members as he smiled, inflating his chest and chuckling arrogantly. In the pathetic hope that blood might spill, Pat's buddies stood by in false allegiance, giving Pat some perverse sense that they were somehow behind his cause.

"Hey, Welch, I'm just going to ignore you. I hope you don't mind," Cody said as he focused on his game of chess.

"I don't mind. I guess we can wait," Pat said, with the same smirk that he often used when he thought he was impressing his buddies. Just about then, the bell signaling the end of the lunch period rang out. "Hey, Chinaman, shouldn't you be going to class?" said Welch. Cody, showing no concern, stood up and started his trek to class. As he passed by the antagonist, Cody tumbled to the ground, having been tripped by Pat.

"What are you going to do now, boy?"

Slowly, exhibiting the highest form of discipline, Cody picked himself up and rose to his feet, where he calmly walked over to Pat and connected a left-cross to Pat's mouth that was so destructive that several of Pat's teeth careened about the asphalt as if they were so many dice being tossed to the pavement. Then, as if he were possessed by a demon, Cody delivered repeated kicks to Pat's head with such fury that he nearly caused Pat to lose sight in one eye.

From that moment on, it might have well have been "Mr. Fletcher" from the standpoint of every member of Oakdale High School's cowboy clan, as the fray and its outcome became permanently etched in the minds of the entire campus community.

Initially, the cowboy culture of Oakdale made a strong attempt to smear Cody and to represent him as the aggressor, but it quickly became patently clear that such a portrayal just wasn't consistent with the facts associated with the matter. In the end, the school district had no choice but to discount reports that Cody was a short-fused tinderbox who beat his aggressor with *nunchaku* (Japanese fighting sticks joined with chain) while he lay sprawled on the ground unconscious. When it was all said and done, the school board suspended Cody for five-days as an appeasement to disgruntled community members.

In some perverse manner, Dwight was proud of his son. Gail, on the other hand, wished that the entire conflict had never come about. She greatly disliked the idea of exposing Cody to any of the hatefulness associated with racism, prejudice, or oppression of any construction. She was very conscious of the entire gamut of struggles experienced by minorities in their battles to gain acceptance in American society. She knew the history of her American relatives, and she had a good idea just how hateful men could be toward one another, with or without reason.

As far as Gail was concerned, Cody had done what was within his power to avoid the conflict with Pat Welch, just as he had told her he had. Still, perhaps being a product of the time she spent with antiwar activists and pacifists during her student days at San Francisco State College, she believed deep in her heart, with great conviction, that violent conflict could most always be avoided. During the time that Cody was suspended from school, Gail dutifully picked up his class assignments such that he'd not fall behind in his coursework. *Surely*, Gail thought, *this didn't need to happen. If only Dwight would or could act more like a father — than a drillmaster. If only Dwight would spend more quality time with Cody, maybe this matter might have had a different outcome.*

Deeply troubled by the crisis, Gail spoke with Dwight. "I think that you need to spend more time with Cody, time sharing the wisdom that you've acquired over the years. I feel that you should explore the idea of taking part in some sort of father-son activity, an activity that is totally removed from this farm. I truly believe that if Cody could have come to you, as a resource concerning the bullying he experienced at school, the incident would not have escalated as it did."

"I've been thinking quite a bit about the matter myself, and I do wish that he had told me about the issue with this Pat Welch fellow. Still, I'm just not so sure of the advice that I would have given Cody after that bully tripped him to the ground."

"You're missing the point, Dwight. You need to spend more time with him. For God's sake, Dwight, he will be in college soon, and then how much time will you spend with him? I know that you love Cody with all of you heart. Now follow my advice and make it happen."

"Gail, I can't do it this week. I need to make a bunch of repairs to the irrigation pipes. I need to do some welding on the flatbed truck's suspension, and I've got to adjust the furnace. I just don't think it is burning fuel efficiently."

"All of that work can wait, Dwight. You need to go on a day trip or, better yet, an over-night trip with Cody."

"Where should we go? Should we just hop in the truck and go somewhere? We can't go camping. It's freezing. It's the dead of winter!"

"For goodness sake, take him to the Exploratorium or the Monterey Aquarium or somewhere. Be creative! Taking Cody on a trip would be a really nice surprise for him. Heavens, I just can't believe Cody's going to be seventeen next week. Where have all the years gone, Dwight?"

"You're right. I guess we could go to the Monterey Aquarium. I think Cody would like that."

Friday morning of that week, Cody and his father packed some clothes into Dwight's truck for the drive to Monterey. Once on the road, the pair talked like father and son, though at times, it wasn't particularly clear who was taking which role. "You know, Cody, there was a very famous writer named John Steinbeck who wrote a book —"

"I know, Dad, *Cannery Row*. We read the book in English class when I was a freshman. It's about a bunch of guys who try to set up a surprise party for this guy named Doc who is a biologist. And, during the party, the guy's house and his laboratory get completely destroyed."

"Gosh, I haven't thought about that story for close to thirty years. How about this: did you know that Monterey, California was the site of the Bear Flag revolt?"

"Actually, Dad, the way I remember it is that after the United States declared war on Mexico, some Navy commander raised the American flag at the Custom House in Monterey. I think that the Bear Flag revolt took place in Sonoma, but I'm not sure."

By the time the pair reached Turlock, Dwight was beginning to realize just how out of touch he'd become with Cody and that he'd not played much of a role in his intellectual development. As Cody and his father continued to advance through the farmlands of the Central Valley in their trek toward the aquarium, Dwight, wisely, let Cody play a larger role in leading the conversation.

"So, buster, what can you tell me about the Monterey Aquarium?"

"All I know about it is that it is the biggest and the best of the world's marine parks. I've heard that they have tide pools where you can actually pick up live sea urchins."

"I didn't even know that you knew what a sea urchin was."

"Mom says that people eat sea urchins and that in Japanese they are called *uni*."

"Did your mother tell you if she had ever eaten a sea urchin?"

"Yes, she said that she and her Japanese friends would go out for sashimi and order them before you were married."

"You know, I don't think I have ever been to a Japanese restaurant with your mother."

As the pair motored along, it became very clear to Dwight that he stood to gain every bit as much as did Cody from the fruits of their outing.

Through the towns of Hollister and Prunedale, the pair continued their course towards the aquarium. By the time they'd reached Castroville they could smell the briny sea breeze and they knew that the ocean would soon be in sight. Shortly after reaching the blue Pacific, Cody and his father found themselves on Cannery Row, overwhelmed by the beauty of Monterey Bay and the excitement of having reached their destination.

"Hey, son. What do you say that we get lunch before we visit the aquarium?"

"Yeah, okay!"

"Hey, look! There's a restaurant called *Sakura*."

"Mom says that *sakura* is Japanese for 'cherry blossoms' or 'cherry tree.'"

"Where did that come up in a conversation?"

"Mother once told me a story called "Grandfather Cherry Blossom." It is a Japanese story about a greedy, evil old man who tries to take advantage of his neighbors after their dog digs up a bunch of gold and silver coins. The greedy old man ends up taking the dog from the husband and wife and tries to force the dog into digging up another treasure. But when the dog doesn't find more treasure, the evil man kills the dog. Anyway, in the story, the dog's ashes are spread near the base of a long dead cherry tree and then — right before the kind man and his wife's eyes — the tree comes to life and bursts forth into full bloom."

"Wow! That is quite a story," Dwight said as he developed a further sense of the degree to which he had become an outsider in his son's life.

"Yeah, Mother has told me many memorable stories."

Once inside of the restaurant, Cody and his father were greeted by a kimono-clad hostess. "*Konichi wa*," said the waitress as she greeted the pair.

"Good afternoon. I'd like a seat for me and my boy, please."

"Would you like to sit at a table or at the sushi bar?"

"What do you think, son?"

"Let's sit at the bar and watch the guy make sushi." Cody said with a sense that he wanted to learn everything there was to know about preparing sushi.

"Okay, you heard it. Two seats at the bar, please."

After climbing atop his stool, Dwight said, "Wow, you know, come to think of it … I don't think that I've ever been to a Japanese restaurant at all. How about you, son?"

"Mom and I once went to a Japanese restaurant in Berkeley, when we went to visit Uncle Peter."

The sushi chef eyed the pair, before speaking. "Hey, you want miso soup?"

"Yes, two please," said Dwight. "Boy, look at all of these choices."

"I know what I'm going to have, Dad. I'm going to have the mixed tempura and a California roll."

"I know what tempura is. Your mother makes tempura with sweet potato and other vegetables, but what is a California roll?"

"It is rice, avocado, cucumber, and little shrimp wrapped in seaweed."

"Okay, I know what I'm ordering. I'm going to have the tempura prawns, a Dungeness crab roll, and two orders of uni — one for each of us."

When their meal arrived, Cody and Dwight were delighted by the elegance of the presentations of their dishes. The colors were so lively and invigorating. The uni, which possessed the most beautiful hues of California poppy orange, glistened with moisture as if it had this very moment been removed from its spine-fortified shell encasement. *The smell was wonderful*, they thought, full sea-fresh tones with a hint of what they could only describe as a "nutty" sensation. And the tempura was prepared to absolute perfection, possessing a thin light crunchy coating that complemented the crispness of the prawns, the al dente firmness of the carrots, and the richness of the sweet potato. Dwight and Cody had never spoken so much about food in their lives, and never in such glowing tones. "We should call up your mother right now and tell her what we are doing, don't you think?"

"Yeah, let's call her now!" Cody said excitedly.

"Let's settle our bill, get some change, and we'll give Mom a call."

At that point, the waitress stepped up to the bar. "How was your meal, sir?"

"Cody, you tell her."

"We loved it! It was excellent. I'd definitely like to come back again."

"*Domo arigato gozaimasu,*" said the waitress.

"What's that?" said Dwight looking at the waitress.

"She said, 'thank you' in Japanese," said Cody as he exchanged a smile with the graceful woman.

"Well, thank you, ma'am. We really enjoyed our meal."

With pleasantries exchanged, Dwight settled the bill, and the pair made their way to the phone booth and directed their call. One ring, two rings. "Hello," said Gail.

"Hello, dear. We have reached Monterey and we just had lunch."

"Is it cold there? It's getting really cold here."

"No, it's kind of sunny. The sun is breaking its way through the clouds. It's not too bad. Guess where, or should I say, what kind of food we just ate."

"Oh, I don't know."

"Just guess!" Dwight urged.

Being as Dwight had never played the guess-what-I-just-ate game with her, Gail just took a stab at the answer. "I don't know — Japanese food?"

"BINGO! How did you know?" Dwight said with mild disappointment that Gail had curtailed the game so effortlessly.

"I didn't know. I just guessed."

"Well, you guessed right! Here, talk with Cody."

"Hi, Mom. We just went to this really neat Japanese restaurant."

"Are you two having fun?"

"Yes, Mother! We are having a great time. Do you know what we had for lunch?"

"No, Cody, tell me."

"We had uni."

"You had uni?" Gail replied with great surprise. "Do you remember when I told you about sea urchins?"

"Yes, I told Dad that you used to eat them with your Japanese friends."

"And what did you think about eating uni?"

"Dad and I loved it. It tasted kind of salty and fresh, like the ocean."

"Did you go to the aquarium yet?"

"No, we are going right now."

"Have a good time. I love you, Cody. Let me speak with Dad.

"Well, well. I hear the two of you are having a great time. Are you surprised?"

"Mom," Dwight said as he looked toward Cody. "I'll talk with you about that later, but for now just understand how glad I am that we made this trip. I love you, dear, and my only regret is that you aren't here to experience this with us."

"Dwight, you well know that I wanted this to be a father-son thing. I will talk with you when you get home. Are you still planning to stay the night?"

"Yes, dear, that is the plan. I'll see you when we get home. I love you."

"Cody, say goodbye to your mother."

"Bye, Mom. I love you!"

"Goodbye, Cody. Have a good time with your father."

Off to the aquarium they headed, Cody and his father, two men on a quest to explore the mysteries of the ocean world.

One of the oddest species of fish that the pair discovered during their adventure was the bizarre looking *mola mola*, or ocean sunfish. Never had they viewed a seemingly more unlikely sea creature in their lives. The ocean sunfish looks much like a monstrous elliptical slab of flesh with one large dorsal fin affixed atop its body, a rudder-like structure attached to the base of its torso, and two ridiculously inconsequential miniaturized fins attached to either side of its lowest extremities. Examining the anatomy of the mola mola, Dwight commented, "That looks more like a flying side-of-beef, than any fish I've ever seen."

When Cody eyed the great beast he simply smiled, thinking to himself just how pleased the Mountain Kami would have been in the presence of the supremely curious looking ocean sunfish.

Next the pair visited the tide pool exhibit. "Hey, look there, Cody. There's our lunch," said Dwight pointing to a purple spiny globe-like shellfish. So that's what a sea urchin looks like up close. Well, I'll be darned."

"Hey, Dad, do you think you can eat starfish?"

"Probably can, son, but they look kind of bony to me. I bet your mom could make one taste good."

"Yeah, Dad, I bet you're right. Mom's a great cook."

"Cody, just to be on the safe side though — I think we should just leave these ones be."

"Yeah, I think you're right, Dad," Cody said with a wry smile.

Throughout the remainder of the day, Cody and his dad took in every exhibit possible, from watching the playful sea otters floating on their backs breaking open what appeared to be sea urchins, to viewing a wily octopus as it lurked among the shadows of its enclosure in pursuit of its next meal.

At the Fletcher home that evening, Gail decided to bake a chocolate cake. She felt that her boys would enjoy such a treat, and that the confection would serve as a fine culmination to a couple of well-spent days for the two most important men in her life. It was particularly cold that night so Gail cranked up the heat and turned on some music and went about the task of measuring the flour, sugar, cocoa, baking powder, and salt before mixing the aggregate until it was of uniform composition. In a separate bowl, she measured the wet ingredients. In went the milk, the butter, the eggs, and the vanilla. After mixing the wet ingredients together, she added the dry ingredients and combined the conglomerate until it was of uniform consistency. Finally she poured the cake batter into a buttered cake pan and placed it into a 350-degree oven. Then she sat and read the recipe section of one of Dwight's agricultural monthlies. The house was getting quite comfortable by then, and Gail was feeling peaceful, albeit a little tired. She could smell the cake as it baked in the oven, *such a comforting smell*, she thought, as she went about her reading.

Meanwhile, Cody and Dwight were playing a game of dominos that they had checked out from the front desk of the hotel. "Let's see here, Charley Spud, that's four plus five plus six plus two, and with this two-five that makes twenty. Ha ha! Beat that," said Dwight as if he'd just clouted Cody into submission.

"You haven't called me 'Charley Spud' since I was a little kid."

"Yeah, I don't know, Cody. I guess you're right."

"Let's see, Dad. I think this double-five makes twenty-five. How do you like those potatoes, Charley Spud?"

Feeling somewhat beaten-up by Cody's strong command of the game, Dwight replied, "Hey Cody, it's getting late. We have a long drive tomorrow. I think we should get some sleep."

"Yeah, okay, Dad. Whatever you say. I guess this way you'll be sparing me the punishment of beating you in another game."

"It's just —"

"Yeah, I know Dad. We have a long drive tomorrow. You know, you should consider yourself lucky that we're not playing chess."

The next morning Cody and Dwight woke up with the rising sun, which on this tenth day of January meant around 7:30 a.m. After casually attending to their hygiene regimens, they enjoyed a leisurely breakfast and discussed taking another trip in the near future. The day was of particular beauty and there was a certain stillness in the air that spoke of a sense of calm of the highest order. Since it was Saturday, the road was expected to be relatively empty, and it seemed likely that their return trip would take considerably less time than their trip out to the coast. Upon making their inland turn off of the coastal stretch, they waved goodbye to the ocean and bid that they'd soon return. "Dad, I want to go up the coast north next time. I want to go up to where the redwood trees are, and I want to go to those tide pools up in Mendocino County, where the aquarium guide said they have those really big red abalone."

"Yes, son, we should do that one day."

The drive home was a quiet, solemn affair, the excitement and beauty of coastal Monterey Bay being greatly dampened by the monotonous uniformity associated with the plainness of the desolate lands that skirted along either side of the roadway from Prunedale to the city limits of Oakdale. As the pair pulled onto the long driveway that led to their home,

Cody and his father smiled at one another. Cody said, "Do you think Mom with have lunch ready?"

"Knowing your mother, I'd say absolutely, son. Absolutely."

Pulling up alongside of the workshop, Cody and Dwight grabbed their bags and headed into the house.

"Honey, we're home," said Dwight as he accelerated through the front door.

"Dad, something smells burnt. Mom, what's burning? Hey, Dad. Look. Mom is sleeping."

"Hey, honey, wake up. Something is burning. Oh, my God. She's cold! Cody, get your mother's legs. We need to get her out of the house. I think the house is full of carbon monoxide. I think the furnace may have failed."

With Cody at his mother's feet and Dwight at her shoulders, the two carried Gail's impliable body to the garage, where Dwight kicked open the door. "Let's lay your mother on the hammock while I call 9-1-1."

"Dad, I'm scared. Is Mother going to be all right?"

"Cody, I don't know. I don't know. We just need to be hopeful. We need to remain positive," Dwight said, realizing that his son was too wise, and he too respectful of Cody than to provide him with anything other than an honest assessment of the matter. When the paramedics arrived, the only thing that they could do was to confirm what Cody and Dwight already knew in their hearts. Their dear mother and wife had passed on to a better place.

By that evening the entire Yoshitaku family had assembled at Dwight's parents' home, since Dwight's home had been rendered temporarily uninhabitable due to the presence of carbon monoxide and the noxious odor of burnt cake. Cody's Aunt Alice and Uncle Peter were the first to arrive, along with their spouses. To ease some of the stress felt by Cody and Dwight, Peter picked up enough food and beverages on his way out of Berkeley to sustain the pair for several days.

Throughout the night and well into the wee hours of the morning, the mood was somber. As the evening progressed, everyone present took the time to relay a personal story that involved Gail. The evening was spent in tears, sadness, reflection, and laughter. The following Wednesday, Gail was put to rest near her parents' home in Turlock, having passed at just forty-six years of age.

Over the ensuing months, Dwight fell into drinking, more than he ever had. Cody returned to school and found that that no one really seemed to know of the immense sorrow that his mother's passing had inflicted upon him. In many ways, he became somewhat of a nowhere man, a man without a refuge from his pain, and a man without anyone to offer him the emotional support and solace that he sorely needed. Still, Cody pressed on through high school. If he could just keep his eye on the ball, he would graduate in five months, at the age of seventeen.

Within a week after his mother had been buried, Dwight readdressed to Cody the plan that he had introduced the previous fall. "You know, Cody, you're no longer a boy anymore. You're nearly a man. After school, I want you to start working with Tomas and Hector in the fields. In the fall you'll be starting college, and by then, I want you to be taking on greater responsibility around here. Is that understood?"

"Yes, Father, I understand."

Cody's life over the next several years could only be described as one of utter devastation. If Cody's mother's presence in his life was analogous to the comfort and security offered by a plush fleece rug, then that rug had been pulled right out from under him, sending Cody tumbling and rolling in despair along a treacherous rock pile at the base of an unstable cliff. To Cody, his mother wasn't just a source of comfort and security, his mother was his personal well-spring of wisdom, hope, and inspiration. In Cody's mind, his mother was the very embodiment of light and all that was good. Perhaps most importantly, relative to Cody's general wellbeing, Gail served as the counter-balance that kept Dwight's expectations of Cody in check with reality. Now, he had no one in his corner to keep his father in check, and Cody was completely vulnerable to Dwight's over-reaching schemes. Cody's life had become so precarious that an outsider might rightly wonder whether Cody would have been in a more favorable position had he been adopted and raised by a she-wolf after his figurative abandonment.

If it had not been understood by Dwight's parents and the entire Yoshitaku family that Cody was college-bound, and if Uncle Peter didn't check in on Cody every couple of weeks, it is entirely possible that Dwight might have tried to hold Cody on the farm, much as if he were a perpetually indentured servant.

For the remainder of his senior year in high school, Cody attended to a full schedule of classes and then worked in the fields with Hector and Tomas until dark, when he would head up to the house to get something to eat before settling into his homework.

By the time fall rolled around, Cody started to develop a new sense of optimism in his life. Yes, he would be attending Stanislaus State University in Turlock, which was just twenty miles from Oakdale, but at his mother's wake, his Grandfather Yoshitaku pledged to house him during college at the family home. It was this single simple family offering that likely made the difference between Cody earning a college degree and not earning a college degree.

Still, Cody looked after his father, making bimonthly trips to assist on the farm during the school year and spending much of the summer with his father during the summer recess.

During Cody's five years at Stanislaus State, it became clear to him that his father was gradually slipping into the depths of chronic alcoholism, and he wondered just how long his father could manage such a lifestyle while continuing to pay his bills, including Cody's college tuition, and moving ahead to grow his business. It wasn't really that Cody had ever observed his father ripping drunk; it was just that his father seemed to bumble along in the garage with increasing regularity.

Dwight was a very broken man without Gail. And not a single day passed where Dwight didn't blame himself for Gail's death, a senseless tragedy that took place because he had spread himself too thin to properly attend to the unsound furnace that extinguished Gail's life with a dense blanket of carbon monoxide. This truth that Dwight kept to himself provoked and haunted him for the remainder of his life.

In 2002, Cody completed his Bachelor of Science degree in Agricultural Science. After an additional year at the university, Cody obtained his teaching credential. By the end of this fifth year, out from under his father's roof, he had lined up a full-time teaching position as an agriculture instructor at Turlock High School. For more than eight years, Cody taught agricultural science courses by the academic calendar and worked on his father's farm during the summer, where he straightened out the business's financial records and worked with Tomas and Hector in the fields, carrying out nearly every conceivable production task.

While Dwight's enterprise was largely stable, Cody wondered how much longer his father would be able to turn a profit, without one form or another of product diversification. Too many people in the valley were now growing sweet potatoes, and it seemed that each year his father's efforts increased, yet his profits either remained flat or of marginal gain. From Cody's perspective, his father either needed to take on another crop, in addition to sweet potatoes, or he needed to find a strain of sweet potato that offered a higher yield or that was in some fashion unique or different from anything else anyone in the valley was producing. Either way, Cody knew that times were changing, but his father's approach to farming and production remained stagnant.

During 2011, Cody found himself traveling with increasing frequency to Berkeley to visit his Uncle Peter. It was Peter who watched closely over Cody during the first few years after his mother's passing. Peter was employed as an executive for a large outdoor equipment retailer based in San Francisco. He was connected in the business community, and he was connected with the Japanese community in San Francisco, Portland, and Seattle. In Cody's eyes, Uncle Peter was the only Japanese-American he personally knew who seemed to walk the fine line of maintaining his Japanese cultural identity while being successful in the world of capitalistic American enterprise. More importantly, it was Peter who was Cody's closest tie to his mother, both in a cultural and spiritual sense.

One day when Cody expressed to Peter the sense of cultural numbness he felt and the sense of drudgery that his life had become, Peter suggested that he look into teaching opportunities in Japan. "It would be a long shot if you were able to go to Japan to teach agricultural courses," Peter counseled. "But you should be able to line up a position teaching English with not much difficulty." To Cody, this thought opened up a whole new world of options.

Within a couple of months, Cody had made dozens of inquiries, and in short order he sent completed application packets to seven language institutes and academies. By late January, Cody had received but a single offer, an offer with a severely limited window of opportunity. After discussing the potential danger of a mid-year resignation with Uncle Peter, Cody decided that he was at a turning point in his life, a place where if he didn't act, he'd forever be cursed for not having taken the opportunity to implant meaning and fulfillment in a life characterized by intolerable disappointment and emptiness.

In initiating the separation from his teaching position at the high school, Cody simply walked into the administrative office of his school district and informed his principal of his decision. "I'm going to need to go on leave for the remainder of the school year to attend to some personal obligations in my life. I'm not asking for permission. I am simply providing the district with notification of my decision. I am willing to remain in my teaching position until the district can locate a suitable replacement. That is, assuming the process can be completed within a month."

"Cody, I'm not sure what to say, or what questions to ask. You've been an exemplary employee in every regard. I guess, I should just say that you will be sorely missed and that if there is anything that I can ever do for you, well — you just let me know."

Hearing the response of his supervisor, Cody was absolutely amazed at how easy it was for him to detach himself from the district. The principal asked that Cody stay on until a suitable replacement could be found and further, that Cody serve on the interview committee, a request that Cody felt honored to fulfill.

The power of a heartfelt truth is perhaps the greatest of all resources.

Immediately, Cody notified the Ikemoto Academy that he would be accepting their offer and would enter the academy as an English instructor, as requested, during March of 2012.

CHAPTER THREE:
FINDING RAPPORT

Hallowed are the grounds of the venerable Ikemoto Academy. Since its inception in the early 1920s, the academy has been the secondary school of choice in the greater Tokyo area. For four generations prominent businessmen, politicians, academics, and other notables have sent their offspring to the Ikemoto Academy toward becoming groomed for success in an increasingly competitive world. Beyond the generalized educational coursework associated with secondary schools, the Ikemoto Academy prides itself in its operation of a highly coveted language school that offers an array of foreign languages, all of which are instructed by native speakers.

While the academy offers foreign language courses in French, Italian, German, Spanish, Russian, and various dialects of Chinese, it is only the English language that is compulsory for every student throughout their entire six-year term. Since the private school operates year-round, it is not uncommon for new faculty members to enter into a contract at most any point during an academic calendar. The academy maintains a seven-person teaching contingent in the English department, where each instructor is retained for no more than one academic year. Cody and Cynthia were among the entering group of English instructors at the academy during 2012.

Cody started teaching English at the academy in early March. He was assigned to senior students at the academy by virtue of his very weak Japanese speaking skills. By this design, Cody was delivering instruction to students who already possessed substantial English language skills. It was these more advanced courses that placed great focus on the development of writing skills.

From the beginning, Cody enjoyed working with the students under his care. He had never worked with students who were more intent on learning. Cody soon learned that whether he was blowing his nose or presenting a complex dialog, each student, male and female, tracked his every move. The situation provided him with one of the strangest sensations he'd ever known. It seemed there was virtually nothing he could do, or not do, to disinterest his student clientele. Each day that Cody entered the classroom, his self-confidence and vigor increased. He grew to love the students and they grew to think of their instructor as a radical alpha-male who was as dynamic as anyone they had ever met. Much to Cody's discomfort, the students treated him no less than as if he were a demigod. There was never any question in Cody's classes who was in charge, and there was never any question that every student in the classroom possessed deep interest in his every word, action, deed, or nuance. For Cody, however, none of this made much sense, and on most days he wondered how long the jig would last, and more importantly, when the administration would catch on that neither he nor his lessons had any substance. While Cody had his doubts, the fact was that Cody, through some mysterious pathway, inspired his students and it was largely this single characteristic of his persona that put Cody in high graces with every individual associated with the Ikemoto Academy.

When Cynthia Martin arrived at the academy in early May, she received great praise from of the entire language faculty by virtue of her *summa cum laude* status as a graduate from the University of Minnesota. While the youngest member of the Ikemoto faculty, her academic prowess and successes immediately placed her in high regard with her teaching peers. Cynthia looked at the opportunity to work at the academy as the culmination of her studies. She believed, absolutely, that living and working in Japan was going to offer her the truest of tests concerning the quality of her academic work over the preceding five years.

When Cynthia first noticed Cody, she was nearly certain that he possessed Japanese ancestry, but was surprised to discover that his language skills were so underdeveloped. Never shy, Cynthia introduced herself, *"Watashi wa Cynthia Martin desu. Hajime mashite."*

"Oh, hi, I mean hello, Ms. Martin. I mean, *Watashi wa Fletcher Cody desu. Dozo yoroshiku onegaishimasu"* (please be kind to me).

Now, in general, there is good reason for presenting a surname before one's given name in a self-reference — that is, if one is a native speaker of the Japanese language; however, for Cody, in this instance, doing so was merely a social blunder associated with the pressure he felt in making the acquaintance of a very attractive and classy female. In over-correcting, Cody continued, "Ms. Martin, before you go too much further, I must tell you that, short of simple pleasantries, my Japanese is very poor."

"That is quite all right, Mr. Fletcher. May I call you Cody?"

Wiping the sweat from his brow and feeling as if he were regaining some balance, Cody replied, "Please, please call me Cody. May I call you Cynthia?"

"Yes, you may. And, Cody, if I could ever be of assistance to you with your Japanese, I would be so honored."

"Oh, yes. I mean, thank you. I mean — *onegaishimasu.* I mean — *domo arigato gozaimasu*! Cynthia, I just think that I might take you up on that," Cody said nervously realizing that an opportunity to be able to actually hang out with Cynthia might be on the horizon.

As the ensuing days elapsed, Cynthia increasingly found her place and her voice in the classroom environment. Where Cody was assigned to instruct the older students,

Cynthia taught ninth and tenth grade students. Cynthia was very pleased to teach the level of students that her assignment presented to her. In Cynthia's eyes, instructing students in these earlier years of language development provided the greatest opportunity for her to provide the critical foundation and structure that was required to master the English language. Her view was that students assigned to her courses were just developed enough in their English speaking skills to possess a good foundation, yet not so advanced that they felt headstrong in their knowledge.

It would be very difficult to find flaws in any aspect of Cynthia's being, but it might be true that some of her strongest attributes were undervalued in the classroom venue at the Ikemoto Academy. Further, while youth and beauty are perhaps among the most coveted of all of life's treasures, beauty can be a distraction and youth an impediment. Cynthia's intelligence and savvy nature allowed her to successfully navigate in her world, regardless of the venue. In her classroom, Cynthia ruled the roost. From the beginning, her students responded to her as if they were competing with one another to maintain in her favor. Where Cody worked tirelessly to ensure success in his classroom, Cynthia managed similar success with minimal preparation.

You just can't explain these things, but Cynthia was set on Cody, in some manner, from the moment their eyes first met. Similarly, Cody developed an understanding about Cynthia himself, that being that she was the hottest, most accomplished young lady he had ever spoken to. The stark difference between the impulses of Cody and Cynthia was that Cody was going to try to parlay his interest in Cynthia into friendship, whereas Cynthia was going to investigate Cody's potential as a suitor. Later that first week, Cynthia approached Cody with a request.

"Cody! Cody!" said Cynthia as she tried to catch up with him in the main hallway of the academy. Calm, cool, and collected Cody, all it took were the tender straight-forward words of a beautiful lady, and his demeanor could be instantly transformed into sudden, albeit less than terminal, clumsiness.

"Oh, uh, hello! I mean, uh, good morning, Cynthia. *Ohiyo gozaimasu.*"

"Good morning, Cody! I was wondering, sometime when you are available, if you could show me around Tokyo."

Cody, while standing speechless, looked about the nearly vacant hallway, much as if he were looking for another person named Cody, as he thought to himself, *Could she be talking to me?*

"Cody?" repeated Cynthia.

Cody, while still flustered, fumbled, "Uh, yeah. You are going to Tokyo?"

"No, I want you to show me around Tokyo. Specifically, the Ginza district."

Cody, now having regained his composure, stated, "Yes. Yes, I would love to go into the city with you. When would you like to go?"

"If you are available, let's go this afternoon. I know it is short —"

"No, no! I'd love to go this afternoon."

It was only Friday, Friday of Cynthia's first full week as a faculty member at the academy, and she had asked Cody to enter into an adventure with her in the world's premiere mega-city. After having settled specific details regarding their departure, Cody stood silent, alone in the breezeway, thinking to himself, *Why on earth would this girl want to be seen walking around Tokyo with me?*

Late that afternoon, Cody and Cynthia stepped off the train and into the Ginza district. As late May days go, it was quite warm and humid as the pair walked among the bustle that tends to saturate Tokyo's most important shopping district. As they maneuvered through the seething and pulsing crowds, the two became acquainted.

"You know," Cody said, "I've never been to Seattle. My Uncle Peter has told me a lot about it, and it sounds very much like a place I would like to visit one day."

"Well, Cody, if you like the ocean, great mountain ranges, beautiful waterways, and the vibrancy of a great city all rolled up into one geographic location, then you would love Seattle. Also, Seattle has one of the finest Japanese markets and specialty stores in the United States. If you love good food, you will love Uwajimaya. In fact, if you love Japan, you'll love Uwajimaya."

"Perhaps, one day, you can give me the grand tour around Seattle."

"We'll have to do that one day," Cynthia said with the casualness of certainty that such a time would come.

"Cynthia, did you know that the best food markets in Tokyo are located in the basements of department stores?"

"Yes, I've heard that. But, I can't wait to see them. I want to take a look at some of those grocery extravaganzas later. I hear that the markets almost take on the character of food-theater. Even an ordinary stalk of celery can secure a leading role."

"Yes. It's amazing the extremes the stores will go to to market their products. We most definitely will have to visit a couple of them. There is a lot to see in the department stores that is unlike anything you normally see in the United States. It's really crazy what you find on the top floors of the department stores," Cody said from his small-town perspective.

"What do you mean?"

"Let's just say that offerings become progressively more deviant or odd as you go to higher numbered floors in some of these department stores. I've seen strange kinds of smoking pipes, and other items that I couldn't even identify. One can't help but wonder what they smoke in those pipes. Some of these Japanese people are really crazy."

"Uh, maybe we should just stay on the lower floors for now," said Cynthia as she shied away from commenting on Cody's offbeat ponderation.

"Yeah, you're probably right."

As the afternoon progressed, Cynthia and Cody visited stores that supplied, seemingly, every purveyance imaginable. The pair perused stores that sold only tea, many varieties of tea, stores that marketed what seemed to be every description of tea known to man. They visited toy stores with inventories so vast that one couldn't possibly survey each item, toy stores where a child would grow old and grey were he or she to attempt to experience each product. At one point, Cynthia took the stage with a floor mat that was fashioned into a giant piano keyboard where she pounded out a rendition of "Mary Had a Little Lamb."

"Wow! That was nice, Cynthia. Do you really play the piano?"

"Well, I haven't played in years, but I did take lessons up until I entered high school. Do you play an instrument?"

"No. No, but when I was a kid my father used to rib me and say that I should take up the harmonica, in case I ever found myself in the slammer."

"I don't get it, Cody," Cynthia said with a troubled look on her face.

"You would have to know my dad. He is kind of sarcastic and he sometimes uses his negativity as a tool to influence certain behavior. When my father didn't think that I was working hard enough on my studies, or in the sweet potato fields, he'd make low-level suggestions that if my ways didn't change, I'd likely find myself 'locked up' as an adult."

"I don't know what to say, Cody. I've never been exposed to that style of parenting."

"A lot of my father's lessons were unorthodox, but I think that deep down he means well. Tell me about your parents," Cody said, with a certain sense of escapement from the painful topic of his mother's death.

"There isn't really much to say about my parents. I mean, they treat me well and they are generous. But there really isn't much of a storyline. My mother can be a little over-extending in her mothering, but that is about as interesting as it gets." Tending to more primal instincts, Cynthia said, "Cody, what do you say that we look for a noodle-house and get something to eat?"

"That sounds like a great idea. I've discovered in the Ginza that some of the most interesting and tasty food is found in some of the most unlikely places. I've discovered some really inexpensive hole-in-the-wall places that serve really excellent food. Are you interested in exploring the underbelly of the city of Tokyo?"

"I wouldn't ever go searching in alleyways alone, but I guess that I'd feel safe doing so with you."

"Yeah, Cynthia, finding a place to eat with you is going to be a lot of fun. Usually I'm at the mercy of my luck when ordering a meal. But with your skill in the Japanese language, this will be the first time that I know beforehand what will be arriving at the table."

Bure & *Boke*: Blurry & Out of Focus

The lights of Tokyo rage against the dying of the light in a manner like no other city. One look at Tokyo's explosive neon glow and the average *gaijin* (foreigner) becomes hopelessly entranced, much like a lowly moth that enters into its demise by circling, until mesmerized, a source of light. The extravagance and illumination of twilight Tokyo seems to allude to universal prosperity for the totality of the city's inhabitants. This illusion deviates, dissipates, and dissolves as one ventures into Tokyo's alleyways and underpasses.

"I'm not sure if it was in this underpass or not, but I found a fabulous *udon* (a thick Japanese wheat noodle) joint somewhere around here. Do you like udon, Cynthia?"

"Yes, absolutely," said Cynthia with genuine accolade for the scrumptious noodle concoction and its serving variations.

Each of the small streets that protruded under the various overpasses seemed to maintain a constant littered and unkempt state. Piles of garbage seemed to stack up beyond what could possibly accumulate in a day or two. Further inspection suggested that under these bridge structures, the city tolerated long-term curbside rubbish, whereas in areas of major foot traffic it did not.

As Cody and Cynthia snaked through this underworld, from street to street, from business to business, in search of the elusive udon restaurant, it became increasingly clear that activities that wouldn't be acceptable on the cosmopolitan streets of Tokyo flourished in these subterranean recesses. Here and there were men, and sometimes women, too drunk to stand or too content to even consider such an inconvenience. Some rolled about in the soupy aggregate that dripped and seethed onto the concrete from the various packages of perishable restaurant discards. Aside from an underlying rancid odor reminiscent of the back-end of any restaurant or cafeteria, the odors associated with the chasmal regions were not overtly offensive.

"This might be it, Cynthia," said Cody as the pair walked up to an establishment with a sign that featured photographs of various meal preparations. "Shall we give it a try?"

"I'm game if you are," said Cynthia in a manner that suggested a mild sense of apprehension.

Once inside the restaurant, which was little more than a dimly-lit chamber positioned with several rows of picnic-like tables covered with cheap vinyl covers, all eyes were on the pair. One man took a long look at Cody, who was dressed in his trademark double-breasted black suit, and mumbled something inaudible to an associate. For several moments, the pair stood wondering when or if someone working at the establishment would offer them a seat. Thinking that the restaurant was closed, the pair turned around to exit. "*Konban wa*" (good evening), a feminine voice called out from behind. Spinning back toward the interior of the room, Cody and Cynthia watched as a slender gray-haired woman, outfitted in a worn kimono, approached.

"Konban wa," replied Cynthia and Cody in unison.

"We would like two seats for dinner," continued Cynthia in Japanese.

After providing Cody and Cynthia with a thorough visual inspection, the woman nodded and led them to a table that was located at the farthest point away from the group of men sitting in the opposite corner.

"Cody, I have no idea why, but for some reason you've become the topic of conversation of those men we observed when we arrived. Did you forget to leave a tip when you were here last?"

"You know, I'm not really even sure that this is same place I came to last time. I swear, this city is so large and so complex that a guy needs to wear a compass on his wrist and carry a GPS."

Within minutes after submitting their order, the waitress returned with the most beautifully presented noodle dishes imaginable. Cody ordered an udon dish that was lavished with fresh oysters, scallions, ginger, and enoki mushrooms. Cynthia was delighted with her pleasant udon that danced in a tasteful sea of broth that coaxed umami (pleasant savory taste) from the dried scallop, white scallion, and mushrooms gracing its surface. "I had no idea that you could get such a fine meal in a place like this," said Cynthia as she spooned the rich liquor from her soup into her waiting mouth. "Cody, I hate to keep bringing this up, but are you sure you don't know those fellows over there? They sure look like they think they know you."

"No, I have no idea who they are. They must think that I look like someone they know."

After finishing their meals, Cody and Cynthia were blissfully content and restful. They spoke about how they loathed the idea of standing up and heading back to their housing units. As the pair reflected upon the success of the evening, two men entered the restaurant and pulled up chairs before handing a package over to the senior figure in the group of men. Each of the men sitting in the group somehow appeared considerably more affluent than one might have expected to find in an eating establishment that seemed to amount to little more than a dive, albeit a dive that served good food. When the bill arrived, Cody settled his account, making sure that he left a sizable tip, if for no other reason than to ward off potential ill-will, were the seated men proprietors of the establishment.

"I think that we had better plan to visit the basement food stores next time," Cody said hedging his bet that he would have another opportunity to spend time with Cynthia.

Throughout the journey back to the Ikemoto compound, Cody tried to make it appear that he thought nothing of the curious group of men who silently studied him and Cynthia as they ate. He tried to convince himself that the whole situation was a simple matter of mistaken identity. *Surely, the men simply must have found a resemblance in my appearance to someone they knew or once had known*, Cody thought to himself.

The following week at the academy was relatively uneventful. On several afternoons Cody casually met with Cynthia in a common area regarding his Japanese language and grammar skills, and each time the pair quickly found that they'd navigated to other topics of discussion. On Friday of that week, the pair made plans to spend Sunday in the Ginza where they would explore the fabulous department stores.

In a number of ways, Cody fully appreciated the bachelor life. It offered ample opportunity for self-reflection and nearly endless freedom, an unrestricted existence where a man was only held answerable to himself. Cody had no difficulty finding entertainment in the vast and diverse city of Tokyo. Due in part to Cody's lone-wolf status and lack of general worldliness, his bachelor lifestyle afforded him opportunities generally undertaken only by fools, the uninhibited, those who sensed immortality — or those who felt they had nothing to lose. Unbeknownst to Cody, his pathway was greased with an abundance of naivety and, at times, the luck of fools.

Late Friday afternoon, Cody decided that he would make a solo trip into the Roppongi district of Tokyo. Some Japanese people say that you can leisurely walk to the Roppongi district from the Ginza in well under an hour, but that the return trip is often one of great treachery. As a bird flies, Roppongi is less than two and a half miles due west of the Ginza, but in terms of the neighborhood's general profile, it is worlds away. Where the Ginza is largely upscale and respectable, the Roppongi district is largely shady and of ill repute. Known for its nightclubs, hostess bars, restaurants, and strip clubs, the Roppongi is a haven for the younger generation and gaijin of all ages. It is the "in place" for tourists who desire both cheap drinks and cheap thrills, and it is the place where greater Tokyo's young-at-heart or soul take to the drink and the dance floor.

If you've got the money, most anything is possible in Roppongi. You can find a girl who will listen to you as if you're the most fascinating individual she's ever met, or you can pay a girl to yell at you at the top of her lungs or to break into a hysterical crying fit with you. There are clubs where women dress as if they are young girls from parochial schools or dress as young wenches sporting the attire of Victorian-era French maids.

Some establishments offer all-you-can-drink specials where you can imbibe until you've either had enough, you fall on the floor, or someone swindles you out of your money and the proprietor sweeps what is left of you into the alley. Often these establishments are fronts for various forms of organized crime. Sometimes patrons of these all-you-can-drink establishments fall victim to the Japanese version of a Mickey Finn, a liquid sucker-punch that replaces chloral hydrate with Rohypnol. Apparently, Rohypnol isn't just for date-rape anymore. In short, this section of Tokyo offers many of the same dangers that San Francisco's Barbary Coast offered to lonely argonauts during California's Gold Rush era.

The Roppongi district was once visibly controlled by the yakuza, but in the management of today's yakuza, syndicates typically take no interest in the debauchery of the throngs of feral foreigners who sweep through the area close to twenty-four hours a day. Today, the yakuza are generally content with collecting kickbacks from the small-time foreign thugs and criminals who own or manage the bars, sex clubs, strip joints, and other adult entertainment establishments that pockmark the Roppongi landscape. The last thing that any self-respecting yakuza organization would want is to become embroiled in an international incident involving a foreigner. It should not go without notice that many foreign embassies are located in the Roppongi district, including the facility operated by the United States. As far as the yakuza are concerned, most everything goes in the Roppongi except violent attacks on foreigners and blatant drug trafficking. The yakuza may stand in the background of certain business ventures, but no one in Japanese society ever forgets who it is that actually runs the show.

Since Cody had discussed the matter with his colleagues and carefully reviewed a 2009 United States Embassy bulletin that outlined the threat to embassy workers and American visitors participating in Roppongi's night life, he practiced elevated caution when out alone. Cody regularly recycled in his mind the bulletin's most important directive. "Remain extra vigilant of your surroundings and maintain a high level of situational awareness." As the recurring theme of youth timelessly refrains, boys will be boys — an undersong that well-applied to Cody, even at thirty-one years of age.

By the time it was 10:40 p.m., Cody had been to three bars and two pachinko parlors, and he was feeling a little restless. The night was warm and there was a pronounced presence of moisture in the air. *A little walk would be nice*, thought Cody. So off he wandered, without any particular goal or destination in mind. Since it was Friday there was much activity in the streets, and it was clear that the evening's energy level was rising.

Past an adult bookstore, past a bakery that sold anatomically correct gingerbread men and women, and forward some more, Cody heard an African man, who he thought was likely Nigerian, say, "Hey, buddy. You looking for a party?"

Hearing the voice, but not hearing the content, Cody said, "Huh, what?"

"Hey, mon. You speak English?" asked the sharply-dressed dark-skinned man.

"Hai! Watashi wa Amerika jin desu" (Yes! I am American), said Cody feeling proud that he could communicate with the friendly stranger.

"Hey, mon, you come with me," said the Nigerian grabbing hold of Cody's arm. "In my club you will have a great time."

"Yeah, okay," said Cody, whereby the dark-skinned gentleman escorted him to a booth and sat him down at a table centered under a dimly lit ceiling lamp.

"You want a drink? It is on the house."

"Yeah, sure. I guess."

Several minutes later a young Filipino woman sat down at Cody's table. "Hey, big guy. Care to buy a girl a drink?"

"I don't know. I really shouldn't. I've got a girl I'm dating," Cody said in self-amplification of the importance of his developing friendship with Cynthia.

"My name is Lulu. Are you sure we couldn't have just one drink?"

"Well maybe one." At that point, Lulu slid a business card with her name printed on it. Cody looked at the card prior to placing it in the interior pocket of his jacket. "Thank you, Lulu."

Unimpressed with the ambience of the club, Cody sat sipping on his drink slower than he ever thought was possible, finally bringing himself to the point of becoming completely sober. As Lulu and he chatted, Cody became increasingly aware that regardless of what he said, the girl would cover her mouth and giggle, without pause, much as if he was delivering the most hysterical monolog ever conceived. Somehow, he knew something just wasn't right. He had never been found to be so funny by others in the past. Cody just couldn't imagine what Lulu could find so captivating about the exceedingly ordinary life he'd led. After an hour he'd scarcely taken more than a couple of very small sips from his complimentary drink.

Lulu on the other hand, had ordered and quickly consumed three drinks, only one of which Cody had authorized. When Lulu ordered a fourth drink, and quickly retreated into the bathroom, Cody knew something was about to happen. As Cody sat back, another man, presumably also Nigerian, advanced to his table.

"Hey, buddy. I'm going to have to collect on Lulu's drinks," said the man as he handed Cody a bill for 40,000 yen (approximately 400 dollars).

"You've got to be kidding me."

"Hey, mon. No joke here. You gotta pay up, mon."

At that point, Cody just sat for a moment as he watched the man walk away. Finally he took one look around, gulped his drink, and headed to the restroom. The lavatory was a raunchy rat-hole with leaking fixtures and a stench that strongly dictated just how long a patron could linger. When Cody exited the restroom he was greeted by two very business-like Japanese men who directed him to a room located at the rear of the club.

"Hey friend, I think that we have a problem. Randal says that you've not paid your bill. I'm sure that there must be some mistake."

"No. Actually there is no mistake. I told the manager, I guess it was 'Randal,' that I was not responsible for Lulu's tab. Really, there is no mistake!"

Point blank, the tone of the room greatly changed and the next thing Cody knew was that he'd been pushed to the floor and sensed that another man was coming up behind him. Immediately, Cody launched to his feet and delivered a series of crushing blows to the unsuspecting Japanese heavies, one following another in rapid succession. Once both men were on the ground, Cody followed through with repeated kicks to the head and gut until each man was rolling about the floor, groaning in agony. Before he knew it, Cody was stomping on each of the men's heads with his dress shoes until his every step transferred blood to the floor, much as if his shoes were freshly inked stamp pads. When he finally realized the damage he'd inflicted on the men, he bolted out the door and into a full sprint that he maintained until he reached the train station.

By the time Cody reached the platform, he started to feel a little strange, much as if he was going to regurgitate. Ultimately, he felt so miserable that he stuck his fingers far down into his throat cavity where he was able to purge the contents of his stomach into a waste receptacle. Still, he still didn't feel quite right. He felt dizzy and was so sleepy that he could barely hold his eyes open. Just as Cody was about to lose his battle to remain conscious, a throng of police cars raced by with their sirens piercing the midnight air with a shrill so unpleasant that he stood up to investigate the source, a provision that raised him to his feet just in time to board the train back to his quarters at the Ikemoto Academy.

"Does this train go by the Ikemoto Academy?" Cody asked with befuddlement, as he stepped on to the train.

"*Hai!*" said a passenger sitting across the aisle in the dimly lit corridor.

Once Cody took a seat, assured that he was heading for home, he again battled the intense desire to sleep that had nearly overtaken him at the depot. But it wasn't to be, Cody had lost and was soon profoundly unconscious.

"Hey, buddy. Hey you! You wanted to know about the Ikemoto Academy," a voice said to Cody. Now the man began shaking Cody's upper body with some vigor. The voice repeated, "Hey buddy! You've got to get up."

"What? Huh?"

"Ikemoto Academy, it's the next stop!" Finally, Cody ambled to his feet, shifting unsteadily, side to side, as he disembarked the train. The night air was now cool, and for the time it took Cody to stumble toward the lights that illuminated his apartment complex, he was marginally functional, managing to turn his key in the lock before stumbling to the floor of his apartment, where he would lie until morning.

When Cody awoke, as is so often the case with Rohypnol, he could scarcely remember a thing about the evening before. He remembered some bars and a pachinko parlor, and he remembered talking to a girl but he couldn't remember the context. On the positive side, he was pleased to discover that he still had his wallet and found that he was able to account for all but 1,000 yen (ten dollars) of the money that he had brought with him into the Roppongi district the previous evening. One thing particularly puzzled Cody. What was the origin of the spattering of reddish-brownish spots on his shoes and on the lower extremities of his trousers?

Later that afternoon Cody ran into Cynthia in the laundry room just as he had completed folding the last of his clothes. "How are you doing on this fine day?" she asked.

"Oh, I guess I'm pretty good," Cody said noting in himself a certain sense of disingenuity.

"What did you do last night?"

"I went down to the Roppongi district and listened to some music in some bars, went to a couple of pachinko parlors — nothing special I guess."

"You were down in the Roppongi district last night? I heard that place is dangerous."

"Well, I don't know about that, but I imagine that a pretty tough crowd calls the shots down there. I guess it's okay to go there if you know your boundaries."

"You know I heard on the news that last night two yakuza guys were nearly killed by some crazy guy at one of the clubs."

"Yeah, I don't doubt it. I guess that those yakuza guys just go after each other, so it is probably safe for people like you and me."

"I don't know, I guess. So are we still on for tomorrow, Cody?"

"You bet, I'm looking forward to some good eats like we had last time. This time maybe we can buy some food in one of the department stores and then have a little picnic in a park."

"That sounds great. What time do you want to leave?"

"I don't know, how does say nine o'clock sound?"

Bright and early the next morning, Cody and Cynthia boarded a train that took them into the Ginza district. Just prior to boarding, Cynthia picked up a newspaper that was sitting on a bench. "Cody, here is that story about the yakuza beating."

"Oh, yeah? What does it say?"

"It says that the two yakuza guys are in intensive care and that the perpetrator might be a foreigner, maybe an Englishman or an American."

"Wow. That is interesting! What else does it say?" said Cody, now keenly interested in the news story.

"Apparently, some waitress or hostess witnessed the assault. It looks like this bar girl named Rurun watched the assailant as he jumped out from nowhere and slaughtered the unsuspecting men."

"Rurun? That seems like a very strange name."

"It does. I wonder if it is a Japanese interpretation or rendition of some foreign name."

"Yeah, I don't know, but the fellow must have been one tough hombre to have come out on top with two yakuza."

"Cody, promise me if you ever go down to the Roppongi district again that you will be very careful. I just don't want my little fella getting hurt."

"As you wish, my dear. I'll be careful. I promise. But, I'll have you know — I may be slender, but —"

"Oh, look Cody. We're just about at the Ginza station."

"Hey, what do you know? We are."

"*Genki desu ka*?" (Are you in high spirits/energized?), asked Cynthia who was visibly pleased with the pair's arrival in the Ginza.

"Yes, I always become energized by the city," said Cody. "We couldn't have arrived at a better time. Most department stores in the city open at 10:00 a.m. Let's go to Takashimaya."

What "the mall" is to America — the department store is to Japan. Where malls tend to sprawl outward, Japanese department stores rise towards the heavens. Due to Japan's limited floor space, the department-store concept is essential to the spatial constraints of its largest cities. The Ginza district of Tokyo is known for its many top-end department stores, emporiums that offer everything that the Japanese consumer could possibly imagine. Upon entering the ground floor of any one of these mega-stores, the patron immediately becomes saturated with the grandeur of the marketing displays and the magnitude of the array of items for sale. Since women form a large majority of the shopping clientele, one should not be surprised to find the ground floor top-heavy with items of a decidedly feminine disposition. It is common to find aisle after aisle of fashionable women's shoes and sandals. One can find a mind-numbing selection of casual foot-ware that ranges in price from 500 to 1,000 dollars.

Cosmetics and other facial products also occupy prime real estate on this single floor that forms a thoroughfare for every customer. In the cosmetic department, consumers find what appear to be endless face-care booths, each manned by skilled technicians who painstakingly dote on a ceaseless stream of eager women. Generally, men's items are found on floors two and above, with household items, such as furnishings and electronic equipment, being located on the floors above that.

If you are an aficionado of fine food, then you most certainly would have interest in spending some time perusing the basement floors of these glorious mega-stores. Once stepping onto the basement level, the shopper becomes delighted with the vast variety of food artistry and olfactory marvels. Stepping off of the elevator into these grandiose supermarkets transfers the shopper to a taste-sensation paradise that can only be described as heaven on Earth.

There are stands that focus only on tempura, magnificent fish and vegetable morsels encased in the lightest crunchiest batter imaginable. In these food courts fit for a king, you will find single cantaloupe that are packaged in custom-designed wooden crates. You'll discover *tsukemono* (pickled or brined vegetables) of every variety and form, including eggplant preserved in the most luxuriant violet-colored brine conceivable. In addition to the mainstay Napa cabbage varieties, kimchee preparations crafted from daikon radish greens, carrots, and a host of other vegetables fill banks of refrigerated cases. There are incredible *onigari* (rice ball) stands, booths specializing in amazing pastries, cakes, pies, and other artistically crafted baked goods, and stalls selling variations of food products that would stupefy even the most sophisticated Tokyo gastronome.

On other aisles, one can find yakitori stands with fish and meat offerings that would overwhelm even the most indulgent of emperors. One can find marinated scallops on skewers, chicken on skewers, Kobe beef on skewers, and everything short of skewers on skewers. It would appear that, for the right price, there is no food that cannot be threaded on a bamboo stick and grilled.

So it was, on this very fine spring morning, Cody and Cynthia walked the several blocks from the train station toward Takashimaya department store, dodging and rolling through the pulsing crowd until they encountered a very old and very unkempt woman. "Hey, are you two Americans?" said a voice that seemed to have sprung from nowhere.

"Yes, we are," said Cynthia as she alternated glances between Cody and the old woman. "I used to work at a military facility in the Roppongi district after the war," the voice continued.

There existed a great sense of honesty, candor, and dignity in the disheveled lady's content and expression as she warmly described the fair treatment she had received from American servicemen during the United States occupation of Japan. With this relay, Cody and Cynthia listened intently to what the lady had to say; still it remained unclear to them how they should respond. Should they offer her money? Would the kind old woman be offended by a monetary gift? Looking deeply into each other's eyes, Cody and Cynthia nonverbally pondered the matter and wondered what they might do to improve the woman's condition. Was the only want of this woman the simple human desire to be appreciated by others?

Tuning out the entirety of the disruptive Tokyo street scene, Cody and Cynthia hoped that the goodwill they felt in their hearts translated to the old woman from their friendly facial and body gestures. When the old woman momentarily paused, Cynthia said something in Japanese that caused the woman such pleasure and delight that Cynthia and Cody, for a single moment, forgot completely about the pity they felt for the short, gray-haired woman and the challenging life it appeared she led.

With great trepidation, Cody and Cynthia struggled for a higher signal that might properly consummate the care each felt in their heart and soul. What is your name, Miss," said Cody.

"My name? You want to know my name?" said the frail woman with certain disbelief. "My name is Koko."

"Koko, would you honor us by sharing a meal?" said Cody, whereby Cynthia started to quiver and shake before sensing a surge of tears streaming down her face.

"Please, do have a meal with us," said Cynthia now visibly moved. "Please join us for a meal."

"I must thank you for the offer, but I need to be on my way. But sometime I hope that we can do this," said the woman with a certain sense of personal pride in her voice.

"I am going to give you my phone number," said Cynthia as she handed a slip of paper to the lady. "I want you to call me one day so we can spend some time over dinner or lunch."

With a smile and a bow, the old woman resumed her trek down the crowded street, pulling her cart of empty cans and bottles behind her as she became absorbed into the masses of nondescript people.

"Cody, seeing that old woman just about broke my heart. I've lived a very sheltered, privileged life — I know this. But, when you offered to take the woman to lunch, I almost completely broke down. I have never been moved concerning the plight of another person as I have been today."

Reflecting on the American experience of his family, Cody replied, "I think that I understand the sense of disenfranchisement that society casts on people due to conditions that are beyond their control and I certainly understand what it is like to feel alone and unappreciated, but I also know that a certain sense of generic goodwill enters the ether with simple acts of kindness directed to those who we sense are less fortunate than ourselves. But, hey. Enough about me and my ideas."

"Cody, that is really deep. That was a really cerebral comment. Where did that come from?"

"Actually, that was Dr. Phil's closing observation from one episode last week."

"Really?"

"No! Not really. It is just a though that I've long recognized and an ideal that I've long worked to uphold in myself. Are you ready to continue on to Takashimaya?"

Had Cody and Cynthia arrived earlier at Takashimaya, they might have been received by a gauntlet of store employees lining either side of the store's entrance waving vigorously to patrons as they entered the first floor showroom. Instead, the pair's entrance was marked by a personal store tour as delivered by Cody.

"On your left you have your sandals and accessories and on your right you have your makeup and other cosmetics," said Cody with the air of a seasoned Tokyo shopper.

"I know it is early, Cody, but I want to go down to the food court. I'm kind of hungry. Please resume your tour at some point."

With Cynthia's mandate, Cody instructed, "Follow me. We'll take the staircase."

Reaching the basement floor food court, the pair was refreshed to find space so pleasingly temperate and inviting. "Oh, it is so cool and comfortable in here, and the smells are so wonderful. Cody, it is everything I dreamed. It is like a stepped-up version of Uwajimaya."

"What is this 'Uwajimaya' place you keep talking about?"

"There are actually four Uwajimaya stores in the Pacific Northwest, three in the greater Seattle area and one in Beaverton, Oregon. Anyway, Uwajimaya is the Pacific Northwest's answer to Japanese supermarkets. If you ever come to visit me in Seattle, we will have to take a trip there.

Oh, my God, Cody, look at all of the different kinds of fish. I think that I have died and gone to heaven. Do you like sashimi?"

"Actually, I had never tried sushi or sashimi until I was about sixteen or seventeen years old. I mean, I really never tried anything too exotic until then. Anyway, I loved it. Have you ever tried uni, Cynthia?"

"Isn't that sea urchin eggs or something?"

"Actually, what is referred to as uni, are the gonads or sexual organs of a sea urchin. It has a taste that is nearly impossible to describe to the uninitiated. I guess, I'd say that it has a rich, almost nutty, flavor with amazing ocean-like overtones. But for uni to be A-grade, for it to be top-notch, it has to be ultra-fresh. Good quality uni typically has the exact color-hue as California's state flower," provided Cody, as he enthusiastically marveled over the culinary virtues of the spiny invertebrate. "Aren't you going to ask me what the state flower is?"

"Isn't it the California poppy?"

"How did you ever know that, Ms. Martin?"

"We have California poppies growing all across the state of Washington."

Quite leisurely, the pair picked up some vegetarian sushi rolls, a couple of chicken yakitori skewers, a package of what looked to Cynthia like Rainier cherries, and some cold green tea. They then set their bearings for a park Cody knew of that was situated on the outskirts of the Emperor's Palace. The park, known as Hibiya Park, is said to be among Japan's first western-style parks.

"Cynthia, tell me what you know about the palace and the palace grounds in general."

"I'm not so sure that I know much more about it than you. I know that Tokyo is referred to as the "eastern capital" to distinguish it from the original capital of Japan which was located in Kyoto."

"What can you tell me about the royal family?" said Cody hoping to glean some of the fruits of Cynthia's knowledge of Japanese history.

"You know what I want to know?" said Cynthia redirecting the conversation to a subject that had been tantalizing her since she became aware of Cody Japanese heritage. "I want to know when your Japanese ancestors left Japan for America. I want to know what the motivation was to come to America. I want to know about your family's early American experiences. And … "

"Hold on a minute, girl. Even if I knew the answers to each of your questions, it would take some time to put the information into concise form."

"I understand," replied Cynthia realizing that she'd shot-off a substantial barrage of inquiries without pause.

"I can tell you that my great grandfather came to America around 1912, and that he left Japan because he sensed greater opportunity existed for him on the other side of the Pacific Ocean. I can also tell you that my family's American experience was filled with many hardships. I can tell you that my grandfather's entire family was interned in a war relocation center for more than three years. And, while I don't wish to complain, even I have been exposed to prejudice, oppression, and intolerance. In many ways I do not feel that I've successfully integrated as an American or into American culture. These concerns form a large part of my motivation to spend this period of my life in Japan. So far, the experience has served as an awakening for me. I've only been here a couple of months, but honestly I can't even begin to express how much richer I've become both spiritually and culturally for the experience. At the risk of placing myself in a vulnerable position, I'd say that meeting up with you has been one of the highlights of my experience here in Tokyo."

"Thank you, Cody. I would like to hear more about the experiences of your family as your thoughts come into form."

As Cody and Cynthia settled into their lunch, the two men who tried to rough up Cody where taking in what nutrients they could via plastic tubes that had been threaded into their stomach via their nose and throat. Ever since the two men were admitted to the hospital, there had been a steady stream of visitors, ranging from relatives and associates to law enforcement officials. Both men were conscious to some degree during their stay at the hospital, but they were severely limited in their range of activities. The Roppongi police directed a battery of inquiries to both men. "Had either of you seen the assailant before? What, if anything, did you do to provoke the assailant? What words were exchanged between you and the assailant? What did the assailant look like? Was the assailant on drugs?"

To avoid making any comments that might alert the police to any suspicion regarding the two men, their answers were limited to yes or no, where possible. Throughout the interview the police seemed to ask all of the right questions and seemed intent on solving the crime. One of the primary challenges associated with the development of top-notch police units in Japan is that most police have very little experience dealing with real-life crime, particularly violent crime. This should not be particularly surprising to those who are aware that Japan has very little crime compared with other industrialized nations. This said, when Japanese cops get together to solve crimes, the good-intentioned police force operates much as if it were assembled from a well-meaning group of Cub Scouts, rather than a seasoned group of veteran law enforcement professionals. Of course, as in the present case, it doesn't help the process when one or more parties fail to provide complete disclosure. Since the two men provided limited details concerning the confrontation, Cody had very little to worry about concerning being confronted by law officials regarding the incident in the Roppongi district.

With the sun directly overhead, Cody and Cynthia reflected on their meal. "That was an excellent lunch. It was filling enough to hit the spot, but not so excessive that I feel like taking a nap," said Cody.

"I totally agree, but as we explore deeper into the culture I want to challenge myself with food of a more exotic nature. I want to step off the beaten path wherever possible," Cynthia said with an air of reflection on the sheltered life that she'd led and a hint of permanence in her friendship with Cody.

"I'm with you on that. I want to take a good look around the Tsukiji Fish Market one of these days."

"Oh, I want to go there! We should do that soon, but I hear that to really take in everything, you have to get there very early in the morning," said Cynthia as the pair hoisted their belongings and set out to explore Hibiya Park.

Hibiya Park is a wonderful forty-acre recreation area located just southeast of the grounds of the Imperial Palace, also known as Edo Castle. Some portions of the park are grandly forested wild spaces of the same mold as American parks such as San Francisco's — Golden Gate Park and New York City's — Central Park. In other places there are wide open areas that under agreeable weather conditions support numerous recreational venues. The space contains two large ponds, expansive grassy fields, various groves of cherry and dogwood trees, and the world's largest gingko tree. There are huge fields for sporting events, and for those with connections with government officials, tennis courts are available. There is an open air music hall, a library, a restaurant, and a large public hall. Very careful inspection of the easternmost corner of the park reveals the ivy-covered ruins of an ancient tower that once stood guard over the grounds of the Imperial Palace.

From where Cody and Cynthia ate lunch near the banks of Shinji pond, at the north-eastern corner of the park, they decided to take the walk to Kumogata pond. This pathway took them through one of the park's two flower gardens where they discovered a shockingly intriguing sculpture. The bronze artwork was titled *Lupa Romana*, a title which refers to a female wolf with a reference to Rome. The sculpture was a gift from Italy in 1938 and depicts a wolf with two suckling infants. It is hard to imagine a piece of artwork that simultaneously stirs up in the mind a more disturbing and compelling scenario. The piece is a recast of an original artwork that dates back to the fifteenth century.

"Oh, my goodness, Cynthia, is that supposed to be Romulus and Remus? That is absolutely crazy. It's unfathomable. It's preposterous! Do you think that children could have been ever raised by a wolf?"

"I don't know, Cody, but it sure makes you think. I heard that in the legend there was this girl who was sworn to chastity. She was a vestal virgin who gave birth to two infant boys. Ultimately, the babies were taken away from her and placed on a river bank in a basket, where they floated away as the river flooded. Anyway, the boys were discovered by a wolf named Lupa and she raised them to be leaders, leaders who each ruled their own city. Sounds kind of crazy, huh?"

"I don't know. I guess I've heard crazier things, but it is rather hard to believe."

"I've read some about this, and while there have been examples of feral children, children who are left to their own devices to fend for themselves, there have been no documented cases of children being raised by wolves. As a linguist of sorts, I do know that these feral children typically never become functional members of society, regardless of the quality or the intensity of the intervention they receive after having been discovered. Apparently, there is a definite window of opportunity in a child's life where the process of developing speech must occur."

"Boy, Cynthia, you've really studied and thought about this a lot," Cody said realizing that he'd likely not be adding much to the conversation from a substantive standpoint.

"You know, it's kind of funny. America doesn't really seem to have many folk legends that capture the imagination and take you away. Sure, we have the Wizard of Oz, Paul Bunyan, and Bigfoot, but they seem so pedestrian compared with the richness of Greek mythology, or even Japanese folk lore."

"Well, what do you expect? The entirety of America's history has taken place subsequent to the Age of Scientific Enlightenment and the Age of Reason."

"Oh, Cody, must we reduce the romantic impulses and essences of folklore to such hard forms?"

"I guess you're right. It does take some of the fun and mystique out of it," Cody provided, realizing the fault in his oversimplification.

With this, the couple stepped back onto the pathway that led to Kumogata pond. The walkway was heavily lined with pines, maples, ginkgo, and dogwood. In places, the canopy became very thick, and in regions off the trail the wild spaces became very brushy, almost to the point where one could conceal him or herself from passing visitors. The park's undeveloped areas were so dense in places that it seemed reasonable to Cody that he could momentarily excuse himself to attend to personal business, just as he had done countless times in the Stanislaus National Forest, near his home. "Cynthia, if you would excuse me for a moment, I need to step off the trail."

"Uh, yeah, okay. I'll just wait here. I'll see you in a second," Cynthia said, with a certain sense of discomfort with the situation.

After a couple of minutes, Cynthia thought it strange that Cody had not returned. Then, when she heard the bushes rustling, she said, "I thought I lost you, Cody." Just as she spoke, an animal about the size of a small dog scurried from out of the brush directly toward Cynthia. The animal very much looked like a raccoon, but possessed facial features that were much more doglike than any raccoon she'd ever seen around her Lake Washington home on Mercer Island. Thinking that she had encountered a small dog, Cynthia said, "Hey, fella, come here. Where is your master?"

Looking at Cynthia, the beast came somewhat closer where it focused intently into her eyes as if to say, "Come and follow me. Come and follow me into the trees." As the creature retreated into the wooded area along an undeveloped trail, Cynthia followed until the animal maneuvered out of sight.

Just then, she heard the bushes rustle, much as if the dog or raccoon or whatever it was, was coming back her way. While she was looking at the scrubby trees and tall bushes in the distance, Cody came into view. "Hey, Cody, I thought that you said you'd be right back."

"What are you talking about? Heavens, I haven't been gone for more than a minute or two."

"Cody, you must have some really deviated conception of time. You've been gone for close to ten minutes. I looked at my watch when you left. It was 12:40 and now it is 12:49, almost ten till."

"Yeah, I don't know, Cynthia, but I'm back now."

"Cody, when you were in the brush, did you see that dog? It must have passed you. It looked like a raccoon. You had to have seen it!"

"No, I didn't see anything. I just took care of my business and immediately came out."

"Oh, my God, Cody. I know what it was! That wasn't a dog and it wasn't a raccoon. I just saw a tanuki. I just saw a tanuki. That was — a tanuki!" exclaimed Cynthia very excitedly.

"What is a tanuki?" Cody said, unsure whether he should be jumping up and down with excitement or evacuating the area.

"A tanuki is a wild animal that looks like a cross between a raccoon and a dog. Some people say it is like a dog and a badger mixed together. The tanuki is often called a *raccoon-dog*."

"I don't know Cynthia. It is awful hard to believe that a wild animal the size of a dog could live a life in — what is in all practicality – the heart of Tokyo."

"I know that it sounds odd, but I know what I saw. It came right up to me and looked deep into my eyes, its nose puckering and expanding as it sniffed the air about near me. I'd swear that it was a tanuki that I saw. I'm going to look up tanuki sightings when I get back to the apartment."

"Yeah, I'd be interested to know myself," said Cody with a hint that he'd need more convincing to fully accept the accuracy of Cynthia's claim.

With the authenticity of the tanuki sighting lacking resolution, the couple continued down the pathway toward Kumogata pond. It was a beautiful warm June day, neither too hot nor too humid. When the pair arrived at the pond they were struck by the mastery of the finely manicured trees and shrubbery that surrounded the small lake. Many of the trees appeared to be shaped into forms suggesting that they were in a perpetual state of exposure to gale-force winds, while others looked as if they had lived a peaceful existence, never having been much altered by human industry.

After taking in the manifest serenity of the lake for several minutes, Cynthia motioned that she felt the time had come to return to the housing complex. "Cody, this has been great fun. I've really had a good time, but I think we need to start back toward the academy," Cynthia said in a detached sense, much as if she had other thoughts on her mind.

Wishing that the day would last, yet not wanting to foreclose future opportunities to explore Japan with Cynthia, Cody said, "Let's go. It has been a rather full day."

With Cody's acknowledgement, the pair reversed their course and headed back to where they had entered the park. From the park boundary, they walked back into the Ginza and to the train station where they would secure transportation back to the academy.

The return trip was largely silent, Cody's thoughts having returned to the fogginess of Friday night and Cynthia's imagination being preoccupied with her encounter with what she thought was a tanuki. By 3:30 p.m., Cody and Cynthia were making a slow approach to their apartments. "Well, Cynthia, I had a fine day. Where should we go next time?" Cody asked as he worked toward receiving a commitment from Cynthia that might solidify a future outing.

Not making any effort toward looking at Cody, she said, "I don't know Cody. I'll have to think about that one. Are you prepared for classes tomorrow?"

In alignment with Cynthia's seemingly aloof response, Cody replied, "I've got a couple of loose ends to synch up, I guess." Smiling at one another, Cody and Cynthia separated for the day.

When Cynthia arrived home she was still strongly affected by her encounter with what she assumed to be a tanuki. A quick search on the internet revealed, that while no tanuki sightings were specific to Hibiya Park, at least one sighting took place in the Shingawa district of Tokyo, two miles to the south of Hibiya Park. The Shingawa incident had occurred the previous year, and its credibility seemed warranted as several people had documented the encounter. In Cynthia's mind it seemed entirely reasonable that tanuki could coexist in the city alongside the uncountable masses of people. After all, raccoons were routinely observed in the heart of Seattle's business district during the more shadowy portions of the day. Why couldn't tanuki find adequate cover and food in a city as massive as Tokyo? Further, if tanuki can swim, couldn't they swim across the moat that surrounds the Imperial Palace grounds, thus securing a wooded niche where they could thrive in relative obscurity? Employing her research and her chain of logic, Cynthia was able to convince herself that, even if Cody didn't personally see the beast, she was sane and what she saw must have been a raccoon dog.

When Cody arrived home his thoughts returned to the brownish spots on the slacks he had worn the evening he spent in the Roppongi district. Were the spots oxidized-blood that he'd perhaps transferred to his pants while walking through bushes or through contact with some other blood-laden substrate? When he emptied his backpack Cody unloaded a half-eaten sushi roll that he put in the refrigerator, Cynthia's newspaper, and the sport jacket that he'd brought.

After hanging up his jacket, he prepared a cup of green tea and turned on the television. The only station that Cody fully understood was CNN International, but sometimes, as in the present case, he'd test his skill at trying to decipher the programing on one of the multitude of Japanese stations he had at his disposal. Flipping through the channels, Cody found one news station that appeared to be showing a region of Tokyo that he'd visited at some point, but he couldn't quite identify the location, beyond that it was somewhere in the Roppongi district. Then it clicked. The place that the news station was filming was outside of one of the drinking establishments that he'd been to two days earlier. Unbeknownst to Cody, it was that same club where he had been served the drink that nearly incapacitated him. All that Cody could make out from the story was that a crime of one sort or another had taken place, and that it had something to do with either the yakuza or some other classification of criminal element.

As Cody sipped his tea, his eyes focused on the article that Cynthia had brought to his attention earlier that day. From what he could understand from the article, it appeared that the report he'd seen on the television might have concerned the identical attack that was written up in the paper. In scanning the article, his eyes caught site of the very curious name — *Rurun*. For some reason the name seemed eerily familiar, but that was as far as the thought unfolded in his mind.

Later that evening, Cynthia's mind got the better of her and she found herself sketching in a notebook, as she so often did when she had things on her mind. She often used her artwork as a means of fleshing out hidden meaning in her life that just didn't seem to show its face along ordinary channels. She sketched a drawing of the old lady that Cody and she had met earlier that day, but took the liberty of portraying her dressed in a fine kimono rather than the grimy garb she had been wearing during their encounter. In drawing in the lady's facial features, she replaced her sullen expressions with a sly look that made it appear that she knew some fantastic secret that no one else knew. In another drawing, Cynthia outlined a sketch of several well-dressed men in black suits who were standing around in a parking lot leaning against luxury cars near what looked like a park or a ball field. By the end of the evening, Cynthia had sketched into each drawing a caricature of a sharply dressed shadowy figure that possessed bodily distortions that were suggestive of the unusual creature she'd seen earlier that day, just off the trail, in Hibiya Park.

Over the ensuing two weeks, Cody and Cynthia spent only the amount of time together that could occur in passing one another in the breezeway or through short periods in the faculty workroom or during after school staff meetings. This lack of face-time confused Cody to some degree, but in reality nothing was at play that put his blossoming friendship with Cynthia in any danger of being discontinued. More correctly, Cynthia did like Cody, and in fact liked him quite a bit. During this time, Cynthia was in deep contemplation about a relationship that she felt in her heart could commence at just about any moment. Meanwhile, Cody questioned whether thinking about Cynthia in any other manner than as a colleague really made any sense.

Butchers and Caretakers

Historically, no other group in Japanese society has been at the receiving end of greater ostracism or has been subjected to more discrimination than has the class of citizens known as the *burakumin* or hamlet people. During the Edo period, the caste of people at the absolute bottom of the social hierarchy was the burakumin. In addition to being composed of generalized outcasts, this group was assembled from members of Japanese society who were thought either to be of defiled character or participants in livelihoods that were considered to be vile or impure. It was in the *buraku* (hamlets) that one would find those individuals who were intimately involved with death, the taking of life, or any of its gruesome manifestations. Tactfully stated, the burakumin caste was an assembly of societal members considered to possess less than meritorious virtues.

It seems curious that the Japanese culture, a culture that places such great emphasis upon personal and societal modesty, doing so to the point where it is culturally unacceptable to flaunt personal achievement, would permit its membership to tolerate, or worse-yet perpetuate, the ostracism of any subgroup of its populace, regardless of the lifestyles, ways, or mannerisms exemplified by such peoples. The severity of this judgment and its outcome is apparent in the record of Japanese history as well as within modern-day society, however potentially unwarranted or inappropriate it might be or appear to be. To the credit of the Japanese people, at least these feelings and judgments are out in the open — for all to see — and not harbored secretly or hidden under the cloak of disingenuity or societal dishonesty. There is something respectable about letting people know up front, with full disclosure, of their perceived failings, whether genuine or imagined.

In contrast, in modern-day America, the tendency of the populace is to judge people by what they have, rather than their line of employment, their educational background, or the degree of their generosity, honesty, or benevolence towards others. Overall, America would seem to be populated with the most superficially oriented citizenry of any of the industrialized nations. In America, people couldn't care less what you do for a living or how pure or impure you are of heart. In America, for the average man or woman, what is important is whether or not you shop at Neiman Marcus or Kohl's, whether you drive a Lexus or a Ford, or whether you run with the "truly beautiful people" or the gang down at the neighborhood pub.

For Cody, it was this sort of value system that poisoned his mind and that placed the brakes on many of his dreams. When Cody first set his eyes on Cynthia Martin, he was captivated by her physical beauty and her poise. As he got to know her in her position as sensei at the Ikemoto Academy, he watched her very closely, being especially intrigued by her carefree spirit, her friendly attitude, and her innate ability to navigate through even the most challenging of circumstances.

Each day Cody couldn't wait to see Cynthia, he was so excited by her presence. In his heart he knew that girls like Cynthia didn't become intimately involved with people like him, people of his upbringing, but even this didn't seem to matter. Paradoxically, this realization offered him much comfort, as it served to subdue the feelings that tugged upon his heart with such vigor. Still, Cody wondered. *Cynthia — beautiful, elegant, sophisticated, brilliant, and well-heeled — they could be cordial colleagues at the academy, couldn't they?* Cody knew that he'd never be rich and that, so far, he'd been anything but lucky. He knew that he'd never have the right look to share time with Cynthia, and he knew that he could never introduce Cynthia to his father. Cody was all mixed up — yet he seemed to love every minute of it.

As a distraction, Cody spent his evenings developing his Japanese vocabulary and grammar. More important, he started to invest solid effort into learning the Japanese writing system known as *Hiragana*. Each night Cody would review vocabulary words, written on flash-cards from the previous evening, before moving into preparing that particular evening's set of cards.

Cody's system of learning the new material was very simple. On one side of the flash card he would write the Hiragana symbols, for example: つみ, accompanied with the English translation: "crime." On the card's reverse he would write *tsumi*, the *Romaji* form of the word. The first symbol, つ, represents the sound *tsu*. The second symbol: み represents the sound: *mi* (pronounced "me"). Within a week Cody had mastered the forty-six characters that are considered to be most basic to the Hiragana system of writing.

Sometimes, late at night, Cody would turn on the small television he'd acquired, towards the challenge of trying to decipher the late night news. One night he encountered a particularly interesting story that involved the Japanese crime syndicates known as yakuza. According to the story, from what he could tell, a Tokyo-based yakuza group had been implicated in some sort of wrongdoing in a Ginza pachinko parlor, but he couldn't be sure of the specifics. Cody found something about the power structure of the Japanese criminal syndicate utterly fascinating.

There is something perversely attractive and alluring about this relatively little-known criminal organization. There always seems to be a certain seductiveness associated with entities that are somehow enmeshed in mystery. For Cody — who, in his heart, often felt that he was little more than damaged goods — the thought seemed even more alluring. Cody perceived that there was something about the lifestyle of the yakuza that was glamorous, daring, and against the grain, yet somehow important and worthy. He envisioned that the yakuza was composed of solitary young men, men detached from society and in some instances even estranged from their own families. Strangely, to some degree, this profile seemed to fit his own image. Just before losing consciousness that night, Cody reflected on an old Pony Express recruitment bulletin from the 1860s that had caught his eye on a fieldtrip that his sixth grade class took to the Oakland Museum of California. The announcement read:

"WANTED. YOUNG, SKINNY, WIRY FELLOWS. NOT OVER 18. MUST BE EXPERT RIDERS. WILLING TO RISK DEATH DAILY. ORPHANS PREFERRED."

The Yakuza in Japanese Society

It is important to understand that the yakuza is an integral part of Japanese society. Unlike the Cosa Nostra, whose work is figuratively done under the cloak of night, the yakuza carry out many of their operations in the open, for all to see. In fact, many yakuza organizations have storefront offices that are open to the public in the communities they serve. There exists a unique symbiosis between the yakuza, the citizenry, and law enforcement.

Some say that if any one of the three legs of this structure were to be removed or substantially altered, society in Japan, as it is known, would collapse. It is said that Japan has somewhere in the neighborhood of 110,000 active yakuza members dispersed among less than thirty crime organizations. To provide some perspective, the Cosa Nostra is said to have roughly 5,000 active members worldwide, while the yakuza is almost entirely limited to Japan, a country that occupies an area smaller than the state of Montana, a country with a population (130 million) that is just over forty percent of the population of the United States. The yakuza is said to be the largest criminal organization in existence, yet Japan has among the lowest incidence of crime of any developed nation. The yakuza has such a tight grip on some communities that virtually no street crime exists, whatsoever. No petty small-time hoodlum would dare operate in a community that exhibits a strong yakuza presence.

History suggests that modern day yakuza may have their origin in the *kabukimono*, an aggressively rowdy strain of masterless samurai that prowled the streets in flamboyant garments and who spoke in a manner that was considered vulgar and intolerant. The quintessential outcasts of the day, they felt answerable to no one, yet strongly loyal to one another. The present day yakuza first took on their modern form in the late 17th century. Their contingent was largely formed from the bakuto and the tekiya, the gamblers and the peddlers, respectively. It was in these groups that the so-called *oyabun-kobun*, father-child, relationship developed and evolved. In short, the *oyabun* is the family boss and the *kobun* are the various underlings in a particular yakuza organization.

In Japanese culture, family loyalty is a natural outcome. A father's law is, quite-simply, meant to be obeyed.

An extremely structured organizational hierarchy defines the position and function of each member of a yakuza family. The catalyst for the explosive growth of the present day yakuza was the entrance of the *gurentai* or "violent yakuza" into the bakuto and tekiya populated ranks, an occurrence that took place shortly after the close of WWII. Since many gurentai were considered little more than street thugs, this movement was considered pivotal in that it doubtlessly led to a lowering of the standards associated with admission into yakuza organizations. In short, this lowering of the bar opened the floodgates to some of Japan's most reviled outcast groups, groups including burakumin, *hinin* (nonpersons), and foreigners (most notably those of Korean origin).

Today, the term burakumin refers to individuals with a personal history or family history within vocations that involve death. Examples of such occupations include tannery workers, butchers, undertakers, and other individuals who handled corpses or body parts. The hinin were individuals so low on the Homo sapiens hierarchal scale that they weren't even considered to be members of the human race. Examples of professions that were occupied by hinin included executioner, vocations that involved torture, and tasks such as sawing-off human heads for public display. If it could be said that Japan has reduced the traditional scorn that has been imposed on the burakumin and the hinin, it can only be said that this has taken place because these unjustly treated peoples have become increasingly difficult to spot or identify in modern society.

Even today, association with known burakumin, by the standards of most Japanese citizens, is so repulsive that such interaction is to be avoided at all costs. So intense is the rejection of the burakumin class that Japanese citizens go to extreme measures to avoid contact with this sub-class of

Japanese society. In 1995, after discovering that she'd given birth to a child sired by a burakumin, a Japanese woman became so distraught that she refused to touch or even look at her child. Subsequently, the woman returned to her parents' home, where she vowed eternal estrangement from her husband and child.

It is said that the modern yakuza is disproportionably populated by those considered to be burakumin. Reflective of this trend, the buraku (the hamlets where the burakumin reside) now accommodate extravagant American-style homes outfitted with sprawling porch-like landings and covered carports occupied by Mercedes Benz automobiles and other high-end luxury cars. It is little wonder why so many of the children born into the poverty, depredation, and oppression associated with the reality of the burakumin, seek admittance into the often violent way of life inclusive to yakuza membership.

Regardless of the ethnic, cultural, or hierarchal-class compositions associated with individual yakuza organizations, there tends to be deep internal loyalty associated with such membership. Of course, this shouldn't be surprising as the organizational structure is modeled after the father-child relationship of previous reference. Doubtlessly, a certain portion of yakuza membership is composed of men who have joined the organization, either in part or as a primary motivator, to experience the feeling of reciprocity associated with the father-child relationship. Just as important as the father-child relationship to the yakuza organizational structure are the traditions and rituals that have bound members since the early days of such organizations.

The initiation ritual for new yakuza members is one such tradition. At the initiation ceremony, known as *sakazuki-goto*, of a yakuza inductee, two cups of sake are poured that symbolize the "blood-of-brotherhood." One cup is poured tall with sake and the other is poured short. Fish scales and salt are introduced into each vessel and the two men drink. The yakuza boss (the father) drinks out of the nearly full cup, while the inductee (the child) drinks out of the smaller-portioned vessel. The two glasses are then exchanged, whereby each man consumes the remaining contents of the exchanged volume of the salty fish-scale-laden sake. Empty vessels mark the conclusion of the induction ceremony.

Another tradition associated with yakuza membership is the practice of decorating one's skin with extensively ornate body art. In Japan, these tattoos are known as *irezumi*, which literally means to — insert ink. It is said that it is common for yakuza members to possess full-body tattoos, these tattoos often being applied via the ancient method whereby sharpened bamboo spikes are repeatedly inserted under the skin. When using traditional methods, the practice of completely tattooing an individual can take years to accomplish. At the conclusion of the process, the subject will be canvased in tattoos in such a manner that, when dressed in business attire, no portion of the tattooed region is visible to others. On occasions, tattooed yakuza members reveal themselves to their colleagues when they get together to play the card game *oicho kabu*. When this game is played, yakuza members shed their shirts in a display of the artfully fantastic forms that seem to come to life on their bodies.

Beyond the tradition and ceremony associated with the yakuza, the real business of such organizations is to make money and to maintain the level of honor and respect necessary to protect personal interests from other yakuza groups. For the most part, this means managing and maintaining loan-sharking operations, gambling establishments, and stables of prostitutes, and collecting kickbacks from private and governmental infrastructure projects. In most instances, yakuza groups have their particular jurisdictions in which they operate, and in most instances they do not stray beyond such boundaries.

Sometimes, however, the age-old, unwritten codes of the yakuza are broken, and when violations become sufficiently offensive to the injured party — the most explosive and fiery kind of hell imaginable breaks out.

To illustrate the point, some years back a powerful Roppongi-based yakuza group was in the process of absorbing another, smaller, yakuza group in a peaceful, business-like proceeding. As part of the merger, a lieutenant from the dominant yakuza group redistricted the organization's turf boundaries, much to the dissatisfaction of a lesser known, albeit extremely violent, yakuza group. In protest of the new demarcations, the violent yakuza group sent a message to the dominating yakuza organization, in the form of two motor-scooter-mounted armed assassins, that the lieutenant had figuratively — drawn the wrong line in the sand. Using borrowed terminology, the *Tokyo Times* reported that the *hittoman* (hit man/hit men) routed three shots into the victim's head and stomach, at point-blank range, in broad-daylight, in front of numerous onlookers. Needless to say, when the police arrived moments after the incident, no witnesses were available to be interviewed. To this day, the *chi no baransushito* (literally, blood balance sheet) remains precarious and unsettled.

While much of the code associated with yakuza organizations works toward self-protection against opposing yakuza forces, there are internal codes that work to support the cohesion and welfare of the mother organization from within. One such aspect of the unwritten code involves the age-old yakuza practice of *yubitsume*, or finger shortening. The practice of yubitsume is literally the act of a yakuza member cutting off a portion of his own finger or fingers, starting with his pinky finger on his left hand. It is essential for a yakuza member to perform yubitsume if he has embarrassed his organization or failed to properly execute a directive, or is the cause of a fellow yakuza member's death, injury, or arrest. If such an event takes place, the offender might expect to find his boss passing on to him a string, a knife, and a piece of paper, within which to wrap the dismembered finger joint. The practice has a long rich history that has reference to the days of the samurai.

As anyone who has ever handled a sword or a fighting stick of any description would acknowledge, the pinky finger plays a critical role in the control of a sword or stick. In fact, the three fingers farthest from the thumb are instrumental in maintaining a tight grip on a sword. When a yakuza member offers his boss or another individual his paper-bundled severed joint, he is in effect making an offer of penance or apology. What the offender is essentially relaying to the receiver of his offering is that he has failed, that he is repenting, and that he has accepted responsibility for his actions. Historically, the idea was that a member of a particular samurai brotherhood with a weak sword grip would be of greater loyalty, and thus work increasingly hard to bolster his contributions in other ways to support his mother organization, in result of his self-imposed handicap. As can be imagined, there is a certain stigma associated with missing segments of fingers. In recent years, much to the relief of the psyche of yakuza everywhere, several prosthetic companies have designed very high-quality prosthetic fingers. It has been reported that the highest-quality, albeit the most expensive, digits are manufactured in England.

It is important to note that many modern day yakuza reject the notion that its origin and roots are in the groups of wandering men known collectively as the kabukimono. As an alternative theory, many yakuza suggest that their organizations have root in the *machi-yakko* ("servants to the people") movement, which essentially describes yakuza predecessors as lawful community-action groups whose primary role was service to the people. This suggestion has some merit when taking into consideration the relief role that yakuza groups have assumed in times of emergency in modern-day Japan.

Among other examples, the aforementioned claim is supported by both the massive Kobe earthquake of 1995 and the incredibly calamitous tsunami that struck off the coast of Japan in March 2011 (an event that resulted in the crippling of the Fukushima Daiichi nuclear power plant). In both instances, local yakuza organizations were among the first groups on the scene to offer generalized assistance in the form of evacuation equipment, a supply of food, and other goods and services essential to the relief effort. In short, local yakuza groups served as general caretakers in their local communities, while designated relief organizations flailed in a state of prolonged chaos prior to mobilization.

The origin of the word yakuza is derived from the Japanese words for eight, nine, and three — in exactly this order. This construction has its roots in the card game oicho kabu. The Japanese words for 8, 9, and 3 are respectively — *yattsu*, *ku*, and *san*, and hence when joined together they loosely form the word yakuza.

The game is usually played with a deck of "flower cards" called *hanafuda*, however, an ordinary deck of playing cards can suffice, if a value of "one" is applied to each ace, and every face-card is removed from the deck. The historical reason that the sequence — eight-nine-three is so ominous has its origin in the fact that in oicho kabu, the sequence 8-9-3 represents the worst possible hand that a player can be dealt. This is because the game constructs player-scores from the smallest digit in the summation of the values of several cards, sometimes three. Since the sum of 8-9-3 is equal to 20, and since the smallest digit of the two numbers is zero — zero, is the resulting score. This hand of cards is deemed the most worthless score one can possibly obtain in oicho kabu. Over time, this numeric sequence has evolved to take on the meaning of useless or worthless bakuto, or people who gamble.

CHAPTER FOUR:
PACKAGING PRODUCTS

Omnipresent in Japan is the supreme refinement of its social structures and cultural traditions. If it can be said that the Japanese are among the most polite culture on the globe, then it can also be said that the Japanese apply the product of their politeness and their specific strain of etiquette as if it collectively formed a fence or protective boundary with the design to deter the populace from the commission of interpersonal infractions, or worse. In Japanese culture, attention to detail and proper presentation are the epitome of every undertaking. This essence is at the center of activities as ordinary as the decorum applied to a peanut butter cookie at a bakery, prior to being presented to the customer, to the day-to-day discourse that occurs between ordinary strangers. In fact, the very code of civility of the Japanese nation appears ancillary to a stringent set of decorous presentation procedures.

Two types of language can be said to be in application in Japanese society. The first, and most common, is known as *keigo*. This type of language structure is most concerned with polite and respectful language, rather than getting down to the real nuts-and-bolts of specific matters. On the other end of the language spectrum is *hadaka hanashi*, or naked language. The primary motivation of this second mode of language places little emphasis on politeness or respect, instead placing the focus of discourse upon being forthright and to the point.

When Cody first joined the staff at the Ikemoto Academy, his Japanese language skills were so poorly developed that his preferred form of communication was something close to silence. It wasn't that Cody didn't want to interact with his colleagues at the academy as much as it was his lack of confidence in his ability to communicate in

Japanese. So where Cody came up short in the language department, he tried to compensate by being well dressed and quick with a smile and a bow. Unfortunately this approach gave many of Cody's colleagues at the academy the feeling that he was at times less than forthright regarding his activities outside of the workplace environment. Perhaps unfair, but the notion prevailed.

Conceivably some of Cody's enigmatic habits could be attributed to his background as a loner or simply as being quirky offshoots of his bachelor lifestyle. Either way, no one at the academy ever questioned any aspect of his personal habits or inclinations.

While Cody's schedule at the academy was a very structured affair, it was not unusual for him to keep strange hours outside of his teaching schedule. Some days after work he would go to his apartment and sleep until the very early hours of the morning, at which time he would drink copious amounts of strong green tea and then silently roll his Vespa away from the academy and cruise off into the night. Some mornings he'd roll back just in time to shower and grab something to eat prior to instructing his courses. There was something that Cody found particularly attractive about darkness and about being alone on the road at night.

Some nights Cody rode his scooter down into the heart of the Ginza. Early on, Cody learned that the most opportune time to navigate the city came either very late at night or very early in the morning. He found something quite spellbinding about taking in the night lights of central Tokyo when the streets were vacant. Some early mornings, Cody would travel down to Tsukiji fish market where he would watch the men as they unloaded hulking bluefin tuna from cavernous refrigerated trucks. Almost everything that Cody knew about the configuration of Tokyo, he learned from his twilight excursions.

It was during these late night rides through the city that Cody learned about the cruel disparity that poverty and sickness, mental or otherwise, unleashed upon Tokyo's hidden people. By night, he found Tokyo's homeless population huddled in doorways or under building overhangs. They could be found in makeshift shelters constructed of cardboard on the outskirts of the Ginza and hidden amongst the towering piles of omnifarious Styrofoam, used for packing fish-products, along the waterfront near the Tsukiji market complex.

Cody never discussed his nighttime jaunts with anyone, but whenever he rode into the city he always packed along bean-paste bread to give to the downtrodden men and women he encountered. It seems so very ironic that the most subjugated, if not neutralized, subset of society is as well among its most liberated, if not empowered, subgroup. So emancipated, so set free, so detached from the mainstream is this class of men, that it seldom seems that anyone puts to scrutiny the motivations behind their genius and or madness. Cody gave great thought to the paradox of Tokyo's hidden people. *What is it that drives these men and woman to orient themselves as outcasts? Why can't these people of the shadows package themselves in the mold of the contrived images that control the streets from nine-to-five? Isn't there some specific point in the lives of these men and women where they consciously choose to stand out so conspicuously?*

Cody seemed to recognize that he could only trust people who didn't question or threaten his image, and that people who initiated character dissections could never be his friends or allies. Never in Cody's life had he felt accepted as American or Japanese, or felt loved and cared for unconditionally by anyone other than his dear mother, the one person in his life that he would have ever moved mountains to have pleased, gone from him for fourteen years.

During the third week of June a letter arrived for Cody from his Uncle Peter. While Peter cared deeply for Cody, his relationship with Cody had many of the earmarks that one might associate with a surrogate parent or guardian. So it was that Peter would make it a point to write Cody every couple of weeks to check up on him and to relay family news and information. Usually the letters were short, largely addressing the weather, the status of the lives of his cousins, and other items that could be considered small talk. And had this letter from Peter stopped midway, it too might have passed off as a chatty letter of little consequence other than to maintain open lines of communication. In this seventh letter since Cody had arrived in Tokyo, Peter put great emphasis in relaying the importance of making connections and forging friendships during his stay. As anyone who knew Cody would attest, he had a particular habit of isolating himself from others, sometimes to the point of appearing irreparably introverted. In the letter Peter counseled, "Whatever you do while you are in Japan — create bonds that will bring you comfort throughout your remaining years."

It was after Peter made this latter point that he shifted into a discussion of the challenges faced by farmers. Initially, it appeared that Peter was talking about generalized plights that farmers faced in their efforts to turn water, soil, nutrients, and sweat into a viable livelihood. But soon it became apparent that what Peter was relaying was that Dwight was experiencing the most challenging production crises since the time he had started to work his plot of land in Oakdale. It wasn't that Dwight was going to lose his farm anytime soon, but the general tone was that if Dwight didn't diversify, and do so soon, he would not far down the road be in a very difficult position, both financially and emotionally. If one word could ever be used to describe Dwight, hands-down it would have to be — stubborn. As Peter reported, nearly half of Dwight's sweet potato crop was experiencing symptoms of what appeared to be some sort of blight. As Peter continued, he shared with Cody that he felt that his father seemed to be distressed to the point where he was "working himself ragged and not making any headway." Peter concluded his letter by emphasizing that his father's state of being was not critical, but that "he most certainly would benefit from hearing from you more often."

Perhaps nothing is more stressful on an individual than to sense that a loved one is in a state of crisis or that a loved one is in need of the spectrum of care and counsel that can only be delivered in person. In the very early hours of the following morning, Cody rolled his motorbike out into the darkness and motored about aimlessly. He roamed the empty streets looking for answers under the bright lights and in the secretions of the shadows. When he thought no one was looking, Cody wobbled his Vespa crazily from side-to-side, much as if he was emulating the pattern a snake makes in the sand. Other times, he would turn corners, while leaning so low to the ground that it looked as if he might take a tumble. Ultimately, the night was his; the road was his, or so it seemed. Just when Cody felt sure that no one was out enjoying the morning in any spirit close to his, he was spooked by an entire troupe of scooter riders who passed him dressed in black. Three o'clock in the morning, and a score of what appeared to be young toughs, on a ride into the night, just as was he. Cody couldn't help but wonder if the group even saw him. The crazy thing was that they drove right by him without even a glance, much as if he were invisible.

As the darkened sky gave way to morning, Cody returned to his apartment and took advantage of the weekend by lounging in his bed, watching television until he could no longer keep his eyes open. He dreamed in sepia tones that he was on his father's Oakdale farm. In his vision he could see his father going through the motions as he fought a debilitating battle against loneliness, the mysterious dread that nature had dealt to his sweet potato crop, and a general emptiness that chipped away at the quality of his every conscious moment. Midway through his dream, Cody was suddenly shocked into wakefulness, with a loud series of raps at his door.

"Cody, are you in there? It's me, Cynthia."

"Huh, what?" said Cody as he came to realize that Cynthia was at his door. "Yeah, I'm coming. Let me put something on," Cody said before opening his door.

"Hey, sleepyhead. What are you doing lying around in bed? It's 10:30."

"Uh, I was up late, riding around on my bike. I got home just before daybreak," said Cody as he buttoned up his shirt and stepped onto the sidewalk outside his apartment.

"What are you, Cody, nocturnal? Sometimes you seem to keep the hours of an owl or a raccoon, or maybe a tanuki."

"Yeah, I know. Sometimes I get to sleep too early, and when that happens I wake up and feel like riding around."

"What do you do out there in the middle of the night?"

"I just ride around on the empty streets. Sometimes, I stop when I see people out walking in the night. Sometimes, I try to talk with them."

"What kind of people are out on the streets in the middle of the night?"

"Oh, I don't know. Just people, I guess, different kinds of people."

"What do you talk about?"

"I don't know. Different things, I guess. I sometimes just see people hanging out on the streets or people trying to sleep. Sometimes, I give them some food or offer a word of kindness."

"Well, that's kind of cool, I guess."

"Yeah, uh, thanks," Cody said in a nervous, somewhat self-conscious, manner.

"Cody, you're just like a raccoon dog, like some sort of an American raccoon dog."

"Thanks, I guess."

"Cody, after you catch up on your sleep, I was wondering if you'd like to have dinner. I was thinking that we could take the train down into the Ginza and have some noodles or something."

"Sounds good. I'm psyched, but let's take the Vespa."

"I don't know. I've never been on a bike before."

"It is very simple. I'll take you into the Ginza, and I'll be safe. All you've got to do is to hold on tight."

"Okay, let's do it," Cynthia said, having accepted Cody's sense of confidence in the matter.

"We'll leave around three, okay?"

"I'll be ready."

Even couched among Cody's large array of quirky attributes, anyone who cared enough to take a closer look could see that he was a man of good character throughout his being. However, it takes a good long time to get to know an individual as independent as Cody. You see, in Cody's adult life he was never groomed to think that he needed to ask for permission from anyone to carry on as he saw fit. If it could be said that ever a man marched to his own drummer, it could certainly be said of Cody.

Shortly after 3 p.m., just as the pair had planned, Cody and Cynthia set off on his Vespa toward the Ginza. The day was quite warm and there was a definite heftiness to the air resulting from the high humidity. As the pair motored to Tokyo's glitzy business district, they were refreshed by the rush of air that accompanied their journey. In relatively short order, Cody found a good location to dock his bike and the pair took in the sights as they half-heartedly searched for a place to take in a meal.

As they walked, they window-shopped, occasionally finding themselves wandering in one store or another looking about with no particular aim. At one point they entered a leather apparel and accessories store, and at Cynthia's suggestion, Cody tried on a number of black leather jackets.

"You know, Cody, if you are going to go traipsing around in the middle of the night on that bad-ass motor bike of yours, you really should be wearing a leather jacket that can offer some protection in the event that you fall or have some other mishap."

"Yeah, I guess."

"Here, look at this one. It is a heavy-duty zip-up jacket that definitely has some weight to it."

"I don't know. Its 45,000 yen."

"Cody, you really can't equate your safety with a couple of hundred bucks. Besides, I have a sense how you drive that thing when you ride alone."

"Yeah, I guess I could try it on."

"What size jacket do you wear, a 42, or so?"

"About a 42 long, maybe a little larger."

"Here is a 44 long. I don't think that you want a jacket that's too tight."

Cody liked the way the jacket fit as he posed in front of a mirror. "I kind of like the way it hugs my body and I really like the silk lining. But at close to $500, I don't know."

Looking over Cody's shoulder and into his reflection, Cynthia asserted, "That, sir, is a rad scooter jacket. You just have to get it! Let's ask the salesman if the price is negotiable."

Walking over to the sales counter, Cynthia said something that Cody couldn't quite make out, whereby the salesman responded with a statement that was equally inaudible.

"What did he say?"

"He said that you could have the jacket for 37,000 yen if we pay in cash. So we would have to go to an ATM, if we want to do it."

"You know, I really do like the fit."

"I think you should get it, Cody. I mean Raccoon Dog."

"That's a good one, Cynthia." said Cody as he resumed his general habit of not drawing attention to himself.

"Yeah, well, as you get to know me, Raccoon Dog, you'll learn that I have a lot of good ones like that." And with that, the couple ventured to the nearest ATM and immediately returned to purchase the leather jacket.

"I think that it is way too hot to wear the jacket now. If we stay downtown late, though, you should wear it on the ride home, Cynthia."

Just after 5 p.m., Cynthia and Cody decided to walk to the Daimaru department store in Tokyo's Chiyoda ward, just off the edge of Hibiya Park. Upon entering the mega-store, the pair headed directly to the basement level to grab a snack. After walking down nearly every food aisle in the store, they decided to split a wonderful looking chocolate chip cookie. After pointing at the specific confection of their desire, the attendant gingerly picked up the cookie with a pair of ebony chopsticks and placed it on a piece of pink tissue which was in turn lifted and placed upon a piece of green wax paper that was then artfully crafted into an elegant little package using a circular fan-like folding procedure, an approach that made the top folds of the package look much like a flower bud on the verge of blossoming. After the spiral folding process, the package was upturned on the counter where a magnificent purple ribbon was shimmied under what now was the top of the cookie, and subsequently tied in such a manner where a handsome bow was secured across the flower-like face of the package. At that point, the ribbon-garnished parcel was transferred to a metallic-green box that appeared to have been engineered for exactly the same cookie that Cynthia and Cody had selected. Once placed in the box, the cookie and its multilayers of apparel were inserted in an ideally sized, glossy-red paper bag.

After paying for the cookie, Cynthia looked deep into Cody's eyes and smiled, before saying in a very serious, sober tone, "I think that we should eat this cookie tomorrow morning, over a cup of green tea."

"Doing anything other than carrying it around with us all night would be complete and utter sacrilege," said Cody in observation of the high-level ritual that appeared to have taken place in the packaging of their not-to-be afternoon treat.

After securing the cookie, the pair walked about some more, eventually exploring the various floors of the Daimaru department store, with each step developing a ravenous hunger. "Cynthia, what do you say we go find a restaurant and get something to eat?"

"You read my mind. I'm famished!"

With the idea of food on their minds, the pair headed down to the department store's first floor and into the streets of Tokyo in search of a quaint little place to grab a meal. As Cynthia and Cody walked, they eventually found themselves in the vicinity of the overpass where they had each enjoyed a bowl of noodles earlier in their friendship.

"Cynthia, how do you feel about going to that little restaurant we visited a couple of weeks back?"

"That place had excellent food. Is it near here?"

"I think so."

As Cody and Cynthia wandered about the store fronts located along the short street sections that threaded under the overpass, they found a small restaurant much like the one they had previously visited. "Let's try this place," Cody suggested.

"Okay by me. This looks like the same place," said Cynthia with less than a strong sense of conviction, as she surveyed the restaurant's business front.

Into the restaurant the pair walked, at which point they, unlike their previous experience, were immediately seated.

"Is this the same restaurant we ate at last time?" Cody asked, trying to locate a restaurant feature that he recalled from the previous outing.

"I don't know. It seems like it is in the same place, but it looks somewhat different."

When the waitress brought the menu to the table, one thing became clear — the menu was the same, but the management seemed to have changed. Just after Cody and Cynthia placed their order, a roar of motorcycles was heard in the street directly outside of the hollow little diner. "What do you think is going on out there with all of the noise?" Cynthia asked.

"Gosh, I don't know. It sounds like an army of motor bikes." As Cody stood to investigate the matter, the roar of the bikes completely died, providing the sense that the bikers had simultaneously turned off their engines directly outside of the dining establishment. Just as Cody returned to his seat, the cook poked his head from out of the kitchen, as if he expected to see the restaurant filled with patrons. Several seconds later ten or more loud-talking Japanese men entered the restaurant and sat in the very corner where weeks before the group of men sat who trained their eyes on Cody and Cynthia throughout their meal. When the bikers entered the dining room they completely ignored Cody and Cynthia, much as if they weren't even in the restaurant.

"Cynthia, I think that I saw these guys ride by me today in the early hours of the morning. I'm sure that I saw them, but then there were twenty or more riders."

Each of the men appeared to be in his late twenties or early thirties, and each wore his hair and sideburns in styles that neither Cody nor Cynthia had ever seen Japanese men wear. Another curious aspect of the men was their very unusual dress, the general precedent being loud, colorful outfits with the apparent design to draw attention to the wearer. Perhaps most curiously, each of the men was sporting a leather jacket with his personal moniker emblazoned across the back in large script. One of the men wore a jacket with lettering that read *Sexy Cat*; another's street-name read *Sweat Puppy*. While all of the men wore similar jackets, the only other name that was discernible from Cody and Cynthia's perspective was lettered with the moniker *Monkey Wretch*.

"Are these guys for real? Cynthia asked. "Look at the names on their jackets. I'm not sure if these fellows are biker gangsters with a wild sense of humor or adult delinquents from the class of 2000.

"I guess they find Americanisms really cool."

"In a crazy messed up way, I think I get that the fellow with the Elvis haircut and the mutton-chop sideburns sports' himself as a 'sexy' dude, but does the other guy mean *Sweat Puppy* or *Sweet Puppy*? And is it — *Monkey Wretch* or *Monkey Wrench*?"

"I don't know, Cynthia, but just to be on the safe side, perhaps it would be a good idea not to look over in their direction any more than is absolutely necessary. Besides, I'm not really sure how I feel about you looking at 'sexy cats' when were out together."

"Oh, Cody, you're so funny. I do agree that it wouldn't be wise to appear as if we are making fun of the names on their jackets. I would like to see just one more name, however, if for no other reason than to determine if they're kidding around or not."

"I personally think that they are not joking around, but rather that they have misrepresented what they had hoped their monikers would relay about themselves."

In due time, the orders arrived from the kitchen and again each meal was a gift to the eye and a gift to the palette. After the pair enjoyed a leisurely dinner, they packed up the new jacket and the ornately packaged cookie, and prepared to walk back to where Cody had parked his bike. Upon exiting the restaurant, Cody was struck by the surprising array of motor scooters that had apparently transported the leather-clad diners he and Cynthia had observed in the restaurant. "It's kind of weird that those little machines pack so much noise," said Cody as he and Cynthia ambled out from under the overpass and back onto the upscale streets of the Ginza. By the time they arrived at the Vespa, the temperature had cooled enough that Cynthia decided to wear the leather jacket during the return trip to the housing compound. By 7:30 p.m., the pair arrived home where Cody took possession of his new jacket and Cynthia took control of the elaborately packaged cookie.

Bosozoku: The Speed Tribes

The emergence of Japanese motorcycle gangs coincided with Japan's expansion of the automobile industry in the 1950s. In the early days of the movement, inductees were collectively referred to as *kaminari zoku* or thunder tribe. Recruits in these early gangs were most often young, impressionable men from lower class families who were either unhappy with the government, the system in general, or their particular lot in life. The most distinct common denominator shared by these pioneering gang members was a keen desire to raise hell and to physically violate the welfare of others. In later years, the media coined the word *bosozoku*, a term that literally means speed tribe, as the go-to term that referenced violent Japanese biker gangs. Back in the day, membership in the bosozoku was a stepping stone for many an aspiring yakuza member. In earlier times, just the mention of the bosozoku had the potential to breed fear in the general populace. In the heyday of the group, in addition to parading about town recklessly on their motorbikes, bosozoku members could be found terrorizing entire neighborhoods and wreaking havoc as if it were a sport. At the height of their days of plunder, the bosozuku were known for everything from firebombing to murder. In short, the group was bent on vandalism and mayhem. At the height of the movement, gang members were known for their outlandish hair styles and militaristic outfits. Traditionally bosozoku members were, almost without exception, under the age of twenty, the legal age in Japan for most adult activities. It is reported that the bosozoku movement peaked in the 1990s and has, since that time, steadily decreased in popularity and prominence.

Today bosozoku membership amounts to roughly 10,000 individuals, roughly one-fourth of the historic peak population. Much of the regimen is gone, as is the majority of the mayhem that was typically associated with the group. Gone is much of the structure, most of the violence, and nearly the entire mystique. Still there exists some violence and property damage; still there exists a good deal of wild motor-biking recklessness; and still there exists the organizational hierarchy of membership. But, without question, membership in Japanese motorcycle gangs is merely a shadow of what it once was. Of the 10,000 individuals who are either considered members of the bosozoku or who consider themselves members of the bosozoku, many groups are now seen as rag-tag groups of has-beens or wannabes rather than quality gangsters possessing proper credentials and/or histories of high-level mayhem.

The next morning Cody headed over to Cynthia's where they agreed that they would share the chocolate chip cookie over a cup of green tea. "Knock, knock. It's me, Cody."

"I'll be there in a moment. I'm just finishing up something," she called out.

"Okay," Cody said as he turned away from the door to inspect the morning sky.

"Hey, you, come on in," Cynthia said in a playful manner, as she backed away from the entrance signaling Cody to enter.

"Good morning, little girl. Did you sleep well?"

"Yes. I sure did. How about you? Did you go on any late night adventures with your biker buddies?"

"No. I kept it simple last night. I just did a little reading, and I looked at the Hiragana character book I've been working on. What did you do?"

"Not much, I just did a little drawing. Look there on the wall."

"You've got to be kidding. Is that supposed to be me along with Sweat Puppy, Sexy Cat, Monkey Wretch, and I can't make out the last one, is it App or Apple or? I can't read the last one."

"Yes. It is just a little doodling, I did last night. You're the one whose face can be seen."

"Hey, you've really got some talent. What is this other picture with the raccoon in a suit in a park? Is that, wait a minute, that's Hibiya Park. Isn't it?"

"Yes. Remember when I told you I saw that tanuki when you were into the bushes?"

"Yeah, I guess, but what's with the sport coat and the tail coming out of the back of the guy's slacks? You really are a curious one, Cynthia. I don't know what I'm going to do with you. And what is that picture with all of these yakuza-looking dudes standing around the parked Mercedes in the park, or is that a —? What is that place?"

"I don't know. It's just a sketch that came out of these here hands."

"You better be careful with those hands, girl. They might be dangerous."

"I'm not quite sure what you mean."

"Oh, never mind. It smells nice in here."

"It's the tea. Can I pour you a cup, sir?"

"Please do, madam."

"Are you ready," said Cynthia.

"Ready, for what?"

"Hasn't the anticipation nearly killed you? The anticipation of the cookie?"

"Oh, that! Actually, I am anxious to know if the cookie was worthy of all of the pomp."

"Do you want to do the honors, sir?"

"No. I want you to open it. I wouldn't mind having the first bite, though."

"Cody, I have something to tell you."

"What? I hope that it isn't anything serious."

"Cody, last night I came home and, well, it was really cold in here."

"And?"

"And, I ate the cookie."

"But, you said it wasn't anything serious. You're kidding right?"

"You're right, Cody. I did say that it wasn't anything serious. I do need to confess though."

"Yeah?"

"I wasn't serious about having eaten the cookie."

"Oh, my God! My heart. I thought you were serious for a minute there. Cut the kidding. Break out the cookie now, lady!"

So with the care and ceremony of a present long in anticipation, Cynthia took the boxed cookie out of its glossy-red paper bag; carefully removed the packaged cookie from its green metallic box; untied the magnificent purple ribbon; and finally unfolded the accordion-like green wax paper that harbored the pink tissue-paper-wrapped chocolate chip cookie. Removing the accumulated mound of packing material temporarily to the floor, Cynthia and Cody eyed the pink tissue-wrapped disk centered on the table. Several unfolds later, the naked cookie sat squarely on the tissue, which sat squarely on the table. "Cody, I'd like you to break this cookie in half."

"As you wish. Don't you want any? Just kidding!"

Once divided, Cody carefully studied the two halves and gave to Cynthia the piece that he thought was larger and then, accompanied by the most silent and still moment the pair had ever shared, each engaged in a healthy bite of the treat. "It is every bit as wonderful as I'd dreamed it would be."

"Oh, it is so good. It is too good for this earth. It reminds me of cookies my mother made me as a child. My mother made cookies that were just about this good."

"Hey, Cody, I don't mean to change the subject, but now that I think about it, you have never brought up your mother before. You talk about your father and the farm, but never your mother."

"Cynthia, my mother, my dear mother died when I was seventeen years old in a tragic accident. In many ways my mother was my world, my truth, and my light. She was my beacon of hope and guidance, and my source of strength and perseverance."

"Cody, I am so sorry. I had no idea."

"My father and I went on a trip for a couple of days, and when we returned she had died of carbon monoxide poisoning from a faulty furnace. We spoke to her just the night before and told her that we'd be home for lunch. When we got home we found her dead in a chair and the house smelling like the burnt cake in the oven. I still have days where I wonder if I have the strength to go on. I miss my mother more than I'd ever be able to tell you. Sometimes, I wake up in the middle of the night after having a dream that she is calling out to me or trying to talk to me. Sometimes, I dream of the Japanese stories that she told me as a young child. I dream of Momotaro, the peach boy, and so many other stories. My mother and I were as close as a mother and child could ever be. Someday, I will tell you more, more about my very amazing mother."

"Your mother does sound like an amazing woman. I wish that I'd had a chance to meet her. If you ever want to talk about it, I am here for you, whenever you wish to talk."

"Thank you, Cynthia. I'll keep that in mind."

As Cody got to know Cynthia better, he thought less and less about the prospect that they one day might become a couple. The funny thing was that as long as Cynthia and he maintained a good friendship that was all that really seemed to matter to Cody. The ridiculous anxiety that Cody once felt about the improbability associated with the two becoming friends ultimately became as distant as the past that Cody seemed to have left behind in Oakdale and Turlock. After spending the better part of the morning together, Cody and Cynthia went their separate ways, each attending to the domestic and professional responsibilities required for their upkeep and workplace obligation at the academy.

When Cody got back to his apartment he turned on the television for a minute and then began to sort his laundry into discrete piles based on fabric color and composition. After organizing the laundry that was machine washable, he nested the baskets that individually held his whites, his bright colors, and his dark colors and headed to the coin-operated wash room. After loading his laundry in the washing machine, Cody returned to his apartment and thoroughly cleaned out his kitchen sink in preparation to hand wash one of his black sport coats and several pairs of slacks. After Cody was satisfied that the cleanliness of his sink was up to muster, he carefully ran some warm water into it and added a small cup of Woolite before aggressively stirring the mixture into a sudsy lather. Cody then extended his hand into the pockets of his garments checking for coins, paper, and pens. When he was confident that his pockets were empty, he slowly submerged each item into the mixture and agitated and kneaded the saturated garments vigorously. At some point he discovered what appeared to be a business card at the bottom of the sink that was bleeding-out red pigment. After plucking the card from the wash water, Cody placed it on a paper towel to dry such that he could later try to read it.

When his coat and slacks were adequately laundered, Cody removed his make-shift plug from the drain, allowing the water to exit the basin before he carefully rung the water out of each piece of clothing. He then refilled the sink to rinse the garments, vigorously agitating the laundered clothes in the fresh water before repeating the process, twice over. Once the items were thoroughly rinsed and wrung out, Cody hung the slacks and the coat over his bathtub to dry prior to returning to the wash room to attend to his other loads of laundry.

Later that afternoon, Cody gave a lot of thought to Peter's recent letter, and he began the process of planning a letter to his father. Curiously, he didn't really know what he was going to say. He knew that he wouldn't be able to say that he missed Oakdale, or even California for that matter. Sure, he missed his father, but not so much in the emotional sense that the term usually engenders. As Cody lay reclined on his bed, pondering the letter he'd write his father, his mind started to wander as he fell in to a restful state.

While Cody felt unqualified love for his mother, obligation seemed like a more fitting sentiment where his father was concerned. Where Dwight was lacking in his ability to satiate the emotional needs of his wife and son, he tried to compensate through the provision of material goods and services. Beyond a doubt, much of Cody's social ineptness was a product of his close association with his mother and his general lack of intimacy with his father. Where Gail spent untold quality hours with Cody in a variety of venues, Dwight spent most of his time with Cody in what could reasonably be considered a managerial or supervisory role. Throughout Cody's childhood and into his adulthood, he never developed what could be considered a solid circle of friends. He had never interacted with people his age in any other manner than what would be considered civil and/or aloof. As a result, Cody spent his entire life as a loner with no reasonable prospect of assimilating into any fellowship, brotherhood, or group in any meaningful manner.

In Cody's early years, this sense of isolation caused him deep frustration and pain, but with time he simply accepted his plight and rolled with life's punches as best he could manage. While neither Cody nor Dwight could lay claim to concrete friendships beyond the bounds of family ties, at least Dwight didn't have to contend with challenges associated with being of mixed race. During his youth in Oakdale, Cody was "that Asian kid" or "the shy, soft spoken, Japanese kid" or in his last year — that young man with all of the pent-up anger who ruined that cowboy kid in a violent rage.

In the early morning hours, Cody rustled into wakefulness and turned on the lights in the kitchen. It was 1:33 a.m., and he felt as rested as if the sun were about to rise. As he filled a glass with water, his eyes spotted the faded red business card and he tried to place its origin. Since Cody remembered checking each of his pockets with the exception of his inner sport coat pocket, he assumed that at some point he must have placed the card in that location. Closer inspection of the card revealed the words:

Randal's Place
In the Roppongi

on the card's face and two words that were unreadable on its reverse. It looked like the first word started with *L* and that that word was followed by an *M*. Puzzled by the inscription, Cody placed the business card on the kitchen table and settled in to prepare himself a cup of green tea.

In the back of his mind, Cody seemed to think that he had heard of Randal's Place, and he well knew that he had been to the Roppongi district some three weeks earlier, but beyond that, the card transmitted little meaning. While drinking his tea, Cody turned on the television and began to think. He couldn't seem to shake from his mind that he apparently had been to this — Randal's Place, but he had virtually no recollection of the circumstances or the occasion. *Maybe I ought to make a little trip to the Roppongi district and take a look around*, Cody thought to himself. With the final tip of his cup, Cody put on some shoes and his new leather jacket, and slowly rolled his bike into the darkness, motoring off into the night, bound for Tokyo's Roppongi district.

While not essential, Cody traveled to the Roppongi via a route through the Ginza district. Cody always became captivated by the lights of the business district during the dead of night. On traveling through the heart of the ward, when he thought no one was looking, he weaved through the arterials as if he was a sidewinder moving about through the desert sand. Violently whipping his Vespa from side to side, Cody capitalized on the freedom that was offered by the largely vacant streets. At one point, he stood up on the seat of his bike and rode in a squat position which caused the front wheel of the scooter to lurch momentarily from off of the pavement.

Occasionally he made hyperbolic turns that took him into oncoming lanes. Cody's riding skills were nothing short of remarkable, and he tapped into his repertoire with great vigor.

After reaching a point where he needed to veer west toward the Roppongi he was surprised by a large group of men riding scooter bikes of similar size and appearance to his scooter. Just prior to entering an intersection, the regiment pulled right in front of him as if inviting him to take a place in their ranks. By the time Cody was mid-block, after having passed through the intersection, he decided to wag his scooter wildly, from side to side, prior to veering off the pathway toward his intended destination. After traveling three of four blocks, Cody encountered the same group of riders heading directly towards him, which he found extremely odd, as to do so required that the group motor at top speeds towards positioning themselves for such an encounter.

Just before Cody passed the group, the riders at the front of the pack motioned for him to pull over to the side of the road. Cautiously, with mild trepidation, Cody pulled over. Reaching the side of the road, he was greeted by what appeared to be a group of peaceful men simply out for a ride. Not knowing what to say, Cody called out, "*Ohayo gozaimasu.*" *I guess it is appropriate to say good morning at 2:45 a.m.*, Cody thought to himself.

"Ohayo," chorused several men, who appeared to be about Cody's age or a little younger. After inspecting Cody's bike and smiling, the men left the scene as abruptly as they had entered it, not even taking the time to exchange additional words.

Cody, still shaking with mild fear and excitement, couldn't believe what had just taken place. He had heard that many of Japanese biker gangs were very violent and as such he couldn't help but feel that he had somehow dodged a very menacing bullet. Perhaps the craziest part of the whole situation, however, was that this group of bikers appeared to include several of the same men that he and Cynthia had observed at the restaurant two days earlier. *How could it be otherwise?* he thought. *Surely, there couldn't be another motor scooter gang in greater Tokyo that had members sporting jackets with insignias reading Monkey Wretch, Sexy Cat, and Sweat Puppy.*

Cody was so overtaken by the event that he headed back to the academy compound, appearing as if he had entirely forgotten about his interest in investigating Randal's Place and getting to the bottom of the mysterious business card. By 3:30 a.m., Cody was lying in bed trying to coax a restful state that just wouldn't come.

Perhaps it was destiny. Perhaps it was a tattoo of sorts that could be removed at will, one that didn't break the skin. Or, maybe, it was just a desperate move by a one-man biker gang to place his mark on the map. Somehow, Cody deeply identified with the group of bikers; and in what seemed to be a star-spangled fit of immodesty Cody decided to modify his new leather jacket with a very personal alias.

Later that day, Cody returned to the store where he purchased his jacket to inquire about locating a craftsman to carry out the alteration that he envisioned. Much to Cody's pleasure, he found that the work could readily be performed by an associate of the leather outlet's manager. After providing a detailed colored sketch of the desired modification to his jacket and submitting a suitable deposit, Cody stopped at Takashimaya to pick up a meal that he hoped Cynthia would share with him.

Having washed up in his apartment, Cody knocked on Cynthia's door. "Cynthia, it's Cody. Are you home?"

"I'm coming," Cynthia replied while opening the door. "What are you up to?"

"Well, I know we didn't have plans, and I know that it is a work night, but I picked up some food and I was wondering if we could have a meal together."

"Yeah, come on in. Cody, as far as I'm concerned, we don't have to have formal plans to see each other."

"Excellent. I picked up some kind of a Chinese noodle dish with onions, peppers, garlic, and chicken. How does that sound?"

"It sounds terrific. Let me get some plates."

"You know, Cynthia, I've been thinking about going to Kyoto one of these weekends on a *Shinkansen* (bullet train). Would you be interested in going early next Saturday, if we could return that evening? It only takes about two hours by the train."

"I'd definitely be up for going. I too have long wanted to go to the historic capitol city. What do we need to do?"

"I don't think we need to do anything more than catch the Shinkansen early Saturday. I've heard the trains come every ten minutes, or so. We don't need reservations or anything."

After a leisurely dinner, Cody and Cynthia parted ways. For the first time in Cody's life he seemed to have something close to a partner to share experiences with. Sure their relationship was very casual, but Cody knew that such an approach offered the most sensible pathway to a meaningful and enduring friendship. Later that evening, Cody took to penning his father a letter. What seemed like a solemn and complex activity when alone — seemed like a light project when he felt the invigoration that Cynthia's friendship channeled into him. In fact, one of the largest challenges that Cody faced in writing this letter, and subsequent letters to his father, was to quell the wondrous optimism that was beginning to flood his senses for the first time in his life.

The letter was kept very simple and straightforward. Cody let his father know that he was well and that his work was being met with modest success. Cody downplayed the crisis on the farm and implored that perseverance was his father's only viable response to keeping the farm productive, counseling further — that remaining steadfast and working to diversify his selection of cultivars was the farm's only hope for survival. Cody urged Dwight to keep in contact with Peter, and he promised that he would write with greater regularity. In closing the letter, Cody told his father that he loved him and then he shared the following. "Sometimes when I am alone, on the crowded streets of Tokyo, I find myself scouring the faces of strangers, looking for fragments of the memories of mother and the times we shared."

A Sweet Shift of Fortune

Kyoto, Japan is known for a myriad of things. For many centuries Kyoto was the imperial capital of Japan. During the Edo Period, Kyoto was among the three most vibrant economic centers in Japan, the other two being Osaka and Edo (present day Tokyo).

In 1997, Kyoto received recognition for the development of the Kyoto Protocol, a precise blueprint that provided general targets to industrialized nations regarding acceptable emission rates for greenhouse gases. In addition to possessing many of the earmarks associated with world-class cities, Kyoto, not surprisingly, is found very agreeable to the tastes of those who esteem order, the vigorous life, and what is wholesome, good, and honest. The city is clean, well-managed, and springing with energy and vibrancy.

One of the metropolitan's jewels flows directly through the city-center in the form of a strikingly picturesque river that sources its flow from headwaters that fall out from the lofty reaches of Mount Sajikigatake. This beautiful aqueous ribbon meanders, with arterial purpose, through the day-to-day lives of 1.5 million people. The Kamo River, banked in erosion-resistant concrete, serves as the symbolic life-blood to a citizenry bathed in history, tradition, what is modern, and what is to come.

There is something magical about the city of Kyoto that goes beyond its rich history and tradition as a cultural and economic center, an essence that echoes of a primal-source and of a sense of imperative immediacy, the importance of the moment. Throughout the year, the river gurgles, bubbles, and whispers in soothing tones of resonance as it works its way, north to south, along Kyoto's eastern corridor.

In the spring, the lanes along either side of the river, here and there, are adorned with the pleasures offered by the lacy frilliness of cherry trees heavily weighted by the charity of their exuberance. And in the winter, on really chilly mornings, when your breath appears to linger in the air longer than you have words, just above the river rests a very dense fog.

Every summer, a new run of *sweet fish* transcends the Kamo River. The return of the sweet fish or *ayu* marks the arrival of summer in the minds of many of the people of Japan, much as do the cherry blossoms of spring toward their fulfillment of those promises associated with seasonal Japan. In June, even among the bustle of very urban Kyoto, old men can be seen lofting intricately hand-tied flies fashioned from the feathers of exotic and not so exotic birds with the aid of long bamboo poles outfitted with flat open-spool reels. When a fisherman is able to skillfully deliver an appropriate fly pattern, at the proper time and place, no ayu is wary enough to avoid becoming table fare.

Sweet Potatoes

"Listen, Dwight, you must be reasonable here. The Hannah sweet potato is the best producing sweet potato in California. I just wouldn't recommend that you spend a lot of time searching for a potato that is better suited for the climate of the San Joaquin Valley. For goodness sake, it is little short of a miracle that any sweet potato thrives in a hot, dry climate like we have here. Perhaps in twenty or thirty years other productive varieties will come into being, but Jiminy Christmas, Dwight — this is 1992, not 2012," whispered a voice from the past.

East coast Native Americans were cultivating sweet potatoes when Columbus arrived in the New World at the close of the 15th Century. A native to Central and South America, the sweet potato was unknown in the Old World until Columbus returned to Spain with specimens of the valuable staple. By the 17th century, sweet potatoes were widely cultivated in the North American southeast.

The sweet potato, *Ipomoea batatas*, a food plant that is related to the morning glory, is cultivated for its large tuberous roots. Since the sweet potato is native to semitropical regions, it enjoys only a limited range of production in North America. Typically, sweet potato production calls for warm to hot climates with at least 150 frost-free days.

Virtually the entirety of the world's production of sweet potatoes are propagated by root or stem cuttings or vegetative appendages, called slips, which sprout from sweet potatoes that are stored at temperatures above 60 degrees Fahrenheit. When slips are utilized, the fledgling sweet potato sprigs are planted in the fields immediately after the last frost. If adequate nutrient, sunlight, heat, and irrigation requirements are met, a crop of sweet potatoes is ready for harvest in four to seven months, depending upon when and where they are produced.

Once sweet potatoes are harvested, a small portion of the yield is shipped "green" to market for prompt consumption. The remainder, however, is submitted to a curing process that greatly increases the stability of the tuber as a food product.

Bullet Train to Shapeshift

While Cody didn't mention to his father the budding friendship he sensed was developing with Cynthia, Cynthia freely spoke to her mother about the curious fellow that she was becoming increasingly attracted to. Cynthia described Cody as smart, independent, and affable. She also told her mother that their friendship seemed so casual and comfortable, and Cody so passive, that passion and romance seemed an unlikely outcome. Where Cynthia often felt mobbed with unsolicited attention, Cody spent a lifetime in relative isolation from social venues of any description. For the first time in their lives it appeared that on their individual terms they had each reached a pleasing middle ground.

In Tokyo, near the summer solstice, sunrise takes place about 4:30 a.m. Early Saturday as planned, Cody and Cynthia arose by 5 a.m. and readied themselves for the train ride to Kyoto. On this particularly lucky day, this notably auspicious day, Cynthia and Cody boarded the Kyoto bound Shinkansen at Tokyo's Tōkaidō route station. The distance between Tokyo and Kyoto is 370 kilometers (230 miles), and by typical Nozomi-model Shinkansen speed standards, the trip takes just under two and a half hours. Having boarded the train at just after 7:00 a.m., Cody and Cynthia found themselves wandering about Kyoto just before the sun had driven the last of the morning dew from the blades of grass that rioted, here and there, in landscaped medians.

For those who take stock in the Rokuyo calendar, *Senbu*, the third day in the six-day sequence, should be marked by bad luck in the morning and good luck in the afternoon. The strange thing about fortune and misfortune, good luck and bad luck, is that they are often entities that cannot be distinguished from one another with any sense of direct immediacy. It is most always the case that what might in an instance be perceived as a boon or a bane in reality is an entity of evolving consequence, an intangible metamorphosing along a pathway understood by no one, an essence capable of enrichment, wretchedness, or insignificance.

Meaningful relationships are seldom built on bowls of noodles, small-talk, and sightseeing, but spending time together, in any venue, does have the potential to evince commonalities or compatibilities that can bring into view underlying structure and meaning. Perhaps the most positive statement that could be made concerning Cynthia and Cody's friendship was that it had been conflict free. But of course, they had not yet addressed politics or religion, the legalization of marijuana, the safety of nuclear power plants, or any matter that could be considered controversial.

The day in Kyoto couldn't be more splendid. The sky was virtually cloudless and the sun was quickly transforming an uncommonly brilliant morning into a warm summer day of epic proportion. Upon disembarking the Shinkansen in Kyoto, Cody and Cynthia immediately oriented themselves to the map which would direct them to the Adashino Nenbutsu-ju Temple.

Kyoto, the historic western capital of Japan is, of all things, most known for the many temples and shrines that grace its landscapes. The ubiquitous fixtures associated with Shinto shrines are the vermillion-painted torii gates. One fabulous example of such a shrine is the Fushimi Inari Shrine in the foothills of Mount Inari in southern Kyoto. This shrine is dedicated to the Shinto God Inari, the god of rice. *Inari Ōkami*

(Oinari) is the kami of foxes, rice, fertility, tea, and of course, sake. Inari Ōkami is the Shinto deity that presides over agriculture and industry and is associated with worldly success and general prosperity.

To a visitor, the Fushimi Inari Shrine appears much as if it were a shrine composed of shrines, being said to have within its boundaries more than 32,000 lesser sanctums. A most notable fixture in the Fushimi Inari Shrine are the numerous kitsune (fox) figures staged about the shrine's expansive grounds. Often, the kitsune is depicted with a key in its mouth signifying its service as a messenger to Oinari. While an understanding of the exact service that kitsune provided to Oinari has degraded over time, the association between the two entities, while somewhat cloudy, remains persistent.

The strong association of the kitsune as a messenger to Oinari in the Shinto religion is undeniable; however, the kitsune's most widely known reverence to the people of Japan stems from its ubiquitous presence in Japanese literature and Japanese folklore. Many Japanese tales concern the clever, if not mischievous, kitsune and its ability to transform space and time. Like the tanuki, the kitsune is known for its shapeshifting ability; and like the tanuki, the kitsune is a relatively common Japanese mammal that frequents the outskirts of many cities, towns, and villages. In fact, kitsune can be found in most any region of Japan that possesses adequately dense green-space, an ample food supply consisting of birds, fish, and/or rodents, and a sufficient quantity of clean water.

The plan of the day, for Cynthia and Cody was to visit the Fushimi Inari Shrine in the afternoon and the Adashino Nenbutsu-ju Temple in the morning. However, the day did not progress as expected.

The Adashino Nenbutsu-ju Temple could not be any more different from the Fushimi Inari Shrine. Beyond the clear distinctions in title, one entity being referred to as a shrine and the other a temple; beyond the difference of a shrine offering purification by water and a temple offering a barrel that spouts continuous bellows of smoke believed to possess healing effects; and beyond the distinction that shrines are associated with the Shinto religion and that temples are associated with the Buddhist religion — even the Japanese have a difficult time delineating between the two worship venues. Generally, in name, the two religious and spiritual entities have similar functions and offer similar opportunities for worship. However, in soul, in appearance, in ambiance, in the sense of quiet, in the sense of absolute desolation — the Adashino Nenbutsu-ju Temple stands out in the starkest manner imaginable.

During perhaps the most distressful, most abominable, most forlorn times imaginable, Japanese people of the Buddhist faith carted their dead to the site of the Adashino Nenbutsu-ju Temple. During the Heian Period (794 – 1185), in the thick mind-fog of war, the desperation of great famine, and times of rampant disease of dreadful proportion, the people of Heian-kyō (modern day Kyoto) abandoned their dead to degrade out in the open, blanketed only by the sky, fully exposed to the elements.

For close to 1,000 years, the bones of many of the dead were left to weather and erode. Scrambled by foraging animals, silently beaten by eons of rain, sleet, and snow, bleached white by the action of the sun, were the skeletal remains of a people, remnants of embodiments that were abandoned by men too overwhelmed by their condition to inter their dead in a secure place of rest. It was only during more restful and peaceful periods of time that these sacred grounds took suitable form for honoring the dead. In time, relatives returned to the deposit grounds that held the physical remnants of their loved ones whereby they placed "grave" markers and statues of Buddha, as best they could from memory or historical accounts. The temple took its modern organizational form near the turn of the twentieth century, when the various stone sculptures were gathered and oriented in concentric rings or neat rows about the sacred statues of the temple.

By Cynthia's calculations, the distance from the train station in central Kyoto to the temple was approximately seven to eight miles, a distance that neither Cynthia nor Cody wished to walk. In short order, Cynthia located on the map the proper location to catch a public transit bus to their destination, and in little more than an hour and a half the pair was weightily immersed within the grounds of the Adashino Nenbutsu-ju Temple. Between the looming conifer-forested peripheries, the eeriness of the silent groves of towering bamboo stalks, and the deadened silence ranging the entirety of the landscape, the temple grounds were unlike any place that Cody and Cynthia had ever visited. Even the birds, when they could be heard, seemed to speak in decidedly hushed tones. Visitors didn't talk, the wind was still, and all aspects of the domain were absent of a physical voice. Information and ideas were exchanged, but were unaccompanied by audible dialect.

From a distance, the expansive accumulations of conical stone figures and grave markers looked eerily like an assembly of ancient human skulls gathered from a burial ground. There is something quite strange, quite sterile, and cadaverous that lurks within the deep, dense, dark ether that seems to hover above the solemn encampments that harbor the earthly remains of humans long since departed. Their presence in the temple's compound dampened Cody and Cynthia's chattiness to a flat-line and reduced their communication efforts to pointing, hand-signals, and facial expressions. Sometimes, pointing was met by a nod or a smile, at other times by a look of confusion or a simple horizontal shaking of the head.

After walking around for an hour or more, the couple, without comment, exited the gates of the temple and walked to the transit stop. Inside the temple grounds, quiet was the mandate; outside of the temple grounds, silence was the product of the weightiness that the episode had layered on Cody and Cynthia's collective psyche.

By the time the pair stepped off of the bus in Kyoto, they had largely returned themselves to their normal operating modes. But residue from their experience at the temple would continue to subdue the generalized energy level of the pair for the reminder of the day.

Since it was nearly 1:30 p.m., Cody and Cynthia decided to seek out an opportunity for lunch. The first candidate on their list was Nishiki Market. The market, in one form or another, has been in operation since 1311. First a fish market and now a multi-dimensional complex with more than 100 storefronts, the market prides itself on locally produced foods and other products. In many ways, the market is much like Seattle's Pike Place Market, albeit much larger, more permanent, and increasingly more sophisticated.

After perusing the various handmade kitchen wares, the glorious array of superbly crafted knives, and the fabulously crafted textiles, Cody purchased several skewers of yakitori octopus, a couple of skewers of lightly grilled red onion, a container of *sunomono* (pickled cucumber salad), and some chilled green tea. Once outfitted with sufficient fare, the pair walked alongside the Kamo River until they located a suitable spot from which to launch their picnic.

The day possessed the most agreeable weather since either Cody or Cynthia had arrived in Japan. The sun shone brightly, the sky was absolutely clear, and the humidity was at a level where it seemed much like a warm summer day along the elevated banks of Seattle's Lake Washington Ship Canal. There was the most pleasant light breeze and the water rolling down the river basin looked inviting. In the distance, an old fisherman could be seen casting his wares in the hope of fooling a wary ayu into striking his offering. The man lofted his fly with great expertise, with the aid of a rod that appeared to measure more than twelve feet, gauging its length against the man's height.

As the pair prepared to sit, Cynthia removed a large beach towel from her daypack and shook it about before gently letting it glide squarely to the grassy field at her feet. At first they sat upright as they transferred their food to a common plate. Then they reclined, side by side, selecting morsels of food to put into their mouths much as if plucking grapes from a communal stem. "This is truly wonderful. The best day ever!" Cody remarked.

"It is fantastic. It is surreal," said Cynthia. "The experience at the temple, though, seemed really ominous and macabre to me."

"I agree. I have to say that I couldn't wait to get away from that temple. It kind of gave me the creeps. Did you see that fox that ran in front of us on the trail?"

"Fox? No, I didn't see it," replied Cynthia.

"I pointed to it, and then it darted into the trees."

"I think the word for fox is kitsune. What color was the beast?"

"It looked much like an ordinary red fox with grizzled gray hair dispersed throughout its back and rear. I didn't know that Japanese foxes were red."

"Yeah, I didn't know either," Cynthia said in a tone suggestive that she'd abandoned the topic. "This octopus, this *tako*, is really excellent, and the onions are tasty, octopus and onions — yummy, yummy."

"You should try this sunomono. I taste a faint essence of sesame oil mixed in with the sweetened vinegar."

As Cynthia took Cody's advice and savored a slice of the pickled cucumber, her eyes, for just a moment, focused on the fisherman. There he was one moment and — there he wasn't the next.

"Cody, the fisherman — he just fell into the water and went under. Do something!"

"Where was he? Point exactly where he was!"

"He went down right there," Cynthia said, pointing to a location midstream near a small riffle that extended across the waterway.

"I think that I just saw him flailing an arm." With the sight of the man breaking the water, Cody flipped off his shoes, tore off his shirt, and raced into the water where the old man was last seen, himself disappearing into the depths.

Cynthia hustled to the river's edge, looking for signs of struggle or the emergence of Cody or the man from the water. Finally the water's surface broke, Cody was up for a moment to get air before immediately returning below the surface, whereby he again surfaced, this time pulling and tugging at some unseen object that seemed to be in a tug-of-war with the bottom of the river channel.

Finally, Cody went under again, this time maneuvering closer to the source that worked against freeing the old man from what likely would become a watery grave. Just when it looked like the battle was lost, the two men surfaced, both facing upward, motionless, yet breathing. At that point several men entered the water and assisted Cody and the fisherman to the shore.

Not surprisingly, under the strain of the crisis, Cynthia was in hysterics. "Cody, are you all right?" Slowly, but surely, each man became increasingly responsive.

"Yeah, I, uh, I'm okay. How, how is the old man doing?" Cody said regaining his composure.

"He's catching his breath, but he's okay."

"Are you okay, my friend?" asked Cody in a calm voice. "It almost got us, didn't it?"

"Kappa! Kappa!" the old man exclaimed, before he excitedly relayed something inaudible to Cynthia.

"What does 'kappa, kappa' mean? And what else is he telling you, Cynthia?"

"He says that the kappa almost got him, but thanks to you, he will be able to see his grandchildren again."

"What is kappa? What are kappas?"

"A kappa is a river beast that kills people or eats people. I'd have to look it up. The man says that the kappa grabbed him, and that that is why you couldn't bring him to the surface quickly. The man wants to know your name. He is asking your name."

"Watashi wa Cody Fletcher san," Cody replied.

"Cynthia, ask him his name and tell him that we are from the Ikemoto Academy."

"He says that his name is Nobuo Fujiwara and he would like us to place a call to his wife."

As Cody and Nobuo completely regained their sensibilities, Cynthia served as a liaison to a conversation that provided background information concerning each man. In those broken conversations, Cody learned that both he and the old man had practical and academic experience in agricultural production. Just when the two men were getting a sense of one another, Nobuo's daughter arrived to escort her father back to his home. In the end, the two men nodded and smiled, but said not a word.

With the Nobuo safely under the escort of his daughter, Cody and Cynthia reflected on the near tragedy. "Cody, I think that you most certainly saved the old man's life."

"Aw shucks, it weren't nothing really," Cody said with a bumpkin twang. "I just did what anyone would do. I think that the greatest miracle is that you saw the old man go under. Without that single event — there most certainly would have been a different outcome," Cody said as he and Cynthia returned to their picnic site.

"Perhaps, but I have absolutely no reason to believe that that eighty-something-year-old man would have been able to get himself safely to shore, had you not gone in after him."

"You know, I'd swear that there was something down in the water that was pulling Nobuo away from me. The harder I tugged on the old man's leg, the more the old man was getting away from me. Even Nobuo said that something was down there, trying to take him away or trying to get at him. The old man said that a kappa was trying to take him away, to take him away to another place. This is what you told me."

"Well, I don't know what was holding Nobuo. All I know is that there is a mythical creature in Japanese folklore referred to as a kappa, but Cody — that stuff isn't real. It's just fantasy! Let's put the matter aside for now."

"I don't think that it works that way, Cynthia. You just can't put something like this 'aside' easily."

"Perhaps you are right, but for now allow me to change the subject. Cody, there is no way that we are going to the Fushimi Inari Shrine today. You are soaking wet and you are not in any condition to be wandering about recreationally. I think that we should try to find you some dry clothes and that we should head back to Tokyo on the first available train."

"Oh, Cynthia, I'm fine. Give me a break, I'm a grown man. Besides, I don't want to put a damper on the day, just because I'm a little wet."

"Cody, I don't care about today. I care about you. I deeply care about you. We can certainly come back another day. Cody, please don't struggle with me about this matter. I know that I'm not your mother, but please humor me — let me care about you, just a little bit."

"Uh, yeah, okay. I guess that would be all right."

So it was, the pair picked up the beach towel and the remnants of their picnic and walked away hand-in-hand, with Cynthia subtly leading the way. After a brief stop at Kyoto Takashimaya department store, Cody resumed the role of a dry-skinned terrestrial, and with Cynthia in tow the pair made their way to the Shinkansen station where they boarded a bullet train for the two and a half hour return trip to Tokyo.

Once on the train, Cynthia and Cody took a pair of adjacent seats, Cynthia at the window and Cody on the aisle. "You know once this thing gets going full speed, don't be surprised if you see me dozing off. I know that it's only four o'clock, but I feel that I could take a little nap. That is, if you don't mind," said Cody.

"No, I don't mind at all. I understand after all that you went through. And don't worry about me. I'll make sure that we don't miss our stop."

With just that understanding, Cody quickly fell into a sound sleep and Cynthia followed suit, resting her weary head on Cody's shoulder. It was becoming clear to Cynthia that she was falling for Cody, and it didn't matter that Cody was uncultured or that he kept strange hours or that he lived in, what Cynthia considered to be, a world of his own. Split between two cultures, Cody was trying to find a middle-ground that allowed him to explore and maintain both his American and Japanese identities, while in the process working to merge his solitary identity with a suitable social identity.

As if sensing he was being watched by something from above, Cody slowly opened his eyes to a cascade of Cynthia's blond locks in his face. Her hair smelled wonderful, and he savored the moment. Realizing that the train was approaching the station, Cody lightly nudged Cynthia. "Hey, Cynthia, we're almost in the Ginza." Shaking her head, and discovering that she had fallen asleep, using Cody's shoulder as a pillow, a strange look overtook her face. "I uh, I guess I fell asleep."

Not wanting to contribute in any way toward Cynthia's sense of awkwardness, Cody said, "Hey, it's okay, babe. I'd be surprised if you didn't fall asleep. We had quite a day, quite a long and eventful day. We should have no problem sleeping tonight."

"You know, Cody, I had a dream on the train that I kissed you. Isn't that funny?"

"I'm not really sure that I see the humor. Am I missing something? I've had several similar dreams during the last month, and none of them were comedies. So excuse me — if I don't start breaking up into laughter."

"I don't mean 'funny' — in the funny ha ha way."

"In fact, just for the sake of laughs, how would you feel about me kissing you now?" Cody said feebly.

"How would I feel? I don't know just how I would feel. I guess that I'd have to let you know just how it felt, that is, after you kissed me — if you were to kiss me."

Figuratively realizing that his ship appeared to have come in, Cody reached around Cynthia, interlocking his hands. "Well, see here, I am going to kiss you, and I think that I'm going to kiss you like —" Cody said as he nuzzled Cynthia's neck directly below her ear.

"I thought that you might kiss me on the lips."

"I'm not done yet. First, I wanted to smell your hair and kiss your neck. Now I think I'm going to kiss your lips."

"Oh, Cody, wow! Jeepers. Let's go to that little restaurant that we always go to under the overpass."

"Did I miss something? I just kissed you and you said to me, 'Let's go to that little restaurant that we always go to under the overpass.' What is that, romantic code for — I really like you or I think that we should get married?"

"Oh, Cody, I'm sorry. It's just that I'm a little mixed up right now. I just want to have dinner with you. I don't know just what I feel now."

"I understand. Let's go to the restaurant."

As the pair made their way from the Shinkansen station into the heart of the Ginza and down to the hidden underbelly that harbored their little eatery of choice, they gravitated to one another, again linking hands in an awkward attempt to make sense of the sudden change in the status of their friendship. When they walked into the restaurant, the couple was greeted by a hostess who promptly guided them to their established table.

"Will this be okay?" asked the woman in Japanese.

"Yes, this is where we like to sit," Cynthia answered.

Just then, the roar of motor scooters shook the building exactly as had occurred the last time they'd been in the restaurant.

"I guess they're here again," said Cody in an upbeat tone as he anxiously waited for Sexy Cat and the gang to enter the establishment. "You know, the other day I ran into the whole gang of these fellows while on an early morning ride. There must have been at least twenty of the guys."

"Cody, I don't want you getting mixed up with those fellows. They could be dangerous men. Did they see you?"

"See me? They talked to me!"

"What did they say?"

"It was early in the morning. What do you think they said?"

"I don't know, Cody — Ohayo gozaimasu?"

"That's right. Well, they actually just said —'Ohayo.'"

"I don't know Cody. I just think you ought to be careful. You are a long way from home, and things are different here."

"How are they —?"

Before Cody could complete his question, Sweat Puppy, Monkey Wretch, Sexy Cat, and a few other scooter kings entered the restaurant. Upon stepping into the restaurant they looked around the place and appeared to nod in Cody's direction. Out of the corner of his eye, Cody watched the men as Sexy Cat ordered a complement of large bottles of beer. At that point Cody was able to make out the monikers of three additional gang members, who apparently went by the names of *Meet Head, Check Mate,* and *Double Treble.*

"Cody, right now I don't really know if any of these guys are dangerous or not, I just know that their spelling is atrocious. And I think that I can say that this might just be how to spell — t-r-o-u-b-l-e."

"Oh, Cynthia, don't get upset. Let's order something to eat. I wonder if these guys are any good at ping pong."

"Cody!"

The next morning, Cody could hardly wait to check on the status of his jacket modification at the leather store. Initially, Cody had placed 15,000 yen (150 dollars) as a down payment on the work, with another 10,000 yen to follow upon completion of the alteration. When the store opened at 10:30 a.m., Cody was greeted by the manager as he unlocked the door. "Ohayo gozaimasu, Fletcher Cody san! Your jacket was delivered last evening. I think that you will be very pleased."

"Very good. I can't wait to see it."

"The letters in the monogram are a very deep red-brown, and the stars are a beautiful blue color, just as you specified. It came out very nice!" As Cody stepped up to the front desk of the business, the manager reached under the counter and removed a large glossy black box that was secured with a handsome yellow ribbon. "That will be 10,000 yen, Mr. Fletcher."

"Let's open up the box and have a look," said Cody.

"As you wish, but you should open it."

With no ceremony regarding the effort that went in to packaging the jacket, Cody quickly untied the ribbon and lifted the box top, fully exposing the jacket and its new temperament. In beautiful maroon lettering, which blazed across the back of the jet-black jacket, were the words:

AM RACCOON
DOG

Symmetrically set about the lettering were four magnificently vibrant royal-blue five-point stars, one centered above and below the moniker and one off-set from either side of the first line of lettering. Cody had selected a moniker for himself, on his own leather jacket, that spelled out *AM RACCOON DOG* in reference to American Raccoon Dog, as Cynthia had christened him after the pair had returned home from their trip to Hibiya Park.

One of the rituals of romance involves giving of oneself and absorbing or adopting aspects of the other participant in the relationship; this is one of the age-old hallmarks of courtship. Without this certain give and take, it is rare that a relationship flourishes or succeeds. Cody made a play into Cynthia's description of him as a raccoon dog, without any understanding at the time of the implications of such a transfer of title. At the time, the name adoption only seemed fun; in that moment, Cody was playing into Cynthia's pet name for him, but as well was playing into the comedy of the leather-clad scooter kings that he repeatedly encountered and which were the initiator of good humor for the pair on now two occasions.

After inspecting the jacket, Cody slid its silky lining over his bare arms and luxuriated in the heavenly nature of its form and comfort. He then paid the man and promptly powered his scooter back to the housing compound to share the upgrade of his jacket with Cynthia.

When he arrived at the Ikemoto complex, Cody engaged the traffic horn that outfitted his Vespa. Beep, beep, his bike tooted. He turned off the motor scooter and ascended the flight of stairs before knocking on Cynthia's door. "Knock, knock. It's me, Raccoon Dog."

"Who?" said Cynthia, not recognizing the nickname that she'd coined for Cody.

"It's me, Cody, aka Raccoon Dog."

"Oh, I'm coming — RD," said Cynthia, as she swung open the door. "So, it's Raccoon Dog, huh? I didn't think that would stick."

"Oh, it stuck all right," Cody said as he rotated about 180 degrees. "What do you think?"

"Interesting, I think it is interesting. I like the way the lettering contrasts with the body of the jacket. What does 'AM' mean? Is it like — I AM or something?"

"No, silly. It's like American Raccoon Dog. Get it?"

At that point Cynthia pulled on Cody's jacket lapels, sharply corralling him into her apartment, announcing to Cody, just prior to kissing him, "You're kind of weird, but I think that I can live with it." Upholding the ladylike reputation that she had established at the academy, Cynthia quickly shut the front door before indulging further.

"Several weeks ago, I didn't believe that guys like me could date girls like you, and now I know that wasn't true. I'm beginning to believe that nearly anything is possible. I'm beginning to feel like almost anything that I do can become a successful endeavor, successful somehow. It's really strange, but I sort of feel like I've regenerated an arm or something. For so many years I was all balled up inside, not even wanting to try to do much of anything, and then my mother died. For years it was like I was some sort of spectator in my own life, and that I was intently watching, waiting for the main character of the story to do something, anything. It was, and I guess it still is to some degree — so surreal. You know, in many ways, I think that you have brought me luck, and more important, I am beginning to think that you have brought me love, something that I've never really had, not like this anyhow. It is kind of funny, but I think that before I met you I was kind of a frustrated or angry person. But I don't feel that way anymore."

"Wow, Cody, baby — TMI, man! No, I'm just kidding. That was quite a presentation. Honestly, I think that I'm a happier person since meeting you. I know that I have really grown to enjoy spending time with you. You're the first guy that I've really and truly taken the time to become friends with, without the stress of becoming intimate. Not that I'm ready to become intimate, yet."

"Cynthia, I've said it from the beginning to myself. I've said, 'If I could only become friends with this girl, I'd be the happiest man alive.' So really, I just can't lose on this one."

"Cody, about what I said a minute ago, about being intimate with you."

"Yeah?"

"I'm thinking that what I said might not be entirely accurate."

"Honestly, our friendship is what is most important to me," Cody said relaying his desire to let their relationship develop naturally, without planning or contrivance.

So, as was the pair's general habit on Sunday's, they went their separate ways in preparation for the academic week.

In Japanese folklore the kitsune, or fox, is associated with many supernatural tendencies not limited to altering both time and space, driving people insane, and taking on the identities of objects, other animals, or human beings. Common themes in Japanese tales involving the kitsune focus on the creature's ability to become invisible, its tendency to self-manifest in the dreams of others, and its predisposition and ability to create wrinkles in the fabric of reality that make it close to impossible to distinguish verisimilitude from authentic truths of existence. One tale reportedly even goes so far as to suggest that the kitsune preys on the essence of human souls or the life-blood of humans through sexual intimacy.

A particularly common dynamic involving the kitsune concerns love-based relationships between a human male and a kitsune that takes the form of a human female. Most frequently, the male is unwittingly enticed into a relationship through irresistible powers of attraction attributed to the kitsune. In time, the male marries or becomes committed to the kitsune before he discovers the kitsune's true nature. In some instances the male wakes up from a dream, not recognizing his surroundings and not knowing the difference between truth and fiction. In cases where the fox-wife bears children, it is often an outcome that these human children possess supernatural tendencies of their own.

While Cody wasn't at the time aware of the folklore associated with the kitsune or that he was potentially falling in love with a life form very different than what it seemed, he was aware that a huge unlikelihood was at play in that the most beautiful girl he could imagine appeared to be falling in love with him. That night, as Cody fell asleep, his thoughts coalesced on Cynthia and on the rich potentialities that appeared to be on the horizon for the two as a couple. Somehow it just didn't seem right to Cody that he could be so lucky. After all, he'd never observed much of a pattern of luck in his life before.

In the early morning hours, Cody cleaned up and prepared himself as if he were getting ready for work at the academy, before outfitting himself with his newly monogramed leather jacket. Then he silently rolled his scooter into the darkness and ventured into the night toward the Roppongi district. When he reached the district, he systematically snaked down several streets in search of the area that he, only vaguely, remembered visiting several weeks earlier. All he could remember was that the area had a seedy look about it and that it appeared similar to the location he saw on the television news program concerning the gravely injured yakuza members. He also remembered the business card that he found in his coat pocket that advertised *Randal's Place in the Roppongi*. As he continued to ride about, Cody could see a large group of scooter riders in the distance. As he approached the bikers, he wondered, *Could the group be the gang of riders that he kept running into?* The men continued past him without even acknowledging Cody. They moved right on by as if they hadn't even seen him. Was this the group of bikers in the restaurant? Was this the group of scooter riders with whom he had recently exchanged an early morning greeting? He just couldn't be sure.

After riding around for another forty-five minutes, Cody could see the glow of morning approaching from the east. He'd ridden for well over an hour and he'd not located the mysterious Randal's Place. Could the club have closed in light of the trouble associated with the beating? Cody's memory of the venue was of absolutely no assistance in the matter. Not done for the night, Cody stopped by a group of intoxicated men huddled together in an alley. *"Onaka ga suita desu ka?"* (Is your stomach empty? Are you hungry?) Cody said, pulling a bag of bean paste bread from his bike rack. When the men answered in the affirmative, Cody broke the bread into several pieces, providing each man with a personal hunk of the staple. Cody then asked, "Randal's Place doko desu ka?" (Where is Randal's Place?) In response, the men simply shook their heads from side to side, in indication that they were unfamiliar with the establishment.

Over the next week, Cody repeatedly thought about how he and the old man Nobuo cheated death in the Kamo River. It just didn't seem reasonable that he, a visiting teacher — essentially a tourist — could find himself in a position to save the life of a Japanese citizen. In harmony with Japanese modesty concerning personal achievements and incidents of valor, Cody did not mention anything to his students or any of his peers at the Ikemoto Academy about what had taken place that day on the Kamo River.

While Cynthia didn't say much about what had transpired in the main channel of the Kamo River that fateful day, when her lips met Cody's, she felt strongly that Cody was an unwitting hero in what likely would have been the tragic death of a peaceable old man. From that day forward, Cynthia took great pride in Cody as a man and found herself in modest worship of his mild-mannered character and masculine articulations. In many ways, Cynthia viewed Cody as a very proud and docile beast in need of refinement, a measure of personal civilization that she was more than willing to provide. She knew that nearly everything was perfect about Cody except for some of the rough edges associated with the way he was packaged and the way that he presented himself to others. Another lingering concern that Cynthia harbored was Cody's restless and wandering soul. In as much as Cynthia admired Cody's independent streak, she was troubled by his impulsive nature of wandering about when and wherever he pleased.

One afternoon after work, Cody traveled down to the restaurant under the overpass where he and Cynthia so frequently ate dinner. Cody pulled his Vespa directly in front of the restaurant and entered the establishment and drank a couple of beers as he read an issue of the English language daily, *The Japan Times*. In some manner, Cody was there to meet with the scooter kings that had seemed to monopolize the restaurant on two of the three occasions that he and Cynthia had patronized the diner. After about an hour, Cody picked up and left the restaurant. Outside, he encountered the bikers just as he mounted his Vespa.

"Konichi wa," said Cody as he nodded to one member of the swarm of riders.

"Watashi wa Double Treble desu," said one of the men, bowing very politely to Cody.

"Watashi wa Fletcher Cody desu."

"Cody san, won't you join us in "Curry House" for a beer," said Double Treble in broken, but intelligible English.

"Oh, you speak English?"

"Yes, all of the boys speak some English. We all went to good public or private schools."

"Well, I really can't stay long. I've got to see my girl," said Cody, realizing that this was the first time he thought of himself and Cynthia as boyfriend and girlfriend. "My girl doesn't really like it when I stay out too late." Cody couldn't believe that he had, within seconds, again referred to Cynthia as his girl.

"Surely, you can come in and have one beer with us, couldn't you?"

"Yes, I guess that one beer would be all right."

"Aren't you the guy that we keep seeing riding around the city in the middle of the night?"

"Maybe. I ride around sometimes late at night," Cody said realizing that he had just led the men to believe that his relationship with Cynthia had him pegged as a guy who was tethered on a rather short leash. "Yeah, I think I've seen you guys," Cody said with a large splash of disingenuity.

"So, you're an American. What are you doing here?"

Not wanting to completely blow his cover, Cody, before he knew it said, "It is really something that I can't talk about. You know, I do some things. I've got my racket, if you know what I mean." Cody couldn't believe what was coming out of his mouth. He'd just told the men a supreme lie designed to make him look like a tough guy or some sort of a big shot, and it seemed like now the only way to proceed was to build upon the basic premise that he was here on business of one sort or another and that he wasn't at liberty to discuss the matter any further.

"Yeah, we understand. We don't tell just anyone about our business either. Hey, I'd like you to meet some of the boys. This is Sexy Cat and this is Monkey Wretch. I think that I'll leave it up to the rest of the guys to submit their own introductions."

"It is really nice to meet you fellows," said Cody.

"It is mutual, Cody san," said Sexy Cat.

"Yes. It is good to finally meet you," replied Monkey Wretch.

After having a beer and serving as an object of international show and tell, Cody graciously bid farewell to the men and returned to the apartment complex.

Probably everyone but Cody would have thought it odd that a bosozoku gang would have taken interest in him to the point of formally inviting him to their table for a drink. As far as Cody could tell, this group of bikers was just a group of over-the-hill salary men who got together to ride just for the thrill of it. He couldn't fathom the idea that this group of bikers who appeared to work so hard to draw attention to themselves could somehow be up to no good. It made no sense to Cody that men who monogrammed their jackets with kitschy misspelled nicknames could have anything to hide.

When Cody arrived back at the housing complex, he went directly to Cynthia's apartment. Once inside, Cody found that Cynthia was listening to an American internet radio station and sitting around doodling. "Hey, you. What have you been up to?" said Cynthia.

"Hey. I've just been riding around, thinking."

"What have you been thinking about?"

"About you. Pretty much, I was just thinking about you. Lately, I've been thinking quite a bit about you."

"Did you get dinner?"

"No."

"I cooked a chicken breast and some eggplant, and I hardly touched it. I'll heat it up, okay?"

"That sounds great."

"You know, Koko called about an hour ago. Do you remember Koko?"

"Not really. Is that a student or a faculty member?"

"Neither. Koko is that old lady we met that day we went to Hibiya Park. She was the lady who was dragging the cart, the woman you offered to take to lunch."

"Oh, yes. What did she have to say?"

"That is the funny thing. She didn't really say much. She just asked how we were. Specifically she seemed to be concerned about you. She said that she had a premonition that something happened to you and she wanted to see if you were okay. When I told her you were fine, she seemed genuinely relieved. It was really kind of a strange conversation. She said that she still wanted to share a meal with us, but that the time wasn't right just yet, whatever that means."

"Yeah, that is weird. I hope that she is okay. It may be that Koko is a little bit loopy."

"Well, she can't be that crazy."

"What do you mean?"

"She said that we make a very nice couple and that your loyalty is only surpassed by your appreciation of fine tobacco."

"What are you talking about?"

"I'm just kidding you about that last part. I don't even know why I said that. Kind of silly, huh?"

As Cody and Cynthia moved away from the topic of the old lady Koko, Cody requested that Cynthia provide some definition regarding the particulars of their friendship.

"Cynthia, I don't think that I can go on much longer, not knowing exactly where I stand with you. Honestly, I think, no — I know — that I'm desperately in love with you.

Honestly, I think that I was fine until I woke up on the return train from Kyoto with a face full of your hair. For God's sake Cynthia, can I just smell your hair? You've got to give me a sign, one way or the other. I don't think that I can handle this much longer. I need to know."

"Cody, I am yours for the taking. I fell in love with you some time ago, but I wanted to love you on your time schedule, and not on mine. I decided some time ago that I would not force a relationship with you, but rather that I'd wait until you were ready for a commitment. You see, Cody, the comfort level that I've built up with you has caused me more to think about being the mother of your children, rather than being some girl that you become involved with or date. So, point of clarification, Cody — I'm not much interested in becoming your girlfriend. It is more a matter of wanting to be your life partner."

"I guess that about answers my question. You didn't beat around the bush much on that one," Cody said as he stepped up to Cynthia and embraced her. "I apologize for my strange behavior. I hope that I've not become too clingy. Honestly, I've been thinking about you in a long-term sense, in pretty much a permanent sense."

By Cody's interpretation, his new understanding with Cynthia didn't much change the freestyle life that he had become accustomed to living. This meant to Cody that he could still ride his Vespa when and as he pleased, that he could maintain his strange sleeping schedule, and that he could live much as he had before meeting Cynthia. In a parallel sense, in as much as Cynthia was an intelligent, articulate, and thoughtful woman, Cody's interpretation was to be initially correct.

Cynthia well knew that structure could be supplanted in Cody's life where it had never been before, yet she also knew that the pathway to this end would come about from advances in love, understanding, and responsibility, and not at the hand of rough-and-ready demands or expectations.

CHAPTER FIVE:
END OF THE LINE

For many generations, Nobuo Fujiwara's ancestors worked the soil of the fertile Okayama Plain in Japan's Chūgoku region. Nobuo himself had worked in farming and agriculture for the better part of his eighty-four years. Born to a prosperous family, he was sent to Tokyo University at the age of seventeen, where three years later he earned a degree in agricultural science, with a specialization in botany. When Nobuo's father died in 1963, Nobuo became the eldest male member of his immediate family, a position of responsibility that placed him at the helm of an agricultural empire that farmed close to 200 hectares (500 acres) of land.

The city of Okayama is the capital of the Okayama Prefecture. The metropolis is located midway, west to east, between Hiroshima and Kyoto, and is not far from the Seto Inland Sea, the body of water that separates the islands of Honshū and Shikoku. Self-proclaimed as the "Land of Sunshine," the city and the surrounding region largely live up to this bold billing. As an agricultural venue, the Okayama Plain is largely known for its Shimuzu white peaches, various varieties of melons, strawberries, and pione grapes. In addition, the region produces root vegetables such as carrots, daikon, onions, and ginger, and summer favorites such as cucumbers, eggplant, and tomatoes.

Nobuo's primary agricultural products were cucumber, eggplant, and a lovely, flavorful variety of onion known as the Shonan *akai tamanegi* (red onion), an onion cultivar that was developed at the Tokyo Agricultural Experimental Station. Still, Nobuo liked to tinker in the development of hybrid strains of radishes, beets, and sweet potatoes.

Nobuo remained a bachelor until the age of 53, when he married Masuyo, the much younger daughter of a neighboring farmer. Within three years, his house was full of music, the voices of small children, and the love of a devoted mother and wife. Together, the Fujiwaras raised three daughters, who were the greatest joy and pride of Nobuo's rich life. Still, it was clear to Nobuo that unless one of his daughters married a man interested in farming the Okayama Plain, his family's long history in agricultural production would soon come to a close.

When Nobuo's eldest daughter left the family home to attend Kyoto University, Nobuo came to the conclusion that the time had come for him to divest from his agricultural holdings and commitments. By the time each of his daughters had completed their university degrees, he and Masuyo sold their agricultural business interests and moved to Kyoto to be closer to the grandchildren he knew soon would arrive.

During the colder, wetter months Nobuo divided his time between working in his high-tech horticultural laboratory, where he experimented with the development of various strains of hybrid vegetables and flowers, and spending time in his workshop crafting splendid bamboo fly rods and artfully hand-tied flies and lures that mimicked many of the insects that were residents in the various rivers where he loved to fish during the summer and early fall.

The laboratory was equipped with state of the art humidity- and temperature-controlled growing chambers, each illuminated with banks of high-pressure sodium and/or metal-halogen lamps. In his laboratory, Nobuo was able to cultivate, and ultimately nurture to maturity, any plant species that he or his network of associates could procure. It was not unheard of for Nobuo to propagate new strains of tomatoes in the dead of winter or for him to bring exotic varieties of orchids into bloom during any month of the year. Nobuo, at one time or another in his career, experimented with the propagation of everything from desert cacti to various cultivars of cannabis.

For weeks after his brush with death in the Kama River, Nobuo became completely consumed by the very sobering fact that his days were numbered. It didn't seem to matter anymore that he'd led a cautious existence and that all aspects of his mortal tendencies were undeniably those of a man driven by an unshakable code of honor and morality. Just as it was clear to Nobuo that he needed to mentally prepare himself for the next phase of his journey through the cosmos, it was clear to him that he needed to begin the process of settling his accounts, personal and private. During Nobuo's in-depth inventory and analysis, he made certain decisions that he felt were essential toward securing the present and future contentment and wellbeing of his family. In short, Nobuo was a very superstitious man, a man who was driven by not only what he thought was right from an earthly perspective, but as well he was driven by what he thought would be in agreement with the spirits that guide all men along their personal trails of enlightenment.

In many ways, Cody was concerned with the same forces that guided Nobuo, but he was not in any position to put such thoughts into a concise form of articulation. Cody unmistakably wanted harmony in his life, but his life, his sense of being, tore at him from the perspective of two cultures, one that he had been immersed in his entire life, but still failed to understand, and another that he felt ran through his entire circulatory system, yet remained encapsulated in an impenetrable shell. Nobuo very well knew who he was, while Cody thought that he knew who he wanted to become, yet the proper pathway to this end remained elusive.

There is something positive to be said about the value of planning and putting one's thoughts down on paper, at least in a figurative sense. Cynthia put her thoughts to paper, in the form of her pastel artwork when she wanted to flesh out an idea or, figuratively, make an idea happen. Cody's approach, however, was improvisation from a more or less ad hoc perspective. As such, he didn't always achieve clean outcomes for his efforts; sometimes he found his results agreeable and other times, not so much. One of Cody's main life goals, although he'd been unable to articulate it succinctly, was to be recognized by authentic Japanese people as a comrade or a friend. He just couldn't palate the idea of being that token, inconsequential Japanese guy from America. Cody knew in his heart that there had to be more to his experience than simply being some sort of strange Japanese novelty from the shores of North America.

Beginning the first week of July, Cody started making a habit of periodically dropping by Curry House where, when he ran into the bosozoku group, he'd be prepared to announce that he was just passing by and thought he would just grab a meal and a beer. The curious thing was, short of nodding to acknowledge Cody's presence, there really appeared to be little interest in him, or his activities. During this period, Cody maintained his erratic habit of riding his Vespa around Tokyo in the dead of night.

One night, when he felt particularly carefree and wild, Cody cruised about the streets of the Roppongi district, artfully free-styling his Vespa, as he often had done with his Yamaha 200 in his early teens. Just as he turned onto a street hosting numerous shabby clubs, Cody found himself heading directly toward ten or more bosozoku members from Sexy Cat's gang, whereby he was motioned to pull over. "Hey, look guys. It's that gaijin biker guy."

"Ohayo gozaimasu, Fletcher Cody san," said Monkey Wretch.

"Ohayo gozaimasu. What are you guys doing down here?"

"We're just cruising around. You know — raising hell. That's what we do. That's who we are. Fletcher Cody san, you can ride that scooter pretty good. Where did you learn to ride like that?"

"Please, call me Cody. I learned to ride in California when I used to ride with the Hells Angels," Cody said, again not believing what had come out of his mouth. "Yeah, that was years ago," Cody continued, posturing himself with a grimace on his face, as he looked about the group for approval. "Yeah, just about all of the members of my posse are in prison now. I'm the only one still roaming the streets, from what I hear," Cody added, realizing that he'd reached a critical mass that made it impossible for him to stifle the chain reaction of mistruths that spouted like unstable particles as they escaped from his mouth.

It wasn't that Cody was corrupt of spirit or that he had a natural tendency toward spreading deviant mistruths. What had happened to Cody was that he just, very innocently, maneuvered himself into disseminating a progression of falsehoods that took on a life of their own. So, as it was, the more Cody realized that he needed to stop the story-telling — the more fantastic his stories became.

In light of the rather tall tales that Cody had transmitted to the bosozoku, Cody decided to drop out of sight for a while, that is, as far as his late night scooter rides and hanging out in the city were concerned. This new commitment allowed Cody to spend more quality time with Cynthia in the low key venue of their apartment complex.

Later that afternoon, following work, Cody visited a local convenience store and gathered together some *mentako* (spicy/salted fish roe) flavored yakisoba, tofu, bok choy, cabbage, green onions, and shredded seasoned squid. After procuring his supplies, Cody returned to the apartment complex and ventured up to Cynthia's to enlist her in the preparation of their meal.

Knock, knock. "Hey, babe. It's me."

"Come on in," Cynthia said as she opened the door and gave Cody a kiss.

"I'm going to start fixing dinner downstairs, and I request your presence."

"I'll come down in a moment. I'm just wrapping up a couple of things."

"Okay, then. I'll get things started."

When Cynthia arrived in Cody's apartment, she rolled up her sleeves and commenced slicing vegetables, while Cody heated oil in a wok and sliced and seasoned the tofu. "So how was your day?" Cynthia asked as she transferred the sliced sections of spring onions into a small bowl before placing it on the kitchen table.

"Oh, it was okay, I guess. Nothing really standout occurred. How was your day? Hey, babe — you want to wash that bok choy, don't you?"

"Yeah, you're right. Hey, what's this?" said Cynthia as she picked up the red-leached business card that Cody found when washing his jacket several weeks previous.

"I don't know what it is. I must have picked it up somewhere. The funny thing is that I've been unable to find any club named Randal's Place in the Roppongi district. I even went riding around looking for the place and asked some people if they ever heard of it, but they hadn't."

"Huh. What does it say on the back? Is it "Lu" something "M" or something?"

"I don't know. It got wet, and I can't quite make it out now."

"Whatever it says, it surely isn't a Japanese name."

"Yeah, weird. After you wash that bok choy we've got to dry it so it doesn't spatter in the hot oil."

"I know, dear. I'm getting to that."

"Did I tell you that I ran into the guys from the motorcycle club early this morning?"

"Now when would you have told me that? The only time we spoke was in the hallway during passing period, when you first invited me to dinner."

"Oh? Oh, I guess you're right."

"Well, what happened? Do you have something to tell me?"

"Oh, it's nothing really, I guess. It's just that I saw them and we spoke again."

"What did they have to say?"

"Oh, not much, I guess. They complimented me on my riding skills."

"Cody, I hope that you're not doing anything dangerous. Tell me that you're not doing any dangerous stunts or anything like that."

"No, I'm not doing anything too dangerous, really."

"What on earth do you think those guys want with you?"

"Oh, I don't know. It's probably nothing more than gaijin envy or something like that."

"Please, Cody, could you define 'gaijin envy?' And please, while you are at it, could you explain why they have apparently chosen you as the target of their worship?"

"Yeah, I'm just kidding. I just made that term up. You know, I did tell the guys something that I feel kind of funny about."

"What did you tell them?"

"You know, it is really quite funny. I think that you'll get a real kick out of it. We were just hanging out, doing what guys do, you know for kicks and giggles. I think that it's really going to crack you up what I said, once you hear it."

"Cody, tell me exactly what you said and the context in which you said it."

"I don't know if that would work. I mean, I think that a lot stands to be lost in the translation."

"Translation? How so? You speak English and, at best, marginal Japanese, and I speak fluent English and Japanese. What is to be lost with your translating — what you more than likely said to the guys in English — to me, a native speaker of the English language?"

"Okay, are you ready for a laugh?"

"Yeah, try me out."

"When the men asked where I learned my fancy riding skills … You know, maybe you ought to be sitting down when I tell you this. I wouldn't want you to fall and injure yourself in a fit of laughter."

"Cody, tell me what you said or I'll see you tomorrow,"

"Okay, I told the guys that I learned my riding skills during the time I rode with the Hells Angels. Isn't that funny?"

"Why ever did you tell those men such a tall tale? Somehow, I'm guessing that when you delivered that line, none of the bikers understood that what you were saying was 'for kicks and giggles,' as you put it. Why did you tell those men that big fib? Why?"

"Honestly, I just got caught up in the moment. Even when I was saying it, I kind of took a step back and wanted to disassociate myself from my comments. It was really surreal. I honestly couldn't believe what was coming out of my mouth."

"Well, I guess it is kind of funny in the crazy way that your innocent attempt to relate to the fellows took on a life of its own. Oddly, I think that the best thing that could possibly come of this is that those guys write you off as if you're just some sort of vacuous blow-hard braggart whose words have little connection with reality."

"Yeah, perhaps you're right. I think that it would be wise to hang low for a while, maybe a couple of weeks."

The idea of lying low after one has embarrassed himself or committed a minor social infraction has some merit in ameliorating wounded egos or the hurt feelings of others. Unfortunately, this idea of "lying low" doesn't work so well in the case of assumed truths shared with men who crave high-adventure, street valor, and motorcycle gang bravado. Cody's absence from the street-scene for even a week possessed the potentiality to give additional legs to his emerging narrative as a motorcycle outlaw.

During the second week of July, Cody received two pieces of mail on the same day. After work, Cynthia picked up both packages in the faculty mail room and carried them over to Cody's apartment. "Cody, you've got two pieces of mail, one from Kyoto and the other from your father."

"Who would be sending me mail from Kyoto?" Cody asked as he scanned the address label. "Holy mackerel! It's a package from Nobuo Fujiwara. I wonder what it is."

With the excitement and wonder of a child, Cody carefully tore the brown paper wrapping away from the package, revealing a loosely bound cardboard box. "Hey, this is kind of heavy, kind of dense," Cody said as he removed a finely crafted wooden crate from the box, a hardwood crate that appeared to be custom-made to hold four very fine looking sweet potatoes that were just beginning to sprout.

"Nobuo sent you sweet potatoes, how curious?"

"Yeah, I'm not so sure I get it either."

"Do you mind if I nudge up to you while you read the letter from your father?" Cynthia asked, having lost interest in Nobuo's gift.

"No, sweetheart," Cody said to Cynthia as he gently kissed her on the cheek. "I'm glad you're here. I hope my father is coping okay." Smiling at Cynthia, Cody slid his thumb into the letter's glue-less gap before breaking the envelope's seal.

"Will you read the letter aloud?"

"Absolutely!"

Dear Cody:

I received your letter and I am glad that you are finding your experience satisfying. Your mother would be very proud of you and your commitment to learning about the Japanese culture. I miss you more than you could ever imagine. Concerning this year's crop, I'm afraid that the crop failure is worse than I had initially thought. Something very serious is affecting the strain of sweet potatoes that we have been growing for more than twenty years. Honestly, I don't know if it is something in the soil or if some genetic modification in the cultivar has taken place. Thank goodness that I've maintained my employment at Central Packing for all of these years. Do you know that next spring I will have worked at the plant for 40 years? Time sure goes fast. Gosh, I sure miss your mother. It has been really hard without her, but I'm sure that it has been much harder on you.

Well, I just want to say that I love you and that I miss you something awful. Take care of yourself, son.

I love you,

Dad

"Good grief, Cody, I think I'm going to cry. Your dad sounds devastated and all alone. He really needs you. And I read a lot of love coming out of his words, maybe even some sorrow or regret, regret that you two aren't closer."

"You are right. I've never seen him in this state before. I feel like I really need to do something for him."

"I'll help you think of something, Cody. We can think of something together that will help your dad."

"I've got to think of something, but not tonight. Tonight, I want to just relax and spend a peaceful evening with my sweetheart. What do you want to do for dinner?"

"I've got some food I can get upstairs," Cynthia answered.

"You know, I can't get over Nobuo sending me those sprouting sweet potatoes. Maybe it is some sort of Japanese custom that we don't know about. Is there some hidden meaning with sweet potatoes, like they're good luck or something?"

"I don't know, but I think we better eat them before they've completely gone to sprouting," Cynthia said.

"Yeah, we should cook them tonight."

"Cody, I'm going to go upstairs for a minute and get a pork cutlet and some vegetables. I'll be back in a flash."

Going from Cody's to Cynthia's apartment involved walking all of the way down to the end of the row of units on the first floor, traveling up the staircase to the second floor, and walking midway down the row of apartments to Cynthia's residence. Under normal circumstances it would take Cynthia two to three minutes to get from Cody's apartment to hers. And so it was that Cynthia headed for her apartment from Cody's, as she had done so many times before. This time, however, as she got closer and closer to the apartment her heart began to race. Once inside of her apartment, she ran for the wall and quickly removed one of her pastel drawings from its perch and slammed the door behind her. Nearly sprinting down the corridor, she continued back to Cody's apartment just as he was starting to wash the sweet potatoes. "Cody, my God — do you remember this drawing? Do you remember what you said about the sweet potatoes in this drawing?"

"I said that I'd never seen purple sweet potatoes."

"Cody, if the flesh of those sweet potatoes is the same color as the sprouts and leaves coming out of those sweet potatoes — I have a strong feeling that the sweet potatoes on the cupboard are somehow the amethyst-fleshed sweet potatoes in my drawing. I know it sounds crazy."

"What does this all mean, Cynthia?"

"I don't know what it means, but I think that if we can somehow get these to your father... Cody, let me say that I think that Nobuo has just provided you with an extremely valuable gift, a gift that we almost squandered as food for a single meal."

"Nobuo was a botanist his entire adult life, a plant geneticist. My God, something tells me that Nobuo has just awarded me with his most treasured botanical creation. And he did so in an enigmatic manner, as a check to see if I was really in tune with him. I've got to get these sweet potatoes to California where my father can immediately start to culture them."

"Oh, Cody, I'm absolutely at a loss for words."

"What ran through your mind when you sketched that picture? My God — the packing label on your drawing — this makes no sense whatsoever. I think that I'm going to faint. Please read what the fruit packing label in your drawing says, so I know that this is all real. Please read it, Cynthia."

"It says RACCOON DOG SWEET POTATOES."

"Cynthia, when did you draw this picture?"

"I guess that I drew it about a week after I arrived at the academy. It is dated March 20, 2012."

That next day, after dividing the sweet potatoes into two parcels and insulating the spuds with straw and lofty bags of loose green tea, Cody prepared the packages for shipping, eventually mailing them from two different shipping locations toward the assurance that at least one package would make it to his father in Oakdale. As a further measure to guarantee delivery, Cody mailed the packages under different shipping protocols. On the postal service declaration forms, Cody listed his packages as containing tea and tea cups. Once the shipping process had commenced, all Cody could do was to keep his fingers crossed that neither package would be intercepted by postal or agricultural inspectors. After sending the two packages, Cody mailed a letter to Nobuo that was written by Cynthia, in which he expressed his gratitude for Nobuo's fine gift.

From the information provided to Cody by the postal clerks at the two shipping centers, he learned the express package would arrive in just short of a week's time and the other package would arrive in roughly two weeks. If Cody's hunch was correct, he could expect that the new strain of sweet potatoes might be resistant to whatever it was that was slowly attacking the sweet potatoes varieties in production on his father's farm. What most struck Cody, and what he imagined would strike every sweet potato farmer in California's Central Valley, was the remarkably purple flesh associated with the newly discovered cultivar. If Cody's hunch was correct, this new crop had the potential to infuse new life-blood into his father and potentially save him from his slow, downward, depression-driven spiral into hopelessness.

Inside each packing box Cody placed a very simple heartfelt note:

Dear Father:

I am well and think of you often. I have met a girl. Her name is Cynthia Martin, and we plan to marry. You will like her. She is very smart and caring. I will tell you more about her soon. In the meanwhile, we send our love and a gift that we believe will bring new hope into all of our lives. It is recommended that you immediately culture these potatoes into the production of suitable slips that can be planted and propagated toward the production of additional stock for slip production. An amethyst-fleshed sweet potato — it's a beautiful thing! Contact me ASAP, once this package arrives.
With all of our love,
Cody and Cynthia

Just as the postal clerk had advised, Cody's first package to his father arrived within a week. Immediately upon its reception, Dwight emailed his son of its arrival.

Dear Son:

Your package arrived today in good condition. A few parts broke off of the cups, but the vessels are still viable. I will get right on it. I think you are onto something, and as such I intend to keep it really hush-hush. I'd recommend that you do the same. I will contact an attorney immediately, such that we can control this thing. Don't worry, son — your old man still has some smarts, and my plan is to do this correctly. To expedite the process and to protect our interest, I may take the effort inside — if you know what I mean. Thank you for the tea. I think I'll have a cup or two tonight.

I am pleased that you have found a gal. I can't wait to meet her. I hate that your mother will never meet this wonderful lady, this woman that who you've found halfway around the globe. I love you, son, Dad

When Cody received Dwight's email his spirits were heightened beyond what he'd even thought possible. Cody was so hugely elated that his first package had made it to his father that he could scarcely even begin to think about sleeping. Finally, in the wee hours of the morning, when his mind could no longer carry a thought, Cody slumped into a state of restful slumber.

The next day, after their shifts at the academy, Cody and Cynthia had a heart-to-heart talk about their living arrangements. Cynthia and Cody agreed that they would keep their relationship in as low-key a state as possible any time they were on the grounds of the Ikemoto Academy. They also agreed that both of their rooms would undergo modifications that transformed each living area into venues that jointly reflected their individual needs and personalities. This of course produced two hybrid living environments where either member of the partnership would feel as much at home as possible in either milieu. From Cody's perspective, such modifications were mostly in name, as he lived about as plain a life as imaginable. However, from Cynthia's perspective this meant that each apartment would be graced with various pieces of her wildly creative anime and other pastel drawings.

With the approach of the weekend, Cody proposed to Cynthia that they wake up very early on Saturday to make a trip to Tsukiji Fish Market. Cynthia had long wanted to visit the market, and Cody couldn't wait to venture into the city after having spent nearly two weeks isolated on the home front.

On Saturday, the couple hopped on Cody's Vespa just after 4:30 a.m. such that they could arrive at the Tsukiji market complex in time to watch the daily bluefin tuna auction.

For the uninitiated, the Tsukiji Fish Market is purported to be the largest and most glorious fish market in the world. Tsukiji Fish Market is located in Tokyo's Chuo ward. While the Tsukiji Fish Market may seem like a frivolous, off-beat curiosity to the tourist, it is strictly a business operation to the legions of assiduous fishermen, processors, packers, and shippers who form the nucleus of Japan's seafood industry. For those who navigate the market on their own devices, the expansive grounds of the bustling operation can be a very confusing, if not dangerous, place.

By the time that Cody and Cynthia arrived at the market, a small crowd had formed at the visitor kiosk, where those wishing to view the auction assembled prior to being guided into the cold, wet building where the bidding action takes place. From the perspective of a bystander, the venue is run much like a massive tuna showroom, huge ice-frosted bluefin lying eerily on surfaces rendered smoky by the ever-present ice-fog that lofts knee-high throughout the room. In deep-frozen rest, these football-shaped behemoths lie in wait, poised for shipment to the highest bidders. The tails of these free-ranging sea predators are often seen protruding from a gill flap of each beast, since this segment of the fish is generally removed to allow for the extraction of flesh samples. Prior to bidding on particular tuna, potential buyers roll small samples of tuna meat back and forth in their hands, each buyer an alchemist, carefully and methodically examining the fat-content of candidate fish. It is not uncommon to observe bluefin tuna exceeding 600 and even 700 pounds, and prices for such tuna to draw bids into the hundreds of thousands of dollars. Just three months prior to Cody's arrival in Japan, a bluefin tuna sold at the Tsukiji auction for nearly three quarters of a million dollars, or more than 1,200 dollars a pound. On the average, market bluefin tuna tend to be in the range of 100 to 150 pounds.

Once in the auction room, Cody and Cynthia huddled up to one another to stave off the icy cold permeating the room. Across the floor, the auctioneer acknowledged bidders while clipboard-carrying men recorded each transaction. Amongst the crowd of bidders, Cody noticed a man eying him with great study. As Cody stepped back behind a particularly tall individual, the man maneuvered himself such that he could re-place Cody into his view. Midway through the auction, after discussing the curious man in the distance, Cynthia and Cody decided to abandon the auction and to test the theory that they were being watched. From the auction building, the pair decided to walk among the stalls that housed the various fish vendors who maintained residency in the market.

Upon entering the swap-meet-like setting, it became evident that the venue was solely designed to be a production and packing area for the various ocean products traded in the market. Vendor accommodations consisted of little more than makeshift work spaces outfitted with flea-market-like wooden tables and overhanging rows of daisy-strung wire supporting dimly lit bulbs without the capacity to transform the space from seeming like a cold, dank cave. In short, during the early morning hours, the space was nearly perfect for middle-manning fish products and ensuring that visitors wouldn't linger.

The diversity of sea creatures at the market is nothing short of awesome. Some businesses specialize in mollusks such as squid, cuttlefish, octopus, abalone, whelk, oysters, clams, and more; while other venders center their operations on fin fish including bream, various tuna species, swordfish, flounder, rockfish, and the deadly fugu (puffer fish). Some merchants in the market are even known to specialize in whale meat. As

Cody and Cynthia took pictures of a fabulous arrangement of large steamed octopi, they again became aware of the curious fellow who was eying them in the auction room. This time, when the man appeared to come toward them from around a corner, they walked briskly to where Cody had parked his bike. "My God, Cody — I'm really worried. That fellow looks very intent on catching up with us."

"Don't worry. We're going to be out of here in a moment."

"Why do you think that he's after us?"

"I don't know. Perhaps it is some mistaken-identity thing."

Just as Cody and Cynthia hopped on the Vespa, a voice rang out, "Hey, hold it. Hey, Fletcher Cody san."

"Oh, my God. Gun it! He knows your name," said Cynthia.

"Stop! Cody san. It's me — Swag Tigger, with the bosozoku," said Swag Tigger as he tried to put the couple at ease.

"Cynthia, it is all right. Look. It's just — *Swag Tiger*," said Cody reflecting his belief that the fellow actually meant Tiger rather than Tigger.

"What? Like that's supposed to put me at ease. Who the hell is *Swag Tiger*?" said Cynthia under her breath.

"Hey, *Swag Tiger*. What are you doing here?"

"I work for the tuna auction as a forklift driver."

"Right on. This is my gal, Cynthia."

"It is nice to meet you, Cynthia."

"You're right, Fletcher san. She is a good one."

"Cody? You told this guy about me," said Cynthia whispering.

"Well, yeah, I guess. Yeah, I guess I might have mentioned you. You know, in passing."

"Cody san, I thought that I recognized you in the auction room, but I just couldn't place you. The guys were really impressed with your background as a Hells Angel. I guess life must be much simpler since you stopped running with your posse."

"Yeah, uh, *Swag Tiger*. We should talk more about that later, but I've got to get the girl out of this draft, if you know what I mean. I'll catch you, man."

"Okay, then, I guess I'll see you around, Cody san," said Swag Tigger as he and Cody bumped knuckles as might occur in parting with a close associate.

"Yeah, that *Swag Tiger*. He's a big kidder."

"How well do you know that guy?"

"Believe it or not, I don't recall ever having met him. I remember seeing a guy with a jacket that said *Swag Tiger*, with two g's. But that is all I remember about the fellow."

"Well, you sure seemed to have made an impression on him. Do you think this is another case of, as you once put it, 'gaijin envy'?"

"Cynthia, you know that I just made up that 'gaijin envy' thing as a joke, right?"

"Honestly, I don't know if you thought that you were 'joking' at the time or not."

"Hey, could you give me a break? This entire thing here is just fallout from when I got a little loose with the truth about the Hells Angels thing."

"Are you sure this is all that it is?"

"Positive."

"I don't know, Cody, you guys seemed remarkably chummy for two fellows who never formally met."

"I swear about this. I really do swear on this."

"Cody, if you see those guys again, you really need to somehow minimize the extent of your 'involvement' with the Hells Angels. This thing really has the potential to develop wings of one sort or another. The last thing we need to have happen, is that somehow the 'misunderstanding' elevates you into some sort of folk hero with the guys or something crazy like that."

"Yeah, sure — if I ever see those guys again. I mean this city has something like fifteen million people, doesn't it?"

"Cody, no excuses, you need to hatch some sort of alternative explanation of your association with the Hells Angels. You know, something like: *I think that you misunderstood what I said concerning the Hells Angels. What I was referring to was a group of guys who pretended...* You know, I don't know what you can tell them at this stage, but you must somehow down-play this thing before it turns into some sort of problem."

The following week, Cody received another email from his father. As in the previous dispatch, Dwight's spirits were again high. In the brief note, Dwight commented that the second package of "tea" had arrived and that it looked like it would "likely brew up real nicely." Cody's father stated further that the maiden venture would definitely be an indoor operation. Most importantly in Dwight's note, he wrote, "For the first time in a long while, I feel like I have a good healthy project to work on. It's a very good feeling."

Not truly knowing Nobuo's intent with the gift of the sweet potatoes he bestowed on him, Cody felt some unrest concerning his decision to export them to his father towards their development into a Fletcher family sweet potato cultivar. Hoping to get further information about the purple sweet potatoes, Cody asked Cynthia to draft a letter to Nobuo, specifically asking him about the background of the species. In closing the letter, Cynthia expressed Cody's interest in making another trip to Kyoto and a hope to visit with Nobuo when that time came.

Meanwhile, Cody and Cynthia decided to make a trip down below the Ginza to their favorite little restaurant, a restaurant that Cody now knew as Curry House. In Cynthia's mind, none of her fears were realized concerning Cody's apparent cordial relationship with the bosozoku group. In truth, neither Cody nor Cynthia ever found any reason to believe that the group of bikers posed a threat of any variety. To Cynthia, the men simply seemed like a cadre of full-grown adolescents who reminded her of the various groups of socially awkward boys that could be found on any high school campus.

Taking into consideration the collective lack of inhibition and profound oddness associated with the bosozoku group, it would not be a great stretch to suggest that the men seemed like the kind of guys who would stage a donut-eating contest, dress up like Liberace, or gather to watch a 24-hour marathon of the 1960s sitcom "The Courtship of Eddie's Father." You could almost hear them commenting to one another, "Mrs. Livingston (actress Miyoshi Umeki) was a real babe, man." They were men with wild hair and great flamboyance. They were men who loved women, but who could seldom find themselves in a social setting where they'd become close enough to let any members of the gender know. They were men who were as at home behind a computer or on the shuffleboard court as they were on their motor scooters. They were outcasts of Japanese society on the grandest scale, but to Cody — the zany bikers were the closest he'd ever come to having Japanese friends.

Cynthia and Cody had never before visited Curry House together during the week, however, as was generally the case during each visit, the restaurant was nearly empty, which caused the pair to question when, if ever, the place received any business. "It surprises me that the vegetables, seafood, and other ingredients are so fresh, yet short of the biker guys, the place seems to receive so little business," said Cynthia looking about the empty shell of the dining room. "I'd bet that they get a good lunch crowd from the local businesses, as well as a flush of people just before the dinner hour, by the look of all of the perishable garbage sitting on the sidewalk."

"Perhaps. What are you going to have?" asked Cody.

"I think that I want to have some sort of curry dish. Presumably, curry should be their specialty here. I'm going to ask the waitress what she would recommend."

"I might have a curry dish myself."

Just as the pair closed their menus, the waitress emerged from behind the vinyl curtain that separated the dining room from the kitchen with a tray of *togarashi* (a Japanese red pepper condiment) containers and bottles of *shoyu* (soy sauce). "I'll be right with you," the woman announced in Japanese as she placed the tray on an adjacent table. Poising herself before the couple, the waitress said, "Konichi wa. What would you like?"

"I want to try one of your curry dishes. What would you recommend?" said Cynthia. "The spicy curry *ika* (squid) is good," said the waitress.

"I'll have the spicy curry ika and a Sapporo beer," Cynthia said.

"What do you want, sir?"

"I think I'll have the dried scallop and white scallion soup, with buckwheat noodles. And I'd like some curry added to the broth. Oh, and a cup of sake, *onegaishimasu*," said Cody in appreciation of the waitress's service.

Looking around the room, Cynthia reflected, "I wonder if we'll see your friends tonight."

When Cody started to reply, his voice was drowned out by the roar of what sounded like a dozen or more scooters pulling up to the restaurant. When the noise died down, Cody continued, "I was going to say that it is entirely possible, but I guess that isn't necessary now."

Just as the pair looked in anticipation toward the door, a tall thin figure, silhouetted by the light from outside of the restaurant, appeared. "Hey, look its *Codester*. We thought that we saw your bike outside," said Monkey Wretch.

As the group entered the eatery, Cynthia turned to Cody with a sour expression on her face while mouthing, "Codester?"

"Yeah, uh, it is hard to tell where that came from, but let's just go with it. I'm sure no harm was intended."

Trailing the pack and then walking right up to Cody's table, stepped Swag Tigger, "Hey, Cody san. Konichi wa, Cynthia san."

"Hello, *Swag Tiger* san. It is good to see you again," said Cynthia pulling together a high level of warmth in her words.

"So what are you boys up to tonight?" asked Cody.

"Oh, you know. We're just going to raise some hell, like usual. Maybe someone will end up in Tokyo Bay tonight, maybe not," Swag Tigger said with a wily grin. "No, seriously, I think that we are having a chess tournament at Sexy Cat's pad tonight. We'll probably play some Clash or some Prince albums. Do you play chess?"

With Swag's question, Cody turned to Cynthia to determine whether or not he played chess, where his questioning look was met with a swift, yet gentle, kick from under the table by Cynthia. "Yeah, I mean no, I don't play much chess anymore," Cody said looking at Cynthia.

With Cody's reply, the kimono-clad waitress scurried from behind the curtain with Cody and Cynthia's order. "Hey, well, I'm going to let you two eat," Swag Tigger said as he retreated to the table occupied by the rest of the bosozoku.

"Cody, who am I to stop you from taking part in a chess tournament? If you want to go, then you should go. Motion

Swag Tiger back over, if you are interested in joining the group."

"Yeah, okay, maybe I will, if I can get his attention."

Just as Cody and Cynthia indulged in their meal, Swag Tigger returned to their table. "I'm sorry to interrupt, but I wanted to tell you, Cody, that Monkey Wretch and Sexy Cat say it's okay it you decide that you want to join the chess tournament tonight."

"Thank you, *Swag Tiger*. I'll think about it, but first I'll have to discuss it with my posse, if you know what I mean," said Cody with a wink as he looked at Cynthia.

"Yeah, I understand. Let us know if you decide you want to play in the tournament," replied Swag Tigger as he returned to his table.

"You know Cody, from what I can tell, those fellows seem like a real fine bunch of guys. I can see that they really like you. I think that you should consider going, if the evening is not expected to go too late."

After finishing his meal, Cody caught Swag Tigger's eye and motioned him to the table. "Hey, Swag, about this chess tournament. How late will it go?"

"Well, it can't go too late. I have to work at Tsukiji early in the morning. I don't know. There will just be ten of us if you join in. I guess about three hours."

"Yeah, I don't think I can go tonight if it goes much beyond three hours."

"Well, Cody, if you lose early, I bet you could be out of there in less than an hour."

"Yeah, Swag, that's the problem."

"What's the problem?"

"You see, Swag, if I go — I'm going to have to win. I really can't give you guys much of a break on this one."

"Oh, is that the way it's going to be, Cody san?"

"Yep, I'm afraid so," said Cody with much of the same grimacing look he wore when he told the group that he rode with the Hells Angeles.

"So, should I tell the boys that you're in?"

"What time are you going to start?"

"Let's see, it's 5:30 now. I'd say we'd start around seven o'clock or so."

"Where do I need to be," said Cody.

"Sexy Cat wrote the address down for you and provided a phone number. Do you know the Roppongi Hills well?"

"Not really well, but we, Cynthia and I, can Google it," Cody said.

"Okay, then we'll see you around seven," Swag Tigger said as he backed away from the table.

"Okay then. I guess that we had better get going, my dear," Cody said, turning towards Cynthia.

When Cody arrived at Sexy Cat's high rise apartment, most of the crew had yet to assemble. When Sexy Cat opened the door, he was wearing a glittery purple dress jacket, reminiscent of something that Prince, himself, would wear. Sexy Cat complemented his ensemble with a white faux fur wrap draped around his neck. "Hello. Welcome, Fletcher Cody san. Can I hang up your jacket?"

"Yes, uh, thank you. That's a real fancy outfit you have there," said Cody. "Should I call you Sexy Cat?"

"On the street, yes — that is probably best. But, in my home, you can call me the *Big Ragu.*"

"Really?"

"No, not really. My given name is Toshi. Call me Toshi. Do you like the show *Rabun and Shuri*?"

"Laverne and Shirley? Yeah, I guess it's okay. I haven't watched it in years. I haven't really watched it much, I guess."

"Cody, I see that your jacket says 'AM RACCOON DOG.' What does that mean?"

"The raccoon dog part is my girlfriend's pet name for me, and the AM part stands for American. The AM thing also is kind of like *I am* so it's like: *I Am Raccoon Dog.* It must sound kind of silly to you."

"No. No, not really. I've probably heard of sillier names in the past," Toshi said. "Hey, come to the kitchen with me. Sadao is making some snacks."

"Sadao? Have I met him?"

"He goes by the name *App4That.* You've probably seen him around. He is a real terror on the chess board, if you know what I mean."

"Yeah, uh, I guess. I may not have heard it expressed quite that way before."

"Hey, Sadao, Cody san is here."

"Hey, Cody san. Glad you could make it. I'm just preparing some sashimi. You like sashimi, don't you?"

"Hello, Sadao! Oh, yeah, I do love sashimi. I love all kinds of sushi. Back in California, me and my posse would make runs down by the Monterey Aquarium and go to this little sushi restaurant called *Sakura*," Cody said, recalling the one and only time that he and his father went to a Japanese restaurant and ate sashimi.

"Swag Tigger brought over a lot of fish today from Tsukiji before we ran into you."

"Man, you fellows eat good. What have you got there?"

"What do we have today, Sadao? We have *tako* (octopus), *uni* (sea urchin), *awabi* (abalone), *toro* (fatty tuna), *hamachi* (yellowtail), and some sea bream. I guess that about does it."

"I've never seen such a wide variety of seafood in my life," said Cody, genuinely dazzled by the array of food before him.

"Yeah, we do this all the time," said Toshi. "We do this so often that I've appointed Sadao as head sashimi chef."

"Your apartment is unbelievable. You've got an amazing view of Tokyo Bay."

"Thank you, and thanks to the tech boom. And to think that my father told me that a hand-held digital pet was a worthless invention."

"Cody, help me arrange the tables and the chess boards, will you?" Toshi requested.

"Yeah, okay."

By 7:10 everyone taking part in the tournament had arrived at Sexy Cat's 25th floor apartment. As it turned out, only eight of the ten contestants were present for the event, the other two canceling out at the last moment. After a short visit, the men took part in a proclamation ceremony led by Monkey Wretch. "He who reigns supreme in this, the tenth Sashimi Chess Championship event, will forever be held in high esteem by this group of men, and if ever a challenger wins over the previous champion, he will gain the people's ovation and fame forever."

"Gosh, if you don't mind me saying so, Monkey Wretch, that was really an excellent preface. Did you make that up yourself?"

"Well, not really. It is actually a modification of a script from an old episode of *Iron Chef*. But thanks, it's nice to be appreciated. *Domo arigato*. Cody, please call me by my given name of Akio, if you would. You probably would have recognized the origin of my little speech had I not removed the part of the script that referred to *kitchen stadium*."

"Let's get on with it, Akio," said Toshi.

"All right, all right, don't go on a tirade, Toshi. Before we start, does anyone have anything they wish to add? Anyone? Okay, then with no further ado — let the games begin," said Akio.

The silence was deadening as each man intently studied every move. Cody was astounded by just how serious each man was with what appeared to be a simple game of chess. No small talk, not a single nonessential word throughout the event. By design, the winner of the event would be determined after the victor, whoever he be, won three games.

In the first game, Cody was paired with Sweat Puppy, aka Ichiro, a game that Cody won handily. "Ichiro, you played a very thoughtful game," said Cody as he loaded up another plate of sashimi.

"I don't know about that, Cody san. You seemed to have beaten me with little trouble. What has it been, about five minutes?"

"I don't know, probably a little more than that."

"Hey, Cody, it looks like you're enjoying that sashimi," said Sadao as he inspected Cody's plate.

"Oh, uh, I guess I am, said Cody as he looked about, coming to realize that his plate was piled higher than anyone else's. "Hey, Sadao, you weren't wearing that outfit when you were cutting the fish, were you?"

"No, I wasn't. Would you wear something like this when working with fish?"

"No, probably not. So, Sadao, do you mind if I ask you a question?"

"No, go ahead."

"Where do you guys find these great outfits?"

"Yeah, they're pretty cool, aren't they?" said Sadao.

"They sure are. I'd love to get a hold of a sparkling banana-colored outfit like you've got on."

"Yeah, I don't know about that, Cody. I think that one person in the group with an outfit like this probably about does it. Besides, my grandmother made this outfit for me, so I don't think that there'd be another one out there like this."

"Yeah, you're probably right on both counts."

"Hey, Cody san, you're up. The first round is over. Now you play Toshi," said Ichiro.

"All right. Let's do this thing."

"So we meet again, my Raccoon Dog friend," said Toshi with a friendly smile.

"This is true, Toshi. You may want to loosen up that mink stole of yours for this game, baby," said Cody playfully. "I don't think that even Sheila E. can help you out of this one." Cody said in reference to Prince's percussionist and sometimes-singer from the 1980s.

Again, there was utter silence throughout the competition, and again, Cody won the match, albeit after losing his queen. "You know, Toshi, that was total luck. I was just bluffing about beating you, and by golly — it happened. It must be my lucky night," said Cody, genuinely surprised that he had won a second game. "Are you sure you guys aren't throwing games to me? I mean, no offense, but I haven't played since high school. I remember little more than how each piece moves around the board."

"Cody san, thanks for trying to cheer us up, but I really think your approach is not providing much relief," said Ichiro.

"Sorry, guys. I guess there is a fine line between maintaining a humble disposition and being sensitive to the resolute intensity and care that each of you brings into the game. For what it is worth, I can't imagine —"

"Yeah, we know — that lightning could strike again in the same place," said Toshi as he shook his head in disbelief.

"Yeah. How did you know? Never mind. Gosh, I'm really not being much of a guest, I wonder if I shouldn't leave."

"Don't be ridiculous. You won each game fair and square," Toshi countered.

"Now you must play Sadao for the championship. Recall, earlier, that I warned you about his skill at the game."

In short order, just as he had defeated his previous two opponents, Cody retired Sadao. With little more than a communal nod of approval of sorts, the tournament was over. There was no fanfare regarding Cody's victory, there was no celebration. Almost instantaneously, the theme of the moment changed from playing chess and consuming sashimi, to maniacal dancing about the floor listening to *The Clash*.

"Hey, Codester, let your hair hang down, baby — it's *The Clash*," said Akio.

"Isn't this music totally bitchin', man?" said Toshi.

"Bitchin'? Uh, yeah, it is really bitchin' — daddy-o," Cody said in realization that he had only heard the term *bitchin'* from his father, when he described what it was like living in San Francisco in the late 1960s. The more Cody watched the guys prancing around Toshi's spacious apartment, the looser his inhibitions became. In no time, Cody was jumping around the place pretending to play the guitar and mouthing the words to *Rock the Casbah*. Catching the excitement, Cody thundered, across the room, "This music is totally freaking awesome!"

"Hey, Cody san, shake it, but don't break it, baby!" exclaimed Swag Tigger, aka Ken. "Cody san, do you like Prince?"

"I absolutely love Prince."

Just as Cody mentioned his appreciation of Prince's music, a video of Prince's song *1999* projected onto the wall. "Cody san, I got my inspiration for my purple jacket from this video."

"Right on, Toshi. Your jacket is totally rad, man," said Cody.

"Hey, Toshi, what about all of this sake? Can I open a bottle?" said Ken.

"Open as many bottles as you want. It's party time, dudes."

"Cody san, do you like sake?" asked Toshi.

"Definitely! I do like sake, but, I probably should go. You know, I've got to get home to the girl. I guess I could have a small cup."

Keeping to his word, Cody had a single small cup of sake and then thanked each of the men for the very fine evening and warm welcome. Upon being led to the door by Toshi, Cody graciously thanked his host for his cordial hospitality and expressed his hopes that the group might soon again assemble. Having suited up in his leather jacket, Cody exited Toshi's apartment.

In riding home, Cody reflected on the wondrously strange evening that he had spent with the scooter gang. Each of the guys seemed to have the warmest, most homely sense about them. It was as if the biker fellas existed as they were, as odd, awkward, or strange as they were or seemed, without a care or sense of caring as to how they might be received or perceived by others. The men were entirely free; they didn't put any stock in trying to be anybody other than themselves. They neither knew nor seemed to care that they were outlandish and hopelessly out of touch with the times. The members of the bosozoku lived and let live, and perhaps most important — they seemed to have accepted Cody as one of their own.

En route to his apartment complex, Cody smiled as he reflected on Toshi's reference to the sitcom Laverne and Shirley, as '*Rabun and Shuri*.' The thought also reminded him of the difficult, if not impossible, nature of subjecting English words to the constraints of the sound repertoire associated with the Japanese language. One curiosity that Cody discovered was that in the Japanese language, *l*'s are often pronounced as *r*'s, and *v*'s are pronounced as *b*'s. Hence, the English word "television game" becomes *terebigēmu*, having truncated television to *terebi*.

Continuing down the road toward his housing complex, Cody became increasingly conscious of a weighty sense of wellbeing that his evening with the Curry House boys had produced. The high that Cody felt with the array of positive elements that seemed to be coming together in his life gave him that edgy nervous feeling that people experience just before they sense they're about to lose their footing. Fortunately for Cody, he remained tethered to the ground by the responsibility of his day job and his commitment to the girl that he, at one time, thought could never love him.

Cody arrived at the complex before 9:30 p.m. and immediately headed up the staircase to Cynthia's apartment. Upon hearing Cody's description of the wonderful evening he experienced, Cynthia genuinely partook in Cody's pleasure of being accepted by the group of men with whom he shared a cultural and genetic bond. "So now that you're part of the Tokyo social scene, will you still be able to find time for me?" Cynthia asked wryly.

"It's not the Tokyo social scene that I'm concerned about, but rather the rigorous training schedule I'll have to follow. Hey, I've got to be straight with you, babe. The guys made me promise them that I'd teach them the unspoken code of the Hells Angels, and that includes — the secret blood ritual."

"Cody, you promised you'd stop the charade. Damn it, Cody, what else did you promise them?"

At that point, Cody looked around the room, as if to see if the walls had ears, and he motioned to Cynthia to come close. "I promised that I'd show them how to make Grandma Fletcher's three bean salad," Cody whispered, prior to breaking into uproarious laughter.

"Cody, you had me so mad, I was steaming. You are joking about everything aren't you, including the Hells Angeles' training?"

"Yes, sweetheart, I'm sorry for kidding about such a sensitive issue."

"Have you always had a wicked sense of humor like that?"

"No, I don't ever recall telling fibs like that for laughs in the past. Actually, I don't really remember having much to laugh about in the past. I must have got it from you."

"Yeah, Cody. I don't think so."

"Hey sweetheart, what did you do tonight?"

"Not much. I looked over tomorrow's lessons and doodled a little bit. That is about it."

While she didn't share the drawing with Cody, that night Cynthia had sketched a leather jacketed chess-king riding a motor scooter through the streets of Tokyo, trailed by a v-shaped pattern of scooter riders, reminiscent of a flock of geese flying south for the winter.

When Nobuo's return letter arrived several days later, Cody had to wait in near agony for several hours for Cynthia to return from a trip to the city. As the minutes turned to hours, Cody kept an eye out of his window such that he could immediately usher Cynthia into his apartment to translate Nobuo's note.

Cody learned that Nobuo was well and that he wished great prosperity to Cynthia and him. Nobuo referenced his mortality and the approach of the final chapter of his life. A certain shade of darkness pervaded his letter regarding a sense of sadness in bringing to a close his family's long history in agriculture. In the letter, Nobuo made reference to keeping many of his horticultural triumphs close to his vest over the years, and admitted to allowing many of his genetic variations to fall back into the figurative cracks "from which they once arose, never to be expressed genetically again." Then Nobuo got very specific:

> *Among my greatest triumphs are the sweet potato specimens that were mailed to you some weeks back. I may be an old man, but I am not a blind man. I may be a wealthy man, but my wealth is finite. You, Cody, are young and your potential for wealth and happiness is without bounds. It is my hope that you recognized the inherent value of the sweet potatoes that you received. They are the only survivors of the species, and as such it is my hope that you have somehow found for this candle, this fleeting essence, a place out of the wind. It is my hope that you are gifted with the wisdom that the nature of my offering to you assumed.*

In closing the letter, Nobuo expressed interest in maintaining contact with Cody and Cynthia, stating that they were to come to his home without delay, if ever again they found themselves in the great city of Kyoto. Continuing, Nobuo added:

> *I am an old man with few years to live, and even fewer in which to be productive. You have prolonged my life and you have permitted me to have more time with my family — and that I shall never forget. — Nobuo*

CHAPTER SIX:
YONSEI RIDER

In 1992, the Japanese government implemented a series of measures that provided law enforcement agencies with greater leeway and authority in the means through which they countered organized crime. Since that time, *boryokudan* (gangster organizations), principally consisting of the yakuza, have become increasingly ardent and vigilant in concealing the methods and the efficacy associated with their individual family enterprises. The chief avenue of attack on these criminal groups has occurred through strategies that work to both interrupt boryokudan funding sources and lead to expanded criminal liabilities against such gangs.

As has always been the pattern, criminal organizations continue to be creative and resourceful entities, uncannily situating themselves one or more steps ahead of law enforcement groups. In responding to new modes of crime fighting and lower tolerance levels of criminal behavior, many Japanese gangsters have come to recognize the advantages of membership in criminal organizations of a more informal structure than traditional yakuza groups.

Jun boryokudan (quasi-gangster) is the term given to these new, less-structured organized crime groups. The term *hangure*, from *hanbun* (semi) and *gureru* (turned delinquent), is also used to describe these loosely organized groups of gangsters.

The group of bikers that Cody had come into contact with well fit a proper description of delinquent; what was unclear was whether this presence of being was deliberate or whether it was an inane characteristic inherent to each member of the group. Fundamentally, all men are hard-wired with the capacity to become violent in the face of danger, fear, or unbridled rage, but only corrupt or depraved men act out violently without provocation. As far as Cody could tell, the only hint of danger brought forth by the Curry House boys was their strength in numbers. From what Cody could determine, the group consisted of at least twenty members or associates, who regularly paraded through the streets of Tokyo with a primary purpose of standing out conspicuously toward irritating, in some manner, the majority of those who they encountered.

The majority of the activities in which members of the group partook were no more disruptive or dangerous than disturbing the midnight quiet and riding their bikes just under the threshold that constituted reckless operation of a motor vehicle.

In the weeks following the get-together at Toshi's Roppongi Hills apartment, Cody had the opportunity to hang out with the fellows at Curry House several afternoons after work. One positive outcome of Cody's affiliation with the Curry House boys was that it strengthened Cynthia and his identification of Curry House as their official personal milieu.

During this time, it became clear to Cody that the boys had developed a certain place in their heart for him to the point where they seemed to care about his welfare. This kinship became apparent when the gang insisted on escorting him to his apartment one early morning after a marathon evening of riding about Tokyo.

On the first Saturday in August, Cody and Cynthia visited Curry House for dinner. When the couple arrived at the restaurant, the sun had been down for close to an hour and it was about as dark as it ever gets in Tokyo. Upon stepping into the restaurant, Cody and Cynthia were surprised to see that several of the tables were taken by groups of men they didn't immediately recognize. After standing at the entrance to the restaurant for several minutes, a waitress, who they'd not seen before, directed them to a table that was arranged directly adjacent to the hallway that led to the restrooms. Several minutes later, the waitress returned with menus for Cody and Cynthia. In looking about the restaurant, Cody reflected on the first time that he and Cynthia had patronized the eatery, whereby he came to the troubling realization that he was again being watched by exactly the same group of men who ceaselessly monitored him during their first visit.

Trying not to let on that he was aware that the men were fixated on him, Cody maintained an animated conversation with Cynthia, periodically directing a studied glance at the men. It was clear to Cody that the men had been drinking and that they were more than likely beyond the point of presenting any threat to either him or Cynthia.

Shortly after the waitress delivered Cynthia and Cody's orders, Cody heard the pleasing sound of his biker comrades pulling up outside the restaurant. "It sounds like the Curry House boys are about to enter the building," said Cody with unmistakable mirth as he looked toward the entrance.

"Hey, look its AM RAC and his gal," said Swag Tigger as he smiled at Cody.

"Hey, Swag, I was hoping that you fellows would show up. Hey, Sexy Cat — shake it, but don't break it, baby," said Cody, looking at Cynthia with a slight look of embarrassment on his face. "You would have had to have seen Sexy Cat dancing to "Little Red Corvette" to fully get the joke." Resigned to the unlikelihood that Cynthia would find humor in his comment, Cody shrugged his shoulders in frustration before uttering, "Oh, never mind.

There he is," said Cody smiling and motioning to Monkey Wretch. "See that fellow, Cynthia? That's App4That. He's the gang's sashimi chef and also the guy who let me beat him for the chess championship."

"Hey, what's shaking, Cody san," said Meet Head.

"Cynthia, I'd like you to meet Head, I mean — meet *Meat Head*," Cody said, looking at Cynthia, while giggling like a school girl. "I think that he means *Meat* — as in beef."

"Cody, you're not really as weird as they are, are you?" said Cynthia reflecting on the tender friendship it appeared that the fellows shared with one another. "Never mind, Cody. Don't answer that! I think I know the answer."

After Cody and Cynthia greeted each of the members of the Curry House boys, the fellows retreated to another table, allowing Cynthia and Cody to get down to the business of consuming their meals. Surrounded by the fine bunch of fellows that had become Cody's friends, he felt a great deal of contentment to be relaxing in their presence in what had become his and Cynthia's favorite haunt.

Once having completed their meals and settling the bill, Cody waved goodbye to the guys and walked around the table to intercept Cynthia. Upon reaching for Cynthia's hand, Cody was hit by a hard bump from a man as he exited the hallway that led to the restroom. Instead of apologizing for his misstep, the man pushed Cody out of the way saying, "Get out of my way, *hetare* (sissy)." When Cody turned to approach the man, Cynthia grabbed his arm motioning for him to avoid a confrontation. As Cody and Cynthia walked toward the exit door, the man pursued Cody, in route pushing Cynthia and calling out, "*Hyōhaku no ke panpan!*" (literally, hair-bleaching prostitute).

At that point, Cody, in what appeared to be a slow-motion movie clip, ducked down and slammed the man with his shoulder, carrying the antagonist across the room to the point where the man's upper back collided with the opposing wall. Something in Cody had snapped, and he pummeled the man with his fists continuously, until the man slumped, motionless, against the wall. Cody continued his attack with kicks to the man's head, only ceasing his barrage at the sound of Cynthia's horror-fueled screams. Realizing what he'd done, Cody grabbed Cynthia's hand and the pair dashed out the door and hopped on his scooter, making a hastened departure back to the apartment complex.

Not knowing exactly what to make of the matter, the Curry House boys simply rose to their feet as they watched Cody and Cynthia breeze out the restaurant's entrance. Looking first at the limp figure sprawled upon the floor and then to the man's drunken associates, it became very clear to the bosozoku that no pursuit or retribution would be forthcoming to Cody that evening.

Upon arrival at their residence, Cynthia remained in near unmitigated hysterics. "Sweetheart, it's all right. We're home safe now," Cody said, embracing Cynthia and attempting to calm her.

"Why did you beat the man so mercilessly?" Cynthia said, looking deep into Cody's eyes for the first time since the assault.

"I was scared," Cody said with a hint of disingenuity, realizing that he wasn't much scared of anything. "I became enraged when he pushed you, and my anger became uncontrollable after he referred to you as a bleached-haired whore. I didn't realize it until now, but only two things in the entire world could bring out that level of rage in me."

"What do you mean?" Cynthia asked.

"Since the time my mother was taken away from me, I've had dreams of taking vengeance regarding her death. At least, I thought the dreams were about my mother. I loved my mother more dearly than any boy could love his mother. And now, somehow, my love for you has become so passionate, so all consuming, that I put everything I had into removing the possibility that the man who pushed you would ever be able to do so again."

"I understand that you lost your mother under tragic circumstances. And I understand that the man, the presumably very intoxicated man, insulted me, but Cody — are we going to read about that man tomorrow in the obituary section of the newspaper?"

"Cynthia, I'm sure that the guy will be fine."

"How can you be so sure?" said Cynthia, not sharing Cody's optimism. "This whole situation seems so ugly, so dirty to me," she said still shaken by the event.

After talking late into the night, Cody and Cynthia put the matter to rest, instead investing their energy as only two lovers can, embraced in a bond that would span over two continents and many years.

Cynthia was upset with what had occurred at Curry House, but not critical of Cody for taking a stance in the matter. Cody was Cynthia's man, even with his faults.

The next morning, Cynthia surprised Cody with some instant coffee and baked goods that she had purchased earlier in the week. During a leisurely breakfast, Cynthia wondered aloud how the event might be interpreted by the Curry House boys. "Are you concerned that last night's incident might have an effect upon your relationship with the biker fellows?"

"I really hadn't given it any thought," said Cody.

"The way I see it, a couple of scenarios could develop. One is that the guys will view you as some sort of merciless bastard that they don't want to have anything to do with. Another is that the fellows will think of you as some sort of bad-ass who is worthy of their admiration in some sort of sick, perverse manner."

"I think that the guys probably know that the incident was provoked and that I just acted as most guys would in such a situation. I don't think that they're going to want to rally around me as if I'm some sort of folk hero or as if I just scored the winning touchdown."

"Well, perhaps you are right, but when you see the fellows, if you see the fellows, do me a favor and downplay the event as best you can. Damn it, Cody. They'll surely believe your tough-guy tale of being a made-member in the Hells Angels now! I just hope that the guys don't decide that you are to be their object of admiration. The last thing we need is for them to develop a sense that your persona — the legendary *Yonsei* (fourth-generation Japanese-American) ruffian rider — is some sort of a hitching post for their wagons, or that you somehow become a template to which they hope to aspire.

In reflecting on the event further, a notion of sadness overtook the couple. "Cody, I think that we have eaten our last meal at Curry House for a while."

"Yes, at this point, I don't think that we, I mean I, would be welcome," Cody said correcting himself.

After the event at Curry House, the boys took to the streets of Tokyo wanting to touch base with Cody, yet realizing that he deserved some peace after the personal and social unrest that he experienced. When a week had passed, Monkey Wretch sent Swag Tigger on a mission to contact Cody. When Swag finally caught up with Cody, he relayed, "A few of us have been anxious to check up on your welfare. The boys send their best and hope to meet up again with you soon." Continuing, Swag deplored, "Whatever you do, don't even think about going to Curry House — not now, it might not be safe for you. Oh, and one more thing, Toshi's having a gathering at his apartment tonight and he requests your presence. Drop by if you can make it."

"I'll try to make it to Toshi's. I'll check with Cynthia. What time is the event?"

"The fellows should be starting to assemble between 7 and 7:30. You should definitely try to get there by 7:30," said Swag Tigger.

Having completed his task, Swag smiled at Cody and added, "Take care of yourself, my friend, and say hello to Cynthia." Bumping knuckles with Cody, Swag Tigger straddled his scooter and rode off into the distance.

Cody had never heard such stern and seemingly heavy-hearted words from any member of the biker group. In the past, the group had always seemed so playful, if not frivolous, but now their collective tone had changed. There was no sense of glibness in Swag's demeanor; there was no sense that the matter was anything to kid around with. The message was sincere, sober, and point blank.

Cody wasn't sure, when he spoke with Swag Tigger, whether he'd be able to make it to Toshi's gathering, as he had made arrangements with Cynthia to visit Meiji Shrine in Tokyo's Shibuya ward, in what Cynthia hoped would amount to a cleansing of Cody's soul, retrospective of the violent beating that he had unleashed the previous week.

Arriving outside of the Torii gates just after 5 p.m., the pair reflected on how their plans to visit the Fushimi Inari Shrine, in Kyoto, were dashed weeks earlier with Nobuo's misfortune in the Kamo River. Strangely, it now appeared that the pair was, in some fashion, experiencing a misfortune or an unpleasant setback of their own.

Just as the couple were about to walk through the massive cypress-wood archway leading to the shrine grounds, they observed a familiar face coming their way. Wheeling toward Cynthia and Cody, with her cache of bottles, cans, and other salvaged items, was the old lady Koko.

In what at the time wasn't recognized for its apparent irony, it was Koko who contacted Cynthia regarding some variety of sixth-sense concern that she experienced about Cody in proximity to the time that he battled to save Nobuo and himself from what Nobuo claimed was a kappa.

The afternoon was warm and it immediately became apparent that Koko was several days into her current set of clothes and that her personal effluvium, an aromatic combination of soiled undergarments and stale tobacco smoke, was in stiff competition with the obnoxious odor of the collected garbage cast about in her cart. "It is so good to see you," Cynthia said as she provided Koko with a hearty embrace.

"I am so glad that Cody san appears well. I had a premonition that you met an unpleasant fate," Koko said as she maneuvered herself to hug Cody.

"We still want to get together with you for a meal, Koko," said Cody as he and Koko engaged in a hearty embrace.

"Yes, we must do that soon," Koko said unconvincingly.

"What are you doing this evening? Are you available this evening for dinner?" Cody asked recognizing the lack of conviction in Koko's voice.

"Tonight, I sense that you have more pressing matters to grapple with. I feel that you have people who expect your presence elsewhere," Koko said.

Looking at Cody, Cynthia said, "We have no plans tonight. If you are available, we are available."

"My dear, I am sorry to say that I cannot visit tonight. In fact, I must now go. I will contact you soon." In walking away, Koko professed, "Cynthia, you will soon be a mother. I am so very happy for you both."

As Koko walked away, Cynthia and Cody looked at one another, much as parents look at one another when their child experiences a major lapse in reality. "Well, that was a rather interesting visit," Cynthia said.

"Yes, there is something very different about her that I can't quite put my finger on. She seems like she is on another plane of reality," replied Cody.

With Koko headed who knows where, to do who knows what, Cody and Cynthia resumed their quest to submit a prayer within the shrine grounds towards an apology to an unknown kami or toward a sense of reckoning with unknown forces, for what Cody knew in his heart was an excessive fit of rage. After purifying their hands and mouths, Cody led a silent prayer at the base of a towering conifer, expressing his desire to be forgiven by the spirits, and a wish that the injured man would experience a full recovery.

After exiting the shrine, Cody and Cynthia stopped at a small yakitori cart that they encountered as they motored along the route leading to their residence. After consuming the last bite of a skewer of yakitori octopus, Cody used the pointed end of the bamboo stick to clean his teeth before saying, "You know, Cynthia, I ran into *Swag Tiger* today and he sent a message that I was invited to attend a get-together at Sexy Cat's, I mean Toshi's, apartment in the Roppongi. How do you feel about my going?"

"Hmm, I guess that Koko was right, people do expect your presence elsewhere," Cynthia replied with mild annoyance.

"Uh, yeah, I was going to tell you —"

"Yeah, that would be fine with me. Try not to get home too late."

From the yakitori stand, Cody and Cynthia rode the Vespa directly home.

After washing up from the stickiness of a muggy Tokyo summer day, Cody pondered aloud as he exited the restroom. "I really don't know what to expect tonight at Toshi's. But I do know that I need to find out exactly what my status is with the guys. Just as a precaution, I want you to have Toshi's address and phone number. It is in my top desk drawer, inside the front cover of the Hello Kitty notebook. You should probably call just after I am to arrive to make it clear that my welfare is being monitored, in some sense."

"You don't think that you have anything to worry about, do you?"

"No, not really, but one weak link in the whole chain is that I don't really have any knowledge, at this stage, of the level of street savvy possessed by these fellows. I don't know the degree to which the matter at Curry House has been discussed within the group or among other individuals."

When Cody left the residence it was just getting dark, which in Tokyo, in the middle of August, meant that it was just before 7:00 p.m. After making his way to the Roppongi district, Cody located a place to park his scooter. The air was cool and curiously quiet, aspects of the moment that made Cody acutely aware of his every step and thought as he propelled himself down the block towards Toshi's residence. Making his way to the front of the building, up the concrete staircase leading to the foyer, down the hallway leading to the elevator, and up the twenty-four flights to Toshi's 25th floor loft, added great suspense to the wonderment of what the evening had in store for him and the Curry House boys.

Since Cody couldn't guarantee that the Curry House bikers weren't friends or associates of the fellow who placed himself on the receiving end of Cody's rage, the thought of an ambush even crossed his mind. However, since Cody had been to Toshi's house under very pleasant circumstances, and since Toshi would have to be aware that Cynthia would know of Cody's whereabouts, Cody completely discounted this possibility. Once arriving at Toshi's door, Cody listened intently prior to knocking. Not hearing any sounds whatsoever, Cody proceeded to make his presence known. Knocking quietly before working up to sound-level and intensity that in most venues would have been considered a major disturbance, Cody was surprised when no one answered his call. Looking up to the ceiling and then just above his head at the door-jam, Cody noticed a small note taped to the molding above the entrance of the door. Believing that the note must have been intended for him, Cody removed the message and read what he could of it.

The note, addressed to ARD, seemed to advise that Toshi and the boys had to leave unexpectedly. The message closed with, "If we are not back by eight-thirty, assume that we have been held up and return to the office. We will contact you to reschedule, SC." In reading, and rereading, the note, Cody was not entirely sure that it was meant for him. Cody thought that ARD might be a reference to the AM RACCOON DOG moniker that he had fashioned onto the back of his leather jacket, but the reference of *returning to the office* and *rescheduling* left him somewhat unsure if his assumption about ARD was correct. The only thing about the letter that Cody was relatively confident about concerned the initials: SC. Cody was fairly certain that SC stood for Toshi's street name. To Cody, the letter seemed unnecessarily cryptic in its construction, but his interest was piqued and he decided to wait until 8:30, as the note appeared to request of him.

As Cody waited patiently in the hallway, he could hear a ringing sound emanating from inside of Toshi's apartment, a signal that reminded him that he had asked Cynthia to call him at the residence. Realizing that Cynthia was the likely caller, Cody reached into his pocket for his cell phone, suddenly realizing that he had left it on his night stand. *Just what he needed*, he thought as he came to understand that his precautionary measure had most certainly become a major source of worry for Cynthia. Having neither his phone nor a means of checking the time, Cody waffled between the idea of taking the elevator to the lobby and trying to locate a pay phone and staying put, in the hope that at any moment Toshi and the gang would show up. As time advanced, Cody became increasingly anxious with his inability to provide assurance to Cynthia that he was not in danger.

Just as Cody could no longer stand not being able to contact Cynthia, he heard the elevator door open, followed by the voices of a number of the fellows who had befriended him. "Hey, there's Cody san. Walk him in the door while Ken and Sadao follow up behind us with the package," said Akio.

Cody could now see Toshi and Akio leading the way, followed by a half-dozen of the other fellows. At the very back of the troop, Cody could see two men he didn't immediately recognize who were carrying what appeared to be a horizontal object wrapped in a blanket. After Toshi and Akio greeted Cody with the traditional knuckle bump, Cody explained that he needed to use the phone. Toward granting his request, Cody was led to a room off the hallway where he could "talk without distraction," as Toshi put it. Picking up the phone, Cody observed Sadao and Ken scurrying by the doorway in tote of a long asymmetric object wrapped up in a sheet that was not much shorter in length than he was tall. Largely ignoring his observations, Cody reached Cynthia and explained that he was safe and that he had only now caught up with the fellows. In closing, Cody told Cynthia that he loved her before returning the phone to its cradle.

"Hey, guys, where are you?" Cody said as he walked about the front room of the seemingly vacant apartment. "Hello?" Cody repeated.

At that point, the men heard Cody and came to realize that he had completed his phone call, whereby they funneled out of a previously closed off room in a manner that raised more than mild suspicion with him.

"Oh, hey, how's it going, Cody?" said Akio. "I apologize for our absence, but something came up at the last moment that we needed to deal with."

"Cody, how are you after that horrible incident at Curry House?" asked Toshi.

"I'm okay I guess. I still have a lot of regret for acting out with such rage," Cody said, wondering if the small talk was some sort of cover for what was going on in the back room. "Cynthia and I went to the Meiji Shrine toward atonement for my actions."

"Well, I'll tell you Cody, we are all really glad that you made it here tonight. We weren't sure if you'd come or not. We kind of figured that you had a lot on your mind," said Toshi. "We planned a rather special evening for you. We want to officially welcome you into our group, but we need to know that we can count on you. We need to know that we can trust you. We need to know that you won't snitch us out for any of our deeds."

"First, I should ask — do you want to join our group?" said Akio.

"Well, yes, I guess. I didn't know that the process would be so formal."

"Well, it is formal! See here, we aren't exactly angels or Hells Angels. We have our skeletons in the closet, you know. There are things about our group that can't go beyond this room," said Akio with a backdrop of nervous laughs from other members of the group.

"Yeah, uh, I guess I know," Cody said as he reflected on the apparent secrecy surrounding the sheet-wrapped object.

"Well, in welcoming you into our group, we have a certain tradition. We have a certain ceremony or sorts."

In hearing of the tradition and the ceremony associated with gang membership in the bosozoku, Cody initially thought that the group was referring to some ritual, perhaps a blood oath or some other sort of initiation rite, but he was mistaken.

"It is our tradition, Cody, to provide our recruits with certain, shall I say, essentials to our organization. We call the tradition *omiyage*." With this announcement, the men assembled about Cody and presented packages to him. Meet Head, aka Hiro, presented Cody with a finely wrapped framed portrait of the gang as they knelt by their scooters at a rest stop on a trip that the group had made to Nagoya the previous year. Toshi, aka Sexy Cat, presented Cody with a beautifully crafted gift bag that contained a very elegant pair of racing goggles that were imported from France.

After Cody had received gifts from all but one member of the bosozoku gang, Sadao spoke. "Cody, after giving much thought to an item that reflects the good feeling I have for you, I figured out the perfect gift," said Sadao as he extended a smartly wrapped box that was graced with an exquisite purple ribbon. "Open it," said Sadao.

Carefully untying the ribbon and gently breaking each tape seal with his thumb, Cody found a beautiful satiny black box. Inside of the box was the most delicately folded emerald-green tissue that enveloped something that felt thick, soft, and lofty. Peeling back the top layer of the paper revealed the loveliest, most luxurious woolen muffler that Cody had ever seen. The item smelled of wool, with residual lanolin, and was constructed with what appeared to be the finest lamb's wool that could be purveyed. The scarf-like garment was designed to look like a large banana, its form being hued in vibrant yellow throughout its mainstay, with green on one end giving the appearance of the unripe portion of the fruit and stem.

"Sadao, I'm speechless, I can't thank you enough for this gift. Where would one even be able to buy an unusual item like this?"

"You can't buy one of those. It is one of a kind. There isn't another one like it on Earth. Not long ago, at the chess tournament, you commented on my outfit, and I informed you that my grandmother fashioned it. I told my grandmother about you, and a bit about your story, and she knitted that wrap-around for you. Notice that it is monogramed with AMRD. That is for your street name — AM RACCOON DOG."

"Get out of Tokyo! You can't be serious. What kind of wild story are you feeding me? You asked your grandmother to knit this magnificent scarf for me, a gaijin?" Cody queried in a manner that revealed the level of incredulity he felt.

"No, it really isn't quite like that. Rather, it is that I asked my grandmother to craft the scarf for my friend, Cody san."

"Excuse me, fellows," Cody said, as he held back a flow of tears that seemed like they'd progress to wellsprings at any moment. "Excuse me, I think I need to use the restroom," Cody said as he walked away to wash his face before rejoining the crowd.

"Cody san, we actually have a couple more surprises for you. In fact, we have someone who we would like you to meet. You might have noticed when we walked in that Ken and Sadao were carrying an object wrapped up in a sheet," said Akio.

"Yes. Akio is right. We have someone we would like you to meet. In fact, it is our collective belief that you have long known of this man. In fact, it is he who was the cause of us being late for your visit," said Toshi.

"I don't know about you guys, but I think I want to have a little something to eat before we deal with our little visitor. What do you say, Cody?" queried Ken.

"Yeah, uh, that would be okay," Cody said realizing that he'd probably just been pulled into some sort of criminal pact of sorts, and that he had more than likely gone beyond the point of turning back, whereby at any moment he might be asked to dispose of a body or to take part in some other dastardly or evil deed.

At one point, the gang seemed so friendly and loving toward Cody, and the next they were sharing with him that they had somehow uprooted a man and transported him, wrapped in a sheet, up twenty-four floors before sequestering him in a back room.

"Cody, do you like fried chicken?" said Toshi.

"Uh, yeah, you know, guys — I'm not really hungry now. I kind of think I should probably get home, you know. It's been kind of a long day and, well, I really wanted to give my bathtub a good scrubbing tonight. You know — cleanliness is next to Godliness and all. Hey, I do want to thank you for all of the great gifts, and, well, I really want to meet the fellow in the back room, but, like I said — it has been a rather full day. Maybe I can meet the guy some other time."

"Hey, Cody. Are you running out on us, man?" said Akio.

"Well, uh, I wouldn't really put it that way."

"Cody, we're not going to let you go until you meet our guest." said Akio

"Uh, okay, if you insist — I guess I could stay for a little while."

At that point, Sadao became noticeably angry. "Hey, guys, I think that this little charade has gone on long enough. If you don't stop this nonsense, I'm going to carry out our little visitor on my back for Cody to see right now," said Sadao.

"You see, Cody, tonight we kidnapped the Colonel. I just think that you should know, that is where we were while you were waiting," said Akio.

"Kidnapped? Which colonel? Do I know him?"

"Oh, you know him all right," said Ken.

"Go get him Hiro," said Toshi.

As Hiro walked toward the backroom, Ken grabbed himself a piece of chicken, and walked up to Cody. "Cody, I want you to know that this is the first time we ever did anything like this," said Ken, as he heartily bit into a chicken thigh. Looking directly into Cody's eyes, while smiling, Ken continued, "Origin recipe, excellent! Yeah, I had no idea that this would be so easy, and that the only tools we'd need would be a screwdriver and a wrench. It was so easy! Remove the nuts, pry the mount from the platform, wrap the guy in a sheet, and throw him in the van. Easy!"

"Cut it out, Ken. I don't want to hear you talking like that," said Sadao as he took a bite of a piece of fried potato.

After several minutes, Hiro rolled out a dolly that supported a vertical figure between five and six feet in height that appeared to be wrapped in several sheets.

"Are you ready?" said Hiro.

"Yeah, go ahead and release Mr. Sanders," said Akio, whereby the sheet was removed, revealing a nearly life-size fiberglass statue of Colonel Sanders that the gang had borrowed from a KFC restaurant just after darkness had fallen on Tokyo that night.

"Hey, Cody san, do you still need to clean your bathtub or can you join us for some Kentucky Fried Chicken?" said Ken.

"Man, you guys really had me going. Something is very wrong with you guys. You guys are really messed up. You guys need serious counseling by a certified professional. You Japanese guys, I mean, us Japanese guys are a really crazy bunch of fellows — aren't we? Damn you guys, let's have some chicken. I'm going to have some chicken. Cynthia is going to freak out when I tell her what you guys pulled on me. Damn you all!"

"Hey, Cody, we didn't set out in this direction — but once this thing started, it just took on a life of its own," said

Akio as the other fellows nodded in agreement. "I must admit, however, that it really turned into a rather amusing little drama," Akio continued.

"Let's all have a toast toward welcoming Cody into our little bosozoku gang," said Toshi, as he motioned to Ken to gather cups and a bottle of sake.

After gorging on the Colonel's original recipe and fried potatoes, the gang celebrated with sake, loud music, and zany carryings on for an hour or more. Finally, the bosozoku motor brigade assembled towards escorting Cody and his gifts back to his *office*, as Toshi had referred to Cody's residence in his note.

A popular Japanese tradition, during the Christmas season, is to feast on Kentucky Fried Chicken; and for Cody, this mid-August day in Tokyo was no less celebratory in the shower of gifts and the sense of fellowship that the moment had brought forth.

For Cody and Cynthia, there was great relief in learning that he remained in good standing with the bosozoku gang and that he was not in any apparent danger concerning the violent incident that took place at Curry House. Still, Cody recognized the wisdom of practicing vigilance and the importance of keeping his guard up, and in this sense, nothing had changed.

Short of Swag Tigger's relay, from Sexy Cat and Monkey Wretch, concerning the importance of Cody's avoidance of the Curry House restaurant, the guys never behaved in any manner that suggested that Cody faced substantial danger in the form of retribution from anyone present at Curry House on the day of the assault. In fact, on the contrary — the gang even appeared to go so far as to make light of Cody's notoriety concerning the incident.

A couple of weeks after Cody received omiyage from the gang, previous to an organized bosozoku ride through Tokyo and its environs, the gang got together for a powwow whereby Sexy Cat and Monkey Wretch discussed the potential need to conceal their identities as they motored about.

Rallying and directing the troops, Monkey Wretch relayed, "The plan is that we are going to ride hard around the city in a particularly rowdy and obnoxious manner tonight. It is our hope to ride down most every street in the business district of central Tokyo and the Roppongi district. Now, I'll be in the lead tonight, and the rest of you are to assume your regular positions in the organizational hierarchy. Cody, since you are the newest member and since you have a particular vulnerability due to the incident at Curry House — you'll be riding in the back. Does everyone understand the tentative plan and their organizational position?"

"Thanks for the lowdown, Akio," said Sexy Cat. "There is one more thing that we need to address. In the interest of concealing our identities relative to the incident at Curry House, Akio and I have secured a group-set of disguises that everyone will wear throughout the evening. Is that understood?" Toshi said as he scanned the faces of the men in search of renegades. "Okay then, let's have the box, Akio."

At Sexy Cat's command, Monkey Wretch distributed to each member of the bosozuku group a nose-mustache-eye-glasses ensemble.

"Okay men, unwrap your units and prepare for installation," instructed Monkey Wretch. "Tonight, let's make it clear just how vexatious and troublesome we are." With those final words, the gang mounted their scooters and they rode off into the early nighttime of the Roppongi district.

As the evening progressed, the good-natured group of awkward thirty-something-year-old delinquents puttered through the city streets like a gang of nomad teenagers looking to fulfill indeterminate quotas of innocuous mischief. In skirting down the well-lighted byways, the riders alternated their demeanor between cycles of stoic and purposeful motoring and episodes of *kama kiru* (riding a scooter in a wild zigzag fashion). Parading through the Roppongi district, the riders drew attention from all whose paths they crossed.

In one instance, while waiting for a signal light to change, the group drew the attention of a business owner or manager working to usher clients or customers into what appeared to be a club or a drinking establishment of sorts. As Cody observed the man, he acquired a certain sense that he'd seen him before. During the time it took for the light to change, Cody developed an eerie feeling that the man had somehow interacted with him, at some point, in a manner that compromised his general sense of comfort or wellbeing. As Cody pulled away with his bosozoku comrades, the dark-complexioned man attended to Cody with an unmistakable look of recollection plainly unfurled across his face. In motoring away, Cody took mental note of the business front where he had observed the man, subsequently creating an indelible image of the man, the physical venue, and the moment in his mind.

Since Cynthia appreciated Cody's need to integrate in a meaningful way with people of Japanese heritage, she encouraged him to pursue his friendship with the scooter gang. In her heart, Cynthia knew that Cody was likely forging fellowships that would provide him comfort and enrichment throughout the remainder of his life. She also realized that a time would soon come when Cody and she would return to the United States.

Returning home from his ride with the guys at an early hour, Cody found Cynthia in the act of sketching what appeared to be a pastel portrait of a family. "Hey, babe — it looks like you're planning our future again." Focusing intently on the drawing, Cody said, "I guess I should be relieved that we will only raise three children."

"Well, dear, we'll start with three children and see where that takes us," Cynthia said, indicating that her work was subject to revision. "How'd the ride go, honey?"

"Oh, it went well, I guess. Toshi and Akio duped us all into wearing plastic nose-glasses-mustache disguises throughout the ride."

"Your friends are incorrigible. They're a real riot. They seem like a fun bunch to be around."

"Yeah, I mean yes. I think that I was very blessed to meet up with them. They really are a great bunch of guys, but I don't know —"

"What, Cody?"

"I still can't believe that you have chosen to spend the rest of your life with me. You, my dear, are my greatest treasure."

"Oh, Cody, you are such a kind, sentimental fellow. You, sir, are going to make the coolest dad for our children, every last one of them — even if we have a dozen."

"I'm glad that you have so much faith in me."

"Cody, have you thought much about starting a family?"

"Uh, I've given it a little thought, I guess."

"I want to live near Seattle in a big house situated right on the banks of Lake Washington, or maybe in a house built just off of the beach on Orcas Island or one of the other San Juan Islands."

"Hey, babe, whatever you say — I'm following you. I can be happy and fulfilled anywhere, as long as you are near."

"Cody, I know that you aren't much into surprises, but I think that Koko was right. She was on target when she demonstrated concern for your wellbeing after you saved Nobuo in the Kamo River. She was also correct when she referenced the important gathering at Toshi's on the evening the fellows brought forth omiyage. And now, I have a very strong feeling that Koko was correct when she commented that I'd soon be a mother."

"You've got to be kidding me! That's wonderful news. Are you going to take a test?"

"Yes, I will purchase and take a pregnancy test this week."

Pulling close to Cynthia and gently kissing her cheek, Cody said, "I can't describe to you how happy this makes me feel. But, how do you feel, dear? Are you okay with this?"

"Honestly, Cody, I never envisioned that I'd have a baby so soon after college, but I must admit that it never occurred to me that I'd meet a man I would love as much as I love you."

"Well, let's remain rational and take this thing one step at a time. At this point, we don't even know for sure if you are pregnant."

The man that Cody had seen at the stoplight was the Nigerian named Randal, and, in fact, Randal did recognize Cody. The reason that Randal remembered Cody so well was that Cody had foiled Randal's plans to extract money from him that night, so long ago, in the Roppongi district. Randal remembered Cody because Cody nearly completely ruined two of Randal's most menacing henchmen after the men made the mistake of not anticipating Cody's potential for ferocious reckoning in the face of danger. Morally correct or not, Randal ran a business, and one of his primary responsibilities was to protect his business interests and to not permit any appearance that someone could short him of something that he felt that he had coming. The way Randal figured it, Cody owed him money for a gal's drinks, drinks for which he charged close to 10,000 yen (100 dollars) per glass, and Cody owed him for the damage that he'd inflicted on his bouncers. Now that Randal knew that Cody ran with one of the bosozoku gangs, he would place his operatives on the lookout for that gang. Making the task easier, Randal passed along to his crew and their associates that they should keep a lookout for a gang of men who wore glasses affixed with mustaches.

As Cody and Cynthia were settling down for the night, a thought crossed Cody's mind concerning the dark-complexioned man he'd seen in the Roppongi district earlier that evening. Could the man have some connection with the mysterious Randal's Place that was printed on the business card that Cody had put aside months earlier? If so, what was the connection?

As far as Cody could tell, he had only wandered about alone in the Roppongi district on one occasion, and of that evening he remembered little more than waking up on the floor of his apartment with the door partially open. Thinking back, Cody recalled that the evening in question was a night or two before he and Cynthia spent the afternoon at Hibiya Park. Somehow, Cody couldn't shake the strange feeling that something substantial, perhaps critical, had happened that night, but he had no sense of exactly what had occurred. He vaguely remembered sitting down and being served a drink. And he seemed to remember getting into a squabble, maybe an argument.

Just as he was about to retire the issue for the evening, Cody's attention gravitated to thoughts of the strange brown spots that he discovered on the lower extremities of his trousers and on his dress shoes the morning following the nebulous evening he spent in the Roppongi district. Cody couldn't help but wonder if he'd gotten into a fight or some other physical altercation during the time he was a patron of the club managed by the mysterious Nigerian, if in fact, he ever was a patron of the establishment.

Pushing himself for remnants of information from the night, Cody developed a vague recollection of a young woman.

There seemed to be a girl who was sitting with him, a girl who didn't say much of anything, but who giggled often. Cody recalled that the girl had an unusual name, a curious name by Japanese standards, anyway. It wasn't a name like *Rabun* or *Shuri*, but it was a name that didn't quite possess a proper Japanese pronunciation. Approaching his memory gap both from the forward direction and the backward direction still led to an undeniable void in his accounting of the night.

Prior to falling asleep that night, Cody and Cynthia agreed that he'd pick up a home test kit the next afternoon after attending to his teaching duties.

During the course of Cody's classes that day, it became apparent to him that his appointment at the Ikemoto Academy would likely be coming to a close were it the case that Cynthia was in fact carrying his child. The academy's rules were very clear. Faculty members were not to take part in any activity that could even remotely be construed as lacking proper moral judgment. Of course, carrying a child out of wedlock was included in that amorphous group of activities that constituted misconduct.

When Cody returned from his quick trip to the Matsumoto Kuyoshi drug store, Cynthia greeted him at the door of his apartment. "Hey, baby, Sadao called about this weekend."

"Oh, what did he say?"

"He said that the fellows are getting together Saturday for their summer classic baseball game at Hibiya Park. I took down his number. He wants you to give him a call."

"Yeah, I'll do that later. How's my little girl?"

"She's feeling fine. Did you get my package?"

"What do you think?"

"I think you always do what you say you're going to do. So let's have it. Give it to me."

"I've got it here inside of my jacket. For goodness sake, they are so high-tech now that the instructions take up more room than the actual gadgetry."

Meanwhile, back in the Roppongi district, Randal was able to extract grainy images of Cody and the rest of the bosozoku group from his security cameras, images that he was able to distribute to several of his associates. By Randal's assessment, the best he could hope for was to discover Cody alone or to locate the gang and isolate Cody from the group. Either way, Randal was bent on providing an opportunity for his fallen soldiers to even up the score.

While Randal had no way to gauge the significance of Cody's positioning in the bosozuku entourage, it would soon become apparent to Cody that each man in the hierarchy was beholden in the highest sense of the word to the man on his right or left, relative to the established riding formation. Since Cody was new to the gang, Toshi and Akio thought it wise to pair him with Sadao, a man known for both his intellect and his mastery of Japanese fighting sticks. Sadao gladly volunteered for the assignment.

After touching base with Cynthia, Cody directed a phone call to Sadao. "Hey, Sadao, this is Cody."

"Ah, good, Cody san, I've been looking forward to talking with you."

"Yes, Sadao, I apologize for not getting back to you earlier."

"Don't worry about it, Cody san. Can you make it to the summer classic baseball game?"

"Yes. I think so. It sounds like fun."

"Yes, Cody, it will be fun. But, more importantly it will be informative. Can you play hardball?"

"Well, I haven't played in years, but I'm up for the challenge."

"Good. I am glad to hear it. Cody, before the game we are all going on a wild ride through the city starting at around noon. From there we will go to Hibiya Park and play the game. So, if it is okay with you, we will make a run down by your place around 11:30, and you can join us as we ride by."

"I'll be gassed up and ready."

"Very good. Then we will see you at 11:30 a.m. Saturday."

For a day centered about a scooter ride through Tokyo and a low-key game of baseball at Hibiya Park, Cody thought that the conversation with Sadao had a rather serious tone about it. There of course was no question in Cody's mind that Sadao was decidedly the most regimented member of the group. Just about everything about Sadao was serious, whether the matter concerned business or friendship. Right then, Cody decided that he'd take the matter of outfitting himself for the game seriously. He decided he'd see if he could get hold of a baseball jersey prior to the game, and then it occurred to him that he could borrow a "decommissioned" Ikemoto Academy jersey and remove the Ikemoto lettering.

Realizing that he was alone in his apartment, Cody ventured to the upstairs apartment to see how Cynthia was faring with the pregnancy test kit.

"Hey, honey, it's me. Are you in the bathroom?"

"Yes. I'll be out momentarily."

"I hope you have good news," Cody said, leaving the interpretation of the term "good news" indeterminate. At that point Cynthia stepped out of the bathroom with a rather puzzled look of her face. "What did you learn, baby?"

"I don't really know. The lines are supposed to turn blue for a positive test, but the blue color is so subtle, I'm not sure if I'm imagining that the lines are blue or not."

"Tell me what you think."

"Gosh, Cynthia — it looks bluish, whatever that means. Maybe we should test again tomorrow. I bought the kit with two test strips, didn't I?"

"Yes, you did. I guess we'll test again later in the week."

"How late are you?"

"It has been close to a week," Cynthia said with a hint of discomfort concerning the matter.

"Baby, it's looking bluer from my perspective all of the time. I love you, Cynthia, and if you are pregnant, I'll be the happiest man alive."

"Oh, Cody, you find goodness in every situation. I love that about you."

"Hey, babe, I'm going to play baseball with the boys on Saturday. I hope you don't mind."

"No, I want you to spend time with your friends. For goodness sake, if I'm pregnant, we may not be in Japan much longer."

"I know. I've been thinking about that, too. You know, I kind of picture the boys coming to visit us in Washington someday. I can almost see the fellows trekking up to the top of Mount Rainier or swimming out to one of the islands in the Puget Sound or wrestling a bear or a mountain lion. Maybe when they come to visit, I'll suggest that we just rent some Harleys and ride out to Rainier."

"Hey, babe. Planet Earth to Cody san. Don't you think you are getting a little bit ahead of yourself?"

"I don't know, not really."

"My Raccoon Dog is a dreamer — a jolly, carefree, international man of imperishable optimism."

Saturday arrived with no new information concerning Cynthia's pending pregnancy. And, just as expected, the bosozoku boys rode by and absorbed Cody into their ranks as scheduled. After motoring down the road a mile or so, the gang pulled over and Akio instructed each member of the contingent to install their nose-mustache-eyeglasses ensemble as the group had done in their previous outing.

August 25 was a particularly clear and bright day in Tokyo, a scenario that would ultimately play out into a hot sticky afternoon in Hibiya Park. But in the early afternoon, while riding through the city on motor scooters, the day was comfortable. As the gang maneuvered about the city streets they carried on in their typical flamboyant style, seemingly finding great glee in their obnoxious antics, even to the point of appearing to bask in the attention provided to them by all those whose sensibilities they were able to provoke. As the zaniness continued, Cody wondered what gain could come from the spectacle they were generating. When in the Roppongi district, the gang rode kami kiru, waddling from side to side, directly in front of the establishment where Cody had observed the Nigerian the previous week. When in the Ginza, the crew stopped in for a beer at, of all places, Curry House. While in Curry House, Cody didn't ask any questions; he just took in the moment realizing that any threat that might have existed earlier must have passed. After little more than what it took to pour down a quick beer, the crew was off to Hibiya Park where they rendezvoused with Hiro (Meet Head) and a couple other of the bosozoku members.

Once at the ball park, Cody discovered that Hiro had transferred to the field, with the aid of a moving van, much of the gang's baseball gear. By the time the scooter riders arrived, the fellows had set up a tent that Cody was informed would serve as the score booth, in essence serving as a place out of the sun from where the game could be observed. The tent was green and box-like in construction. The structure stood tall and wide enough for a person or two to stand and observe the game through its heavily tinted screen, a veil that permitted those outside of the tent to only observe an opaque silhouette of the scorekeeper.

Whether or not it was legal to do so, the bosozoku parked their scooters on the edge of the green space located near the third-base line. The scorekeeper's tent, which was located on the first-base line symmetric to where the scooters were parked, offered an unrestricted view of the field as well as distant views along an asphalt roadway where automobiles often parked before being ushered along by park managers.

Hiro, with his early arrival, had been able to chalk the ball field's boundaries and put in place the flat, pillow-like bags that would serve as the bases and home plate. After dividing the bosozoku members into two teams, a coin flip of an old 20-sen piece landed dragon-side up, signaling that Akio's squad would bat first. With this outcome, Akio's players, with the exception of Cody, walked over to their bikes where each retrieved his personal collapsible aluminum bat. As Sadao walked up towards Cody from his scooter, he commented, "You know, we really need to get you one of these." Each bat was telescopic in construction, coming into full assembly with a simple decisive outward thrust, thus pulling the bat body and handle portions into position.

"Yeah, I didn't know that telescopic bats even existed."

"It's a big world, Cody san. I invite you to join it," said Sadao as he loudly snapped his bat into its striking configuration.

"Now, Cody san, I want you to keep your eye on the ball," said Sadao as he pulled out a small pair of field glasses to look into the distance. Looking through the glasses, Sadao continued, "I don't want you to be too disappointed if we decide to call the game early."

"What do you mean 'call the game early'?"

"Let me put it this way. We have been followed here by some very dangerous men, and we may need to soon retreat."

"You've got to be messing with me, Sadao. You're joking, right?"

"I wish that was the case, Cody san. We need to act relatively natural here, but do you see the pair of Mercedes Benzes in the distance?"

"Yes. I see."

"Do you see the three fellows leaning against the automobiles?"

"Yes."

"Well, they are watching us with binoculars right now."

"What are we going to do?"

"Were in luck, Cody. The scorekeeper has a handle on the whole thing. He is in touch with Hiro and some brothers out beyond the men and their Mercedes."

"Why did this happen?"

"Toshi and I had a sense that we might be being watched. And we decided, along with Akio, that it would be best to execute a controlled confrontation rather than to be surprised by an encounter at a time and place that was convenient for our friends out in left field. Okay. Okay, then it's game on?" said Sadao speaking into a small microphone connected to his inner shirt. "Okay, Cody it looks like you'll be batting first. Here, use my club," Sadao said as he handed Cody his personal bat.

With Toshi's team occupying their positions, Cody approached the plate, the infield chanting, "Hey, batter batter. Hey, batter batter..."

Bantering back, Cody baited, "Baseball, hotdogs, apple pie, and Chevrolet — I've got your number, baby."

The first pitch Cody received resulted in a foul ball punched down the first base line. The second pitch whizzed by him for a strike. Count — 0-2. At Sadao's urging, Cody swung and missed the third pitch.

Upon striking out, Cody was instructed to walk over to his Vespa and to park it alongside of the scorekeeper's tent. With this maneuver, it became clear to the scorekeeper that Cody was in fact the object of the attention of the men lingering in the distance.

After three quick innings, with the allowance of a couple of runs to Toshi's squad, which were calculated to make the ballgame appear plausible to onlookers, the scorekeeper decided that the time had come for the bosozoku gang to pack up their equipment and head out. After sportsmanlike handshakes between the opposing squads, the gear that was transferred to the park by Hiro was reloaded into the van. At the direction of Sadao, Cody was instructed to position himself inside the now vacant scorekeeper tent, where he was to remain until receiving further instructions. From a distance, Cody's silhouette could be discerned as a nondescript shadow situated behind the tightly woven nylon screen. When everything was loaded, the van pulled in front of the tent, momentarily blocking it from the sight of the men watching in the distance.

As the van pulled away, the entire gang, with the exception of Cody, hopped on their scooters and motored out of the park leaving the occupied tent and Cody's Vespa sitting starkly alone in a venue that was moments earlier an active ball field. As the gang rode into the distance, they lost sight of the silhouetted figure inside the tent.

Observing that the gang had abandoned Cody in the tent alone, the men jumped into their Mercedes and beat a widely circuitous path to the tent, parking seventy or so feet from its position. Warily, the three men walked toward the tent, one man removing a large knife from the inside of his dark sport coat. Reaching the structure, the knife-wielding man cut through the canvas, only to discover the quite inanimate life-size fiberglass rendition of Colonel Harland David Sanders that the boys had borrowed weeks earlier.

The well-dressed thugs had been duped, duped by the gang of men now swarming about the tent on their scooters like a cloud of hornets. Surrounded, the men stood frozen while Monkey Wretch made his approach. "I take it that you were expecting someone other than the Colonel," Akio mused while removing the menacing knife from the lead thug's grasp. "Something tells me that you've not come to learn the identities of the 11 secret herbs and spices. What is it that we can help you with?"

At that point, Ken stepped up to the center of the confrontation with several bottles of rotten fish entrails that he'd obtained from Tsukiji market. Stepping up to the men and upturning one of the plastic bottles on the head of the apparent leader, Ken said, "You men have been laboring hard in left field, and you are hungry, but we only have fish sauce for you today."

Once finished with the first man, Swag Tigger emptied the remaining bottles on the heads of the lead man's associates. At that point, Sexy Cat stepped up and motioned to several bat-wielding bosozoku assembled about the automobiles. "Make it so these nice men can see through their tinted windows," Toshi said as the scooter riders methodically shattered each pane of auto glass.

"Fellows, we really need to be leaving now, but before we depart I must stress that you being able to walk away from this scene is an act of our supreme benevolence. If you mess around with any one of us, you will once again meet with all of us. Is this understood?"

Looking each man in the eye, Akio walked the line, pacing before the men with his telescopic bat repeatedly being cast into his hand. "Is this understood?" Akio demanded as he took the butt of his club and thrust it deep into the belly of the man who at one time held the knife blade. "Is this understood?"

Recovering from being punched with the bat in the stomach, the man said, at a barely audible level, "Yes."

"I can't hear you," repeated Monkey Wretch.

"Yes," repeated the grimaced-faced man.

"Yes what? I want you to be explicit. I don't want there to be any misunderstanding about this."

"Yes, I understand."

"What about you guys," Akio questioned.

"We understand," said each man as they looked at one another.

"Okay, then it looks like we have an understanding. Now, who sent you here?" Akio continued. "I need to know, fellows. Don't keep me in suspense."

"We have come on our own. We are here to save face for the beating we received."

"What if I told you that I don't believe you, that I think that you are dirty scoundrel liars?" said Akio.

"I swear," responded the apparent leader.

"This is very strange," Akio said as he looked at his associates. Do any of you fellows recognize these guys?" Akio said as he scanned the blank faces of the bosozoku members.

At this point, the thugs seemed to be confused, muddled to the point where they wondered if in fact they had correctly identified Cody as their assailant.

"Okay, gentleman, I'd like each of you to remove your driver's license from your wallet. Please hand them to my associate here, as he passes by," Akio said pointing to Toshi. Receiving the photo identification documents from Toshi, and placing them in his pocket, Akio continued, "You men are free to go, but remember what I said about bothering any one of us, bothering any one of us in any manner. Okay, fellows, I would implore that you obey all safety and traffic laws as you proceed home. I hope each of you have a really bitchin' evening."

With the thugs having figuratively limped away in their damaged vehicles, and with the tent and the Colonel loaded into the van, Cody's eyes welled up with the powerful realization that the men whom he'd befriended had taken him into their lives with the care and devotion that he'd believed was a currency only exchanged between individuals related by bloodline. Having mounted their scooters, the bosozoku resumed their structured riding formation as they peeled out of the park with the van taking a place in the rear of the procession.

Cody was escorted back to his housing complex, shaken, but intact. Entering the complex, he rolled his scooter into the faculty storage room, a precautionary measure in the event that any of the fellows he had just encountered maintained a design on taking him down.

Walking into his apartment, Cody found Cynthia beaming at him. "Wow, what's on your mind? You look like you just won the lottery," Cody said as he removed his baseball jersey and placed it on the table.

"I'm pregnant. We are going to have a baby."

"This is the best news I've ever heard."

"Oh, sweetheart, I'm glad that you are so happy. Now we have to plan our next steps. But first, how was the game?"

"Oh, the game. The game was interesting. Toshi's squad won by two runs. How'd your day go?"

"Cody, I had a phone call from Koko today."

"Oh? What did she have to say? How's she doing?"

"She called to ask about you. She said some crazy stuff about you being in imminent danger."

Realizing that a definite pattern had developed in Koko's ability to recognize instances that concerned his wellbeing and safety, Cody simply said, "That is fascinating, but I think that the danger has passed. I hope the danger has passed."

"What do you mean, 'the danger has passed'?"

"Oh, it's just that Koko seems to sense these things after the fact. The only thing that we don't really know is just how much after the fact it is that her visions have reference. When did she call?"

"It's just after five now. She must have phoned two or three hours ago."

"Interesting. I wish she were here. I would probably have some questions to ask of her. Did Koko say anything more?"

"She said that she had a vision of our child being born in America."

"Koko rides the line very close to appearing crazy or delusional, but that 90-year-old woman seems to have some wild sort of extra-sensory perception. There is something uncanny about her ability to recognize things that bypass the rest of us," Cody acknowledged. "Does she see the future or does she create the present?" Cody wondered aloud.

"Cody, have you ever heard of shapeshifting?" Cynthia asked.

"I think so. Isn't that when a creature or person has the ability to alter their appearance or to alter space and/or time?"

"Yes. That kind of sums it up."

"Have you ever wondered why, when we see Koko, she always has the presence of some sort of foraging animal?" said Cody reflecting on the quantity of trash and other debris that Koko was always seen carting about.

"I never really thought of Koko in that way."

"Have you ever got a big gulp of her aroma? I think that Koko is a dear lady, but she smells as if she spends the bulk of her days scavenging in a dump site with feral dogs, cats, and who knows what else, maybe tanuki and kitsune," Cody pondered.

"Oh, Cody, don't be so harsh."

"Okay, whatever, back to our new addition. Are you ready to tell your mother?"

"Honestly, Cody, I think I might as well. Of course, I'll need to see a doctor pretty quick, but the test seemed definitive this time. For goodness sake, my period is nearly two weeks late now, and my cycle has never been anything but consistent. I'm going to write her tonight. I'm going to tell you though, Cody, she is going to request, or should I say mandate, that I immediately return to Seattle."

"And what about me?"

"Well, of course, I would insist that you accompany me."

CHAPTER SEVEN:
BRINGING IT HOME

As far as Cody and the fellows were concerned, all was good. No one was hurt, and there was good reason to believe that the bosozoku had made their point with the thugs they had encountered in Hibiya Park. The only thing that remained unsettled in the account of the bosozoku was to return the Colonel to his rightful spot outside of the KFC restaurant from which he had been removed. Only when this was done, could the biker posse be at peace with the universe, by their collective reasoning.

With the announcement to Cynthia's parents that their first grandchild was on the way, and that the pair was preparing to return home, Cody and Cynthia initiated the process of tying up loose ends and presenting to the Ikemoto Academy their notice of intent to vacate their positions. Cody and Cynthia dreaded the idea of sharing this news with their students, but each knew that it would be best if the students heard the word from them, rather than gleaning it through other channels.

One very important loose end on Cynthia and Cody's mind was to locate Koko to let her know of their plans, but they knew that finding Koko in Tokyo was much like finding a specific toothpick in a lumber mill. The couple was largely resigned to the notion that the only way they would find Koko was if she found them first. Still, the pair looked for her as they slowly detached themselves from the great city of Tokyo. On more than one occasion they thought that they had seen her in the distance, but each time they discovered that the woman they saw was not Koko.

Before leaving Tokyo, Cody wanted to fulfill one objective that had been on his mind since he took his first steps in the city. While impulsive at face-value, Cody had mulled over the idea of getting a tattoo for more than five months. After consulting Ken, who was no stranger to skin art, Cody started the painful process of ink insertions via the traditional method of bamboo instruments. The image that Cody set his mind on was an intricately designed koi fish surrounded by a blue mosaic pattern consisting of classically styled ocean waves, representative of the violent and mysterious great blue sea. The koi was magnificently toned in hues of orange, yellow, and black, while the boundless ocean was crafted as an elaborate seascape patterned in indigo that was bordered in jet-black pigment. In the upper right-hand portion of the design was a solitary red-orange orb identical to the fiery sphere depicted on the Japanese national flag. As a whole, the design was to cover Cody's entire left inner-forearm extending down to his wrist to the point where it would be obscured by the sleeve of an ordinary dress shirt. In consulting with the artist, Cody learned that the process was to take place in four sessions over two weeks.

With Cynthia and Cody having initiated the task of cleaning and organizing their living spaces, they reflected on the grand adventure that had become a permanent fixture in their lives. As Cody went through the layers of sedimentary paperwork that had deposited in various locations of his apartment, he filtered out what he would retain from what would be discarded.

While he sorted through a stack of old newspapers, Cody's eyes haphazardly caught sight of a particular article that Cynthia had brought to his attention several months earlier. Lo and behold, the article addressed the news story that concerned the Roppongi night club beating, the violent assault that was unleashed on the two bouncers just prior to Cody and Cynthia's initial visit to Hibiya Park. Thinking back, Cody remembered that he acquired the newspaper the same day that the couple first met the old woman Koko, an event that occurred the very day that he first began to connect with Cynthia. Realizing the significance of his find, Cody placed the newspaper amongst the items that he would keep.

Short of the newspaper, several letters from Cynthia, his employment contract with the Ikemoto Academy, and various government documents, including his working visa and drivers' license paperwork, Cody found very little ephemera he wished to retain.

As Cody drew himself a glass of water from the tap, he caught the site of the faded and water-leached red business card that he'd put aside so long ago, the business card imprinted with the words — Randal's Place in the Roppongi, the card with the name on its reverse that he couldn't quite make out well enough to read. Pondering its simple construction for a moment, Cody wondered if the card was somehow connected with the Roppongi night club beating incident. Without delay, Cody honed in on the newspaper article and read what he could of it. Scanning the story his eyes caught the Hiragana script — るるん, pronounced as "rurun" or "ruroon." Apparently, this was the name of the female witness of the assault. Experimenting with the word, Cody formed with his mouth the sound "ru-ru" with an immediate nasal sound "na." He continued several sound variations of the woman's apparent name. Then he looked at the business card. Cody could just barely make out the English letters "L" and "u" followed by a letter at the end that looked like it might be an "M." "Ruru n" he softly repeated, "Ruru n." Then he refocused on the "M" on the business card for the first time realizing that in the Japanese language "N" and not "M" was a stand-alone consonant. *What if it were "Ruru M" in the newspaper article, instead of "Ruroon" or "RuruN?"* Cody thought to himself. Shaking his head in confusion, Cody said softly "Ru" and then looked at the card mouthing "Ru" followed by "Lu." He then voiced "Ruru?" as if applying a question to his analysis before dispatching —"Luru?"

"Oh, my God," Cody exclaimed loudly, as a certain chill overtook him that sent shivers throughout his nervous system. "My God, it's *Lulu M*. It is Lulu with the initial M," Cody exclaimed, in a true moment of high-level satori.

While Cody had experienced an instance of extreme enlightenment, the moment provided him with anything but a moment of calm. Yes, Cody had pieced together a portion of the mystery associated with Randal's Place in the Roppongi, but he also had to grapple with the fact that he was very likely the assailant in the attack of the two bouncers who were so gravely beaten. What troubled Cody most was that he couldn't remember the assault or having met Lulu or Randal. Cody knew that this could only mean one thing, that being that his drink was drugged by either Randal or Lulu.

Several things became apparent with Cody's discovery that he'd been involved in the Roppongi night club incident. For one, the statement the gangsters at Hibiya Park made about settling their account with Cody, being an act to "save face" for the beating they received, now made sense. Cody now knew that the men in the park were not connected with the incident at Curry House. Cody knew this had to be true, as only one man was on the receiving end of his rage when he and Cynthia were accosted. Another result of Cody's revelation was that he now believed that he knew the identity of the curious Nigerian he'd observed on the Roppongi corner weeks earlier, a location that he now felt was the likely site of Randal's Place.

Wanting to surprise Cynthia with his new tattoo, Cody was able to get his final session completed within eight days of his introduction to the bamboo needles. Still, this meant that he'd need to wear long sleeved shirts for more than a week and only undress when he was out of sight of Cynthia.

On the day of his last procedure, he was notified by Sadao that the group planned an early morning run through the city. For Cody, it had been a good while since Cynthia had tamed him of his nocturnal habits. Still, Cody did miss the night, and the freedom associated with the streets of early morning Tokyo, so he agreed to the venture. The crew was to meet in the Ginza at 2:00 a.m., in front of the Imperial Hotel.

Realizing that he'd not visited the men and women who gathered together by night in Tokyo's alleyways in some time, Cody brought along a loaf of bean paste bread. After putting on his leather jacket, Cody walked over to the bed and leaned over to kiss Cynthia. "I'll be home soon," Cody whispered as he walked out the door.

It was early September and the night temperature was a cool 17°C (63°F). Cruising about in the Ginza, Cody encountered a man and woman couple who were sitting up in a cardboard box structure that looked as if it had housed a refrigerator in a previous life. The disheveled pair was huddled together smoking cigarettes when Cody approached. The scraggly, unshaven man looked to be in his sixties, and the woman appeared to be in her late forties. Both seemed as if they might have been professionals of one sort or another at one point in their life; and both appeared as if they had sacrificed comforts they once had known for a life out in the open, drinking in the streets of Tokyo.

"Ohayo gozaimasu," Cody said as he coasted his scooter to a stop.

"Ohayo," chimed the pair.

The couple was very friendly and eager to learn what they could from the young gaijin. "Why are you here?" said the man.

Responding, Cody replied, "I am Japanese-American and I came here to teach English, but now I'm about to return home."

Looking at Cody curiously, the woman replied in well-spoken English, "Was your experience good?"

"My experience was good. I feel like a new man. I came here confused regarding my identity, my race, and my culture. I came here hoping to find out who the hell I was. And I learned that I was no one, simply a hollow shell occupying space and consuming resources. In America, I felt that I wasn't acknowledged for who I was," Cody said as he looked up to the heavens. "Anyway, back in America I was no one — and, honestly, while that may not have changed, I do feel better about my condition. Before I came here, I knew nothing of my heritage or my culture or even myself. A lot has changed, since I came to Japan. So, I'd say my experience was very good, overall."

At that point, with nods from both the man and the woman, Cody said, "Do you mind if I ask you a question?"

"No, that would be okay," said the man with a nonverbal nod of approval from the woman.

"What is it that a man or woman needs more than any other thing?"

Thinking intently, the man and woman pondered silently. "They need a sense that they control their lives," said the man as he looked toward the woman.

Alternating her focus between Cody and her partner, the woman offered, "A person needs to appreciate themselves for who they are, whoever they are or from wherever they came."

At that point, tears came to Cody's eyes and he thanked the couple. "My experience in Japan has generated much personal growth. This moment serves as a perfect example. If I have learned anything from this experience, it is that valuable learning springs forth from the most impromptu or accidental situations. I thank you for this moment, and for this opportunity for me to regain my bearings," Cody said as he handed the bean bread to two of the souls that Tokyo seemed to long have forgotten. Walking over to his bike, Cody straddled his scooter, before dismounting and walking back over to the couple. "My name is Cody Fletcher. What are your names?"

Having lit another cigarette, the man waved the smoke away from his face before saying, "My name?"

The woman then said, "You care to know our names?"

"Yes, it is important to me that I learn your names."

Again looking at the woman, this time in semi-disbelief, the man said, "My name is Jiro and my wife's name is Emi."

Looking deep into the woman's eyes, as if peering into her soul, Cody said, "Emi, what a pretty name. Emi is my grandmother's name, Emi Yoshitaku. Well, I guess I'd better go," Cody said as he turned to walk to his bike.

"No, please don't go yet," the woman said as she stood up and brushed the ashes and unburnt tobacco from her sweater. "I want to say goodbye." Hearing the woman's request, Cody walked up to the box from which Emi stood. "I'm glad to meet you," said Emi as she extended her hand and put forth her upper body into a deep bow which was met with reciprocation from Cody.

Putting his scooter in gear and slowly motoring off, Cody felt as if he was in virtual alignment with the person he wanted to be, experiencing that rare feeling that he'd done everything in his power to make things right with his world and with those whose paths he crossed. As he moved towards the Imperial Hotel, Cody felt a sense of being alive unlike any he'd ever experienced before. He'd come a long way, having gone from being an isolated night-rider who roamed the streets alone, to being a member of a gang of good-hearted fellows who appreciated him for who he was. Coming into view of the hotel, Cody could see that a small covey of men on scooters had assembled along with other riders joining the group from various directions. For the first time ever, Cody had the genuine feeling that he belonged to a group, that he was an integral member of a fellowship, and the sad thing in his mind was that the experience would soon come to a close. He knew that it would be this night that he'd need to mention Cynthia's pregnancy and their intent to return to America.

Coasting up to the fellows, Cody turned off his engine and smiled at his friends.

"Hey, Codester. You ready to ride?" said Akio.

"Stick around for a while, Wretch. You'll find out," said Cody in a sassy tone.

"Hey, Sexy Cat — I like your outfit. I'd have worn a dress if I knew that we were going in drag tonight."

"Cody, one day you're going to fully appreciate flashy gear like this. Mark my words!"

"Yeah, we'll see, Sexy Cat. On the streets they call me Am Rac," he replied. "Where's my main man, App4That?" asked Cody looking about the group.

"He'll be here soon," said Ken as he popped a piece of hamachi (fatty pen-raised yellowtail) into his mouth. "Want a piece, Cody?" Ken inquired.

"Damn rights I do, Swag. It's great to have a connection at Tsukiji," Cody replied as he extracted a piece of raw fish from Ken's open bento box.

Once Sadao arrived, Cody got the group's attention. "I have an announcement that I need to make. First, I want to say that membership in this club has been one of the most wonderful developments in my life. I also wish to share with you that Cynthia and I are expecting a child early next year. Sadly, we will be returning to America within the next month. It is our intent to move to the great city of Seattle, in

Washington State. I don't know how long it will take us to become established, but I want each of you to know that you are welcome in our home at any time. I don't think that any of you know just how important you've become in my life or how difficult it is going to be for me to return to the states, no longer having the option to spend time with my dear bosozoku friends."

"Well, Am Rac. That's a very good little speech. The fact is that once you join our little club, there really isn't a mechanism for leaving the group. So, I guess the short answer is that we will have to deny your request to return to the United States," Akio said sternly.

"He's not serious, Am Rac. Damn, I'm going to miss you. We've become good friends in so little time," said Sadao.

"Hey, fellows, do you mind if we ride. I need the flush of air across my face," said Cody fighting back tears.

"Before we ride, I have something I want to say," said Toshi. "Am Rac, we have not known you long, but what we know of you is that you are honorable and genuine. You will always be a member of our little band, whether here in Tokyo or across the ocean in Seattle, Washington. Everyone, all of you, please step over to Am Rac's bike."

With the men congregated around the Vespa, Toshi placed his right hand palm-down on Cody's seat cushion, where in procession the entire group of men stacked their hands in hierarchal order, in radiating fashion, beginning with Akio and ending with Cody.

"Let us now ride," Akio broadcasted as he winked at Toshi to provide a signal to the men.

Aligning in their establish formation with Akio in the lead, and Cody alongside of Sadao in the rear, the scooter gang rode through the well-lit streets of the Ginza and beyond. Exactly one hour into their run, during an extended episode of wobbly kama kiru, the ranks of the scooter formation tailed off as the riders peeled outward before dropping back. The riding formation had become inverted. Cody, confused at first, now found himself leading the gang, leading the scooter riders with the raucous cheers and scooter beep beeps from the bosozoku group that provided him with the gift of fellowship.

With the light of day quickly approaching, the gang escorted Cody back to his digs at the Ikemoto Academy. "We'll get hold of you soon for a party at the pad," Toshi said as the gang motored away.

As Cody made his way to his apartment, he was overcome by the huge level of satisfaction that his adventure in Japan had provided him. Quietly entering his apartment and stripping down, Cody got into bed and quickly fell into a rich satisfying sleep marked by fantastic visions and wondrous dreams.

In many respects, the morning that came several hours later was bright, beautiful, and full of promise. In the classroom, Cody felt particularly inspired, and this breathed much life into what otherwise might have been a humdrum day of language and writing drills. In the late afternoon, he traveled into the city to pick up food staples to get him and Cynthia through the week. In the moderately-sized store where he generally shopped, Cody picked up some pork cutlets, chicken thighs, udon and ramen noodles, onions, carrots, cabbage, and bok choy. Strapping his groceries to his scooter rack, Cody made a short run to the waterfront where he watched for a moment as the massive shipping vessels moved to and fro between Tokyo Bay and the Pacific Ocean. In reflecting on the moment, Cody realized that in the amount of time it would take a cargo ship to make a round-trip from Tokyo to the west coast of the United States, he would be back on American soil. Understandably, Cody found little comfort in that thought. For Cody, everything that was essential to his wellbeing was in

Japan. Turning his back to the sea, Cody returned to Cynthia and an apartment that was stacked with packed boxes and memories of simpler times.

When Cody arrived at the housing unit, Cynthia had curious news to share. "Cody, while you were away — guess who came rolling up to the complex. You will never guess."

"Let's see. Was it Santa Claus? No, it couldn't be Santa — it's only September. Oh, and sleighs slide instead of roll. Was it —?"

"Cody, be serious."

"Cynthia, you know how I feel about guessing games."

"Okay, I'll give you a hint. She is very mysterious."

"Was it maneki neko? Beckoning cat is a female right?"

"Okay, now you're getting warm."

"I don't know sweetheart, was it Koko?"

"Bingo!"

"How the heck did Koko know we lived here? I guess we did tell her that we were instructors at the Ikemoto Academy."

"Yes, that has to be it."

"I still find it hard to believe that she rolled her little cart of junk all the way out here."

"Well, that is just what she did, Cody."

"What did Koko have to say?"

"Well, she started by asking about the baby and then she asked about you — she always seems to ask about you. She said that you were now in a very disruptive cycle in your life."

"Oh yeah? What kind of disruptive cycle am I experiencing? Am I in danger, again?"

"I don't know, but it is the craziest thing."

"What's so crazy?"

"Koko handed me what she said was "a very special cigarette," a cigarette that you should smoke if you find yourself in a state of imminent danger or turmoil."

"That seems utterly ridiculous to me. God, I hope that she's not mixed up with a bunch of sumo wrestlers."

"What is that supposed to mean?"

"Forgive me. I just read that a sumo wrestler just got busted for like a tenth-of-a-gram of marijuana, or some ridiculously small quantity. Never mind."

"Maybe I should check," Cynthia said, rolling the end of the cigarette back and forth between her thumb and index finger, as she examined the substance for its color.

"What are you doing to my cigarette, Cynthia? Here, don't wreck it. Give it to me before it loses its powers or something."

Receiving the cigarette from Cynthia, Cody placed it in the inner pocket of his leather jacket.

"When did Koko leave?"

"That is the funniest thing, I went inside for a moment to take a phone call, and when I returned she was gone. It was like she just vanished."

"Hmm, that is weird."

"Who called?"

"It was Sadao. He wanted you to call him back when you returned from the store."

"I should probably give him a call now."

"Honey, what did you do with the Hello Kitty notebook? That's where I'm keeping my phone numbers these days."

"I didn't pack it. It is still in the drawer."

"Thank you, sweetheart."

Cody located his phone book and directed a call to Sadao. "Hey, what's *appening*? It's me, Cody. Get it? What's *appening*?"

"Yeah, I get it."

"You know, I don't even know why they call you App4That."

"I'll tell you about it some other time. Cody, I need a hand with something tonight. Can you help me?"

"You know I will."

"Okay, I'll be passing by around nine to pick you up in the van."

"I'll be ready."

"Okay, I'll see you then."

"Cynthia, it looks like I'm going to have to go out for a little while tonight. I shouldn't be home too late."

"What are you guys going to do?"

"Sadao didn't say, but he's picking me up in a van, so he probably just wants me to help him move some furniture or something."

"Gosh, Cody, sometimes you guys seem so secretive."

"Oh, honey, don't let your imagination get the best of you."

"Cody, what is on your arm?"

"What do you mean?"

"I mean — what is on your forearm? I thought I saw some sort of design or something when you reached for the mystery cigarette that Koko brought over."

"Oh, I was going to surprise you, but I forgot with all of the talk about Koko and the distraction of calling Sadao."

"You were going to surprise me in what sense?"

"Honey, I got a tattoo. I got a tattoo on my inner left forearm. I was going to surprise you when I returned from the store."

"Well, let's see it. You know, I'm really not that fond of tattoos."

"I think that you'll like this one. It's of a fish, a koi," Cody said, as he stripped down to his V-neck undershirt to reveal the ornate tattoo which he'd successfully concealed for more than a week.

"Gosh Cody, thank goodness we are headed back to the states."

"What do you mean?"

"Sakes alive, Cody, you are prime recruiting material for almost any credible yakuza organization. Think about it. You are missing the last joints of your two smallest fingers on your left hand, and now you have this huge ornate tattoo of a traditional Japanese carp."

"It's a koi," Cody said, correcting Cynthia.

"Okay, a colorful traditionally styled koi broadcast across your forearm, and if you want to get technical, you might even score extra points for having a father who works in a slaughterhouse."

"What do you mean by that?"

"Cody, the Japanese consider people who hold employment in jobs that involve death or any of its manifestations to be outcasts, and in some sense to be impure. The Japanese exercise serious condemnation for these so-called burakumin. And it is burakumin who sizably populate the ranks of yakuza organizations. I'm not being judgmental, Cody, but I just want you to come home with me in one piece, unscathed."

"I hear you, and I understand your point."

"Honestly, Cody, I think that I will find your tattoo much more favorable on American soil."

Like clockwork, Sadao arrived at the housing complex at 9 p.m. sharp, pulling up in the large white van that was used to transport the equipment to the ball field the previous week.

"Hey, Cody. Lovely evening we're having isn't it?" "Indeed it is, Sadao. What's on your mind?"

"I volunteered to return the Colonel to his place of business. Can you give me a hand?"

"Do we just have to drop him off?"

"Pretty much, although we do have to carry him a little distance before we set him up. I don't think that any risk will be involved."

"Let's go. We can always say that we found him in an alley or something, if anyone should ask."

"You know, Cody, I almost thought that someone was following me until just before I pulled up to the academy grounds, but I guess they're gone now."

"So, Sadao, why do they call you App4That?"

"The label is relatively recent, but the idea is an old one. You see, I use to work for Toshi's company before he cashed in on his stock. I did a lot of the programming for his various digital toy people and digital toy pets. The story is really kind of boring, but I guess you could say that I developed software applications for the various toys and gadgets that his company produced. I still dabble in freelance application development for iPads and other notebook-class platforms."

"Hey, Sadao. I think that someone ahead is waving us down."

"Yeah, I see her. I guess we should stop to see if we can be of some assistance. Roll down your window."

"Konban wa," exclaimed Cody

"Konban wa," replied the woman excitedly.

"Can we help you?" Cody said believing that the lady looked remotely familiar.

"There is a gravely injured man in the back of my van. He needs immediate medical attention."

"I'm going to pull over and check this out, Cody," Sadao said as he pulled to the side of the road.

"Yeah, I'm with you." Just as Cody and Sadao peered into the back of the van, the pair was greeted with jarring blows to the head and body from men wielding hardwood batons.

"I understand that you fellows like to play hardball," said a voice from the dark. Dazed but conscious, Cody and Sadao remained still while each pondered their fate.

"We're going to take you fellows on a little ride to the boss's favorite little underground tunnel."

After a short ride that seemed eternal, the van transporting Cody, Sadao, and their captors pulled into what appeared to be a quiet residential sector of the city. Upon reaching the location, Sadao and Cody were forcefully ushered along a dark, dank, canal-like walkway with an essence that was reminiscent of a grubby, wet mongrel, complete with the representative odoriferous secretions. As the small group, consisting of Cody, Sadao, and the two heavies made their way to a remote chamber, each was brushed with root-like structures that protruded from the walls and ceiling that were similar to what one might encounter were they to navigate through the flaps and bristles of an automated car wash.

Once inside the main room, a large candle could be seen that dimly illuminated the image of a man sitting at a small table. "I'm so glad that you could make it. We had Lulu flag you down tonight. Do you remember Lulu?"

"No, I don't remember anyone named Lulu," Cody said hoping against the odds that he might be freed by his captors.

"What is this name — Am Raccoon Dog?"

"It is just a name that I made up for our scooter club."

"What is your real name and where are you from?"

Realizing that he had better provide answers, Cody said, "My name is Cody Fletcher, and I am from Oakdale, California.

"Write the name of this place down on this piece of paper," the man said in an attempt to gain an understanding of Cody's command of the Japanese language.

Obeying his oppressor's directive, Cody wrote in perfect English lettering, O a k d a l e.

"Where is this — *Oakdayaly*?"

"It is in California, in America."

"You are a liar. You are a very clever Japanese man, a man who will soon meet his end. What do you do for a living Cody Fletcher san?"

"I teach English to high school students."

"Lies, all lies — Cody Fletcher san. You are yakuza. It is written all about your being. The prosthetic fingers on your hand cover up your acts of yubitsume. These marks upon your body are unmistakable."

"Actually, I cut my fingers in a farm accident with a fan belt on a tractor."

"Again you lie. Roll up your sleeve Cody Fletcher san. Show us all of your yakuza artwork."

Having little other choice, Cody rolled up his sleeve to reveal the freshly penned tattoo on his forearm. "What do you think of all of this?" questioned the interrogator as he looked towards Sadao. "What is this name — App4That?" demanded the man, referring to the monogram on Sadao's jacket.

"I have nothing to say," said Sadao.

"Am I to assume that you are also from this — *Oakdayaly*, California?"

"No, no, I'm not from Oakdale," Sadao said as he shook his head in confusion regarding the wild revelations brought to light regarding Cody.

"What is your name?"

"Watashi wa Koizume Sadao desu."

"Let me see your hands, Koizume Sadao san."

Lifting his hands into view, while glancing at Cody with a look of betrayal, Sadao said, "I am not yakuza. I am a computer programmer."

"Again, you men tell me lies."

Walking around the room, in deep contemplation, the interrogator said, "I think we need to try another tactic."

"Cody Fletcher san, who do you work for?"

"I work for the Ikemoto Academy here in Tokyo as an English instructor."

"Let me ask you another question. What does your father do for a living in Oakdayaly?"

"He runs a sweet potato farm and he works at a slaughterhouse during the week."

Smiling and laughing, with his cruel associates joining him, the interrogator said, "Burakumin, now we are getting somewhere. Cody Fletcher san, you are among burakumin. Unfortunately, we are not your friends. Cody Fletcher san, we will now get some answers from you. We will start by cutting off Koizume Sadao san's ear to see what answers you will provide." Walking over to Sadao, one of the henchmen grabbed Sadao by the earlobe and proceeded to slice off his entire left ear with a small paring knife. As Sadao cried out in agonizing horror, the other thug punched him in the stomach toward quelling his incipient wailing.

Seeing his best friend butchered before his eyes and reduced to a pitifully cowering victim, Cody said, "I'll tell you anything, just leave Sadao alone."

"Ah, now we seem to have gotten through to you."

"Yes. I am prepared to tell you everything, but can I first have a cigarette?"

"I am sorry Cody Fletcher san, none of us smoke."

"I have a cigarette inside of my jacket, if you would just allow me retrieve it."

"Not so fast, Cody Fletcher san." Pointing to one of his men, the interrogator said, "Get Cody Fletcher san his cigarette."

Reaching inside of Cody's leather jacket, the henchman produced and handed the parcel to Cody before bringing the candle into proximity where the cigarette could be ignited.

Drawing sharply on the small roll of tobacco, Cody breathed in deeply, but nothing seemed to happen. Taking another prolonged and robust pull, he leaned back and felt a sense of calm, a sense of utter tranquility, if not mild intoxication. Cody looked about the room and drew on the cigarette once more, this time until its glowing embers radiated a bright red-orange as they spit, sputtered, and whistled — whereby the flame-engulfed bindle fell from his hand. Meeting the foundation of the chamber, the thick matted floor covering became enflamed releasing the noxious odor of burning hair, a horrible essence of burning tuft and scorched flesh that was only overshadowed by the agonizing yelps of the wretched and tortured beast as it dissipated into the ether.

Seattle, Washington: Fall 2016

The early fall sun sailed through the window as Cody rested quietly from an ordeal that he'd long remember.

"Doctor, how much longer before he'll come around," asked Cynthia as she brushed Cody's hair away from his eyes as he lay reclined.

"It ought to be any minute," the doctor offered as Cody began to twitch about the eyes and brow.

While Cynthia squeezed Cody's hand, his eyes slowly opened. "Hey, honey, are you waking up?"

"What, huh?"

"Shhh, baby. Take it slowly."

"Did it go okay?" Cody asked groggily.

"They got them all. They were huge suckers too. My big boy had really big, mean, wisdom teeth," said Cynthia playfully. "You look like Vito Corleone with your jaw all puffed out like that."

"Where are the girls?"

"Emi and Kyoko are with Mother."

Making contact with the doctor, Cody said, "Am I free to go?"

"No, not yet, fella. I've got to write you a couple of prescriptions, and I have to write down some instructions so that you can read them when you regain your bearings."

"Hey, mister, you had better 'regain your bearings' pretty quickly. You've got a very busy week ahead," Cynthia counseled. "You've got your father driving up the first load of potatoes, and don't forget we've got visitors coming this week."

"I know. When are they coming?"

"I just received an email from Michiko, and she said they would be arriving at Sea-Tac tomorrow at four p.m. Tomorrow is Tuesday, isn't it? Yes, they get here tomorrow," Cynthia said answering her own question.

"Don't I have to be at the Bellevue Senior Center tomorrow, too?"

"No sir! It is Wednesday that you have to be at the senior center."

"Okay. I have written a prescription for a pain killer and I have written one for an antibiotic, in case you're your gums become enflamed," the doctor said as he volleyed his eye contact between Cody and Cynthia. "Read my notes thoroughly, and call me if any questions arise."

"Thank you, Dr. Clark," said Cynthia as she received the prescriptions and glanced toward Cody.

"Yes, yes, thank you, doctor," Cody said, realizing that some response from him was in order.

"Mr. Fletcher, I do know a man who cuts hair, if you are interested," said Dr. Clark.

"Thank you, doctor, but my little rascal likes to wear his hair kind of long these days. He's on a one-man crusade to bring back long hair to the masses."

"Okay then. Oh, and Mr. Fletcher — congratulations on your new restaurant. The wife and I enjoyed a very fine meal there last week. You do know that *tiger* just has one "g," don't you? Where did you come up with the name — Tigger Swag Sushi, anyway?"

"Doctor, I'd tell you, but it's kind of a long story."

"Okay, then. Call me if you have any concerns."

"Yes, Doctor, I'll do that."

As a wedding gift to Cynthia and Cody — Evelyn and Harvey Martin pledged to buy the couple their first home, but only under the condition, in the words of Cynthia's father — that they "not camp out on our front lawn." What this meant to the fledgling couple was that they were to set up stakes on their own turf. To Cynthia, this meant that they would find a residence in or around Seattle, yet not on Mercer Island.

After a considerable search effort, the newlyweds finally settled on a huge 1920s Greek Revival home that nestled up to Lake Washington. As time would tell, the Laurelhurst residence proved more than adequate for the couple and their growing brood. Of comparable importance, the domicile had the advantage of being close to the city and all of its conveniences, while being isolated from the city and most of its encumbrances.

When Cynthia and Cody arrived home, Cynthia's mother had just put the girls down for a nap. "The twins had such a great time at the zoo today," said Evelyn.

"Do you remember, dear, when I use to take you to the Woodland Park Zoo?"

"Mother, do I remember? You use to pack me up to take me to the zoo into my early twenties. Of course, I remember."

"You were always such a sweet child. You know, dear, winter is approaching. I want you to go out and get yourself a nice warm coat, so you don't catch cold. It gets so breezy out here on the point."

"Mother, I'm getting older now, and I do know the order of the seasons. But, okay, Mother, I'll get a warm coat."

"That's my girl. Cody, make sure she gets a coat. Cynthia has always been such a frail girl, you know."

"Yes, Mother, I'll make sure that our little angel gets a coat," said Cody in the fashion that had become his and Evelyn's signature consortium.

"For goodness sake, Mother, I don't know why you just don't go out and get me a big glass jar to live in."

"Cody, be a dear and look into the glass jar thing."

"Yes, Mother."

"Well, Mother, thank you for watching Emi and Kyoko," said Cynthia as she worked to usher Evelyn out the door.

"You can count on me anytime, dear. Well, I should probably get along and tend to your father. You know how lost he gets without me."

"I think he hides," quipped Cynthia winking at Cody.

"What, dear?"

"Oh nothing, Mother. Have a safe drive back to the Island."

Cynthia's mother was a beautifully distinguished woman. She dressed herself in the finest clothes, rubbed elbows with Seattle's elite, and tended to her husband and only child as would a tenacious mother hen, rarely allowing her brood to sense independence while ensconced in her feathery grasp. With increased success in Cody's various business enterprises, Mrs. Martin fought like the dickens to retain her relevance and authoritative presence.

With the arrival of a late afternoon breeze, a trailer backed into the Fletcher driveway. "Honey, the truck is here," exclaimed Cynthia.

"I'll go tell them where to place the container. What do you think, dear?" Cody said in the realization that he'd need to host the trailer for a couple weeks.

"I don't know. Can you put it on the gravel alongside the pool house?"

"I guess, I just hope that it isn't muddy out there. I don't want them to get all mucky."

Walking out the front door, Cody was greeted by the driver. "Where do you want the crate?" asked the driver.

"Let's put it out by the pool house."

"Yes, sir."

"Of course, I want the doors facing out. Before you drop the container, let me check the cargo to see if it is in good shape."

Opening up the trailer's door, the shipping agent said, "Man, those are nice. What are they, brand-new?"

"Yes, sir."

"One for the wife and one for you?"

"No, I've got two of my dearest friends coming to visit. I guess we'd better deal with the paperwork."

"Yes, sir. Sign here."

Returning back to the house, Cody relayed to Cynthia, "They're here safe, and apparently sound."

"Thank goodness they arrived after Mother left. I don't think that we'd have ever heard the end of it."

"Well, unfortunately, I don't think we are over with it yet. I'm probably going to give one to each of the girls when they come of age."

"Yeah, I don't know about that one, Cody."

"Don't worry. A lot can happen in a few years, believe me."

"Okay, Cody, whatever you say. Are you still under the effects of anesthesia?"

"Perhaps. Let's see how I feel tomorrow," Cody said putting the matter to rest.

Closing the Loop

The next morning, Cynthia rallied the troops bright and early. By 6 a.m. she was working feverishly to spruce up the upstairs bedrooms and attending to the final touches in the bathrooms and communal areas.

Cynthia attended to every detail in her effort to ensure that her guests received the level of care to properly celebrate what she and Cody felt was an important milestone. For Cody, the get-together represented his first opportunity to host some of the Japanese friends that he'd made while working as an English instructor in Tokyo, more than four years earlier. For Cynthia, the visit was to provide a rich opportunity for her to interact in person with the two articulate and eloquent Japanese women who had become her friends through the year-long correspondence that facilitated the festive gathering.

By 7 a.m., Emi and Kyoko had eaten breakfast and were each occupied with paper and a box of crayons in the library, each girl sitting at a small desk in the pursuit of drawing fantastic pictures, much as their mother had done when she was their age. With the twins secured in a safe activity, Cody swept off the dock leading to the cabin cruiser and tended to tidying up the pool area. After a successful white-glove test that signaled that the patio barbecue was up to his standards of cleanliness, Cody walked the grounds to ensure that the compound would pass muster from Cynthia.

By noon, Cynthia finally gave the seal of approval to Cody. "I guess the house is presentable."

"I'd hope so. You worked me like a dog for most of the last week."

"Listen, RD, I am not entertaining our friends in a home that isn't immaculate in every respect."

"Yes, dear."

"We had better get to thinking about heading to the airport."

"Yeah, I know, Sea-Tac is going to be crazy at this time of the day."

"We had better give it at least two hours. Let's start this great experience off on the right footing."

"You're right, dear. You're always right about these things."

Having loaded up the twins in the van, Cody and Cynthia maneuvered on to Interstate 5 and continued south toward Tacoma. The pair made particularly good time until reaching south Seattle, where traffic slowed to nearly a dead stop. "Why does this have to happen today," said Cody, as he looked at Cynthia.

"Hey, honey, take it in stride. You've done what you can. Just remain calm. We will get there when we can."

"Yeah, I know. It is just that the excitement has built up so high."

As the family continued down the road, Emi and Kyoko fell asleep, and Cynthia went over a check list concerning the itinerary that she had assembled for her guests relative to the ten days that they were to visit. At one point, she pulled out her iPhone to check the flight status of the jet. "It looks like the flight is ahead of schedule. More than likely, they'll be waiting when we arrive."

"Damn, I mean — darn it."

"Calm down. I don't want you waking up the girls with your frustration."

"I know. I'm sorry."

"It's okay. Oh good. Look, we're almost at Sea-Tac."

"Finally! It is about time."

Having survived the late-afternoon Seattle-Tacoma International Airport traffic, Cody and Cynthia exited the interstate and veered along the road toward the short-term parking garage. Pulling into a parking space, Cody commented, "This spot is as good as any."

Realizing that there was no way to counter their tardiness, Cynthia calmly awoke Emi and Kyoko, placing them in their stroller, while Cody reached behind his seat to grab his leather jacket. Having safely secured the twins, Cynthia looked at Cody as he straightened his lapel. "You okay, Raccoon Dog?" Cynthia said smiling at her husband.

"Yeah, I'm okay, babe. How about you?"

"I'm kind of nervous, in a way."

"It will be okay."

"Are you girls ready to meet daddy's friends?"

"Yes, mommy," chimed Kyoko

"I want to pet daddy's cat," said Emi.

"I'm afraid it's not that kind of a cat, Emi. Daddy's friend isn't really a cat."

"Let's go, Mom," said Cody.

"Okay, okay, Dad."

With everyone saddled up, the family exited the garage, crossed the stretch of busy road near the passenger pick-up area, walked through the automated sliding glass doors, and proceeded to the baggage carousel, where they expected to find their visitors.

Identifying his guests from the rear, Cody snuck up behind Sexy Cat whereby he screeched, much to Cynthia's horror, "Hey. Shake it, but don't break it, baby!" and then, focusing on his riding partner, he cawed, "Hey, who dresses you — your grandma?"

Cody was in absolute delight. Toshi and Sadao, two of his dearest friends in the entire world, had come to visit him and Cynthia with their wives. As Cody, Toshi, and Sadao shared a gang hug, their respective wives, Kamiko and Michiko, and Cynthia assembled around the twin girls. Crouching down to greet Emi and Kyoko, the strikingly elegant and refined Japanese women spoke as if they were the adoring big sisters of the young girls. Intently studying the friendly, albeit foreign faces, Emi and Kyoko seemed to recognize that within the travelers there existed a common bridge that somehow connected the small aggregation as a family.

With things seeming much like old times to Cody, he talked incessantly about all that he wished to share with his visitors. "I want to take you to my home and go for a boat ride on the lake."

"You've got a lake, Cody san?" said Sadao.

"Well, I can't really claim it as mine. I share it with the fine folks of Seattle."

"Is it a big lake?" asked Toshi.

"Well, let me see. To put it into perspective, it has roughly one-eighth of the surface area of Lake Biwa, near Kyoto."

"Oh, I see," said Toshi.

"I also want to show you the Jimi Hendrix Museum."

"Right on, Cody san. Can you get us some *purple haze*?" said Toshi.

"You mean some *acid*?"

"Yeah, I just want to wrap a couple of dozen hits in my *hachimaki*" (bandana).

"Yeah, Toshi, I don't think so."

"Really? You can't get it?"

"Yeah, I don't know. I'd have to check around," said Cody. "You know, you Japanese guys, us Japanese guys — we are really crazy!"

"Yeah, I know. *Everybody kinda crazy. Now you crazy too*," said Sadao making reference to an old George Thorogood tune.

Changing the subject, Cody said, "Hey guys, I want to take you on a Seattle run. Are you fellows interested?"

"What are we going to do, buy a couple of bikes for a single run?" said Toshi.

"Not quite. I've got things worked out. All we need to do is get you guys a couple of international licenses. Then we'll be set. That is why I said to bring your driver's identification."

"Let's do it then," said Toshi with a nod of agreement from Sadao.

Arriving at Cody and Cynthia's home, the boys carried in their luggage and settled into their respective rooms. Rather than unpacking, Toshi and Sadao suited up into their swim trunks and surprised Cody by racing down the boat dock, simultaneously assuming the cannonball position before plunging into the water. "Cody, come on in, the water is great!" exclaimed Sadao.

"Yeah, I know," Cody said, as he ran inside of the house to find some shorts. The funny thing was that Cody, in his nearly three years living in the home, had never jumped into the lake. The fact was that he'd do it a couple of times a week, most every week, for the remainder of the years that he lived in the Laurelhurst home. There was just something about the strong bond that was formed among these close friends who lived on opposite sides of the globe. As individuals, they would probably jump into an open sewer if it meant that they could carry on with one another as they had grown to love to do.

The next day, bright and early, Cody and Cynthia began the preparation of a morning meal suitable for royalty. It was Cynthia's hope that their guests would appreciate the marriage of an authentic Japanese breakfast with that of its American counterpart. The party was to dine on miso soup, rice, salted salmon, and brined eggplant, as well as traditional American fare including sausage, flapjacks, and scrambled eggs. Once Cynthia had secured Emi and Kyoko in their highchairs, their guests slowly filtered in.

Michiko and Kamiko arrived at the table dressed with the elegance and restraint of meticulously prim cherry trees in early bloom. Upon their arrival, the pair immediately offered to assist with the preparation of the pageant of breakfast offerings.

As Michiko sliced oranges and Kamiko measured out a quantity of green tea, Sadao and Toshi, pajama-clad and disheveled, plopped down at the table. "Good morning, fellows," Cody said. "We've got a full day ahead of us. I hope that you're raring to go."

"We're all over it, Cody san. Right after a swim in the lake, we'll get down to the business of getting ready," said Sadao with a nod of approval from Toshi.

"You know I think that I might have something for each of you to wear today," Cody said, as he walked toward a hall closet. Returning from the closet, he said, "Here, Toshi, I think this is about your size," Cody said as he presented Toshi with a flashy green jacket that glittered and pulsed as it furled in the light of the morning sun."

"Where did you get this? I want a dozen," said Toshi as he canvased the kitchen and then the living room, in search of a mirror.

"You might look at the label," Cody said with a prideful smirk on his face. "Read what it says."

"Sexy Cat? It say's Sexy Cat, Kamiko."

"Read the rest."

"It says, 'Sexy Cat® — Tokyo & Seattle'."

"Did you have this label fashioned for me?"

"No, not quite, Toshi. I'll tell you about it in a moment, but I want to get something for Sadao."

"Sadao, I'd like to let you wear one of these," Cody said returning from the same closet that housed Toshi's jacket. Lifting up a heavy burgundy colored muffler, constructed from thickly woven wool ellipses joined together in such a fashion that they collectively resembled a large clutch of grapes, Cody said, "What do you think? It's a wool neck wrap designed to look like a bunch of grapes. See how it comes down along the neck, before dropping down across the shoulders toward the waist? If you stand back it looks like a vest. And look, it even has a green extension off the back of the neck that looks like the stem of the grapes. Pretty wild, huh?"

"Now, Cody, I know that my grandmother didn't knit this. I love it. Where on Earth did you find this?"

"As I said to Toshi — read the label."

"It says, 'App4That: Woolen-Fruit® — Tokyo & Seattle'. Nice label, Cody san, but where did you get the wrap? Where did you purchase the muffler?"

"See, that's the thing, guys. These garments are produced by my employees in Bellevue, Washington. It is a startup operation of my clothing line. I put senior citizens living on fixed incomes to work. I named the company *GrandmaWorks*. Kind of catchy, huh?"

"Cody san, you are a man of many surprises."

After the group of friends shared a leisurely breakfast and the boys had taken a brisk dip in Lake Washington, the phone rang out, whereby Cynthia received the call.

"Hi Dad. Yes, Cody is right here. Cody, it is your dad. He is calling from Vancouver, Washington, and he says he'll be at Uwajimaya in about four hours."

"Let me talk to him," said Cody. "Hey Dad. How's the drive going?"

"It's going fine, son. So are you and Cynthia going to be able to meet me at the market as planned?"

"Dad, I wouldn't miss it for the world. Cynthia says you'll be there about two o'clock. Is that correct?"

"That's right, buckaroo. I should get there maybe a little early. Bring your gloves."

That afternoon, with Cody, Cynthia, Emi, and Kyoko; Toshi and Kamiko; and Sadao and Michiko all loaded into Cynthia's van, the party on wheels weaved its way out of Laurelhurst, through the University district, through Wallingford, Fremont, and Queen Anne, before traveling down First Street to South Jackson and then on to 6th Avenue South, finally reaching Uwajimaya Market. The crisp fall day was accented with ample light, and while only midday, the day seemed rich and full. When the group arrived, they could see that Dwight was backed up to the loading dock. Jumping out of the van, Cody called to him, "Hey, Charlie Spud. I brought along some help from Japan."

"Well that's just fine, son. I hope they're prepared to work."

Not knowing anything about why they were at the curious market, Sadao and Toshi simply looked at one another, shrugging their shoulders. "Hey, Toshi, I've got a couple of pairs of gloves for you and Sadao under the front seat. Please get them."

Opening up the trailer door, with the entire troop peering in, brought to light a huge haul of boxes. Climbing up on the landing to join his father, Cody reached above his head and grabbed the first of many boxes of product that would lay a foundation for many fruitful seasons of a very special Japanese sweet potato with the most remarkable amethyst-colored flesh.

Emblazoned on each box, the trade label read:

Raccoon Dog
Sweet Potatoes
Oakdale, California & Seattle, Washington

ABOUT THE AUTHOR

TIMOTHY P. REGAN is a career educator with undergraduate degrees in chemistry and mathematics and a master's degree in education. As a writer, Mr. Regan is drawn to story venues that focus on foreign, little-known, overlooked or seldom addressed locations or life-style niches. For more than a decade, Mr. Regan has been entranced and allured by all things Japanese, and this essence is evident throughout his recently completed novel: AMERICAN RACCOON DOG. Mr. Regan resides in the Humboldt Bay region of Northern California.